So

The

The Killing Interviews

Gavin Horrocks

This book is dedicated to the people
who inspire me.

Contents

Prologue / Chapter 1

Part One
    The Setup
    Chapters 2 to 13

Part Two
    The Emotional Rollercoaster
    Chapters 14 to 27

Part Three
    The Hunters and the Hunted
    Chapters 28 to 48

Prologue / Chapter 1

"Daddy, I don't want to do it." The young boy looked around the dusty barn nervously, shuffling his feet in the loose hay that littered the floor. The secrecy of what he was about to do was all too confusing. After his father had tried explaining this to him the evening before, he tried to be excited. But now he was finally here, any excitement he had had, was now evaporating quickly.

"Look, Charlie, we've spoken about this, and I've explained why it's important."

"But, Daddy, it's so heavy and I don't like the noise."

"Zack did it all by himself yesterday, Charlie. So be a good boy and be brave," his father said.

"But Zack is fifteen and I'm only ten."

"So that'll give you the chance to be brave like him. You're always saying he gets to do things you don't. Think of it as your turn for an adventure."

Both Charlie's body language and look of utter confusion said *'why am I doing this?',* but Bernie was hopeful his son would carry it out even if he had been unable to fully explain to him exactly why it was necessary. All he could do was make it as easy as possible and add a bit of mystery in the hope to make the horrible ordeal seem exciting in some macabre way.

He checked the loaded shotgun was still pointing at the drugged and unconscious man he could view through a small hole in a huge dark blue tarpaulin sheet he had strung up across some rafters and had fixed in place with nails. It was all designed to hide the sight from his son. Charlie didn't know there were people behind the huge curtain. Better he didn't watch what was about to happen. A small video camera was also carefully mounted high in the roof space. It could see the unconscious man and whoever was using the gun. This was a necessary part of the rules, so Bernie had been told. He understood.

"I'm going to hold the gun for you, Charlie. All you have to do is pull the trigger," he said. "Try to think of it like how you play with your toy guns at home. But you're going to have to squeeze really hard, like I showed you at home. Okay?"

"Okay. And you're gonna hold it up so, it won't be heavy, right?" he asked, as he stood there nervously, fidgeting and shuffling his feet.

"Sure, son, I'll take the weight, and I've got it rested on this stand, too. Don't forget to wear the big ear protectors."

Charlie picked up a pair of oversized orange ear defenders which reminded him of the headphones his father put on when listening to music. Except these ones muffled the sound and there was no music to listen to. They slipped forwards on his head. Twice. But he finally got them on, so they didn't slip about.

"Come over here, then."

Charlie walked over to where the gun rested on the stand his father had painstakingly rigged up the night before, but it needed a pair of strong hands to hold the shotgun steady and Bernie duly obliged. One last check through a tiny hole in the tarpaulin. It was still aimed at the man's head.

"Okay then Charlie, time to be a big boy." But his voice was on the verge of breaking. His hands were wanting to shake and his legs felt like jelly. Somehow, he managed to steady the shotgun for his confused son. Charlie put his finger through the trigger guard, looked at his father and thought he saw a tear in his father's eye.

"Why, Daddy? I don't understand what I'm doing. And you look so sad."

"Please son. Just do what we talked about. And if you do it quickly, we can go to that shop like I promised you. Maybe we can get an Action Race Track set as a reward."

Charlie took a big breath like his father had shown him earlier and squeezed the trigger; and though it seemed to move a bit, he couldn't pull it all the way back.

"I can't make it fire, Daddy."

"Put the finger from your other hand on top of the finger and use both hands."

"Like thi..." BANG. The shotgun rudely interrupted him as it released its load. Meanwhile, Bernie managed to absorb the recoil. Unexpectedly Charlie, rather than being surprised, shocked or startled, actually started laughing uncontrollably. Bernie almost fainted as soon as he heard the explosion but seeing his son now rolling on the floor in fits of giggles added an even more sinister angle to what was occurring.

"Well done, son", he somehow managed to say, hiding any lies or subterfuge from his voice. "Now, do you remember the next thing we both have to do, like we talked about?"

"Yes. I have to wait here and count to a hundred out loud, while you make some bangs over behind that blue wall."

"You're a good boy, Charlie. And make sure you keep wearing those ear protectors all the time."

Bernie walked several paces to the right to where the edge of the tarpaulin hung. He peered around the side to where the drugged man had been perched and partially tied onto a chair. The man was now fully slumped forwards and there was little left of his head. The shot had been a total success. But how on Earth could he justify calling it a success when he had all but forced his youngest son to execute a complete stranger?

Anyway, he reminded himself, he had no time to think or dwell on any of this. He dragged the remains of the man away from that part of the floor. With all his strength, he then dragged another unconscious person into view of the video camera who sat tied to another chair into the exact same position where the first had been just moments before. He cursed himself for not having mounted the camera within easier reach. It would have been easier to move the camera than to lug dead or drugged people about.

And all the while, he could hear from the other side of the tarpaulin, "Fifty six, fifty seven, fifty eight...'

No time to dwell. Satisfied he was in view of the camera and sure that his face could clearly be seen, he then raised the gun to the head of the slumped person in the chair and without any feeling for who it was, pulled the trigger. The sound of the shotgun blast stopped Charlie counting.

"Carry on counting, Charlie", Bernie called out as loudly as he could so Charlie would hear through the ear protectors, "I've got to do it once more." And with that he shoved the dead body out of the way and started back to where the third was still unconscious.

This would surely break his heart. He tried not to look at the last person, an old woman whose head lolled forward toward her chest, just like the other two had previously. But it looked as if she was coming around. Yes, indeed, she was starting to wake up. Bernie almost passed out. But he had come too far to pull out now. As speedily as he could, he dragged her to the same position as the other two, assumed the video camera was still in the right place for it and raised his gun. For the briefest moment before he pulled the trigger her eyes met his. And what he was convinced he saw was not anger or blame, and what he saw fell some way short of forgiveness, but instead there was a look of complete understanding.

But the flash from the muzzle obliterated not only the image but brought instant death, dimming those beautiful eyes forever.

Bernie sank to his knees. If he had been a religious man, he'd have started praying. Instead, he started sobbing.

"Ninety two, ninety three..."

Bernie stood back up. He brushed loose hay from his shirt, wiped his face with one of the sleeves and rushed back around to the Charlie's side of the tarpaulin. He gestured to him to take the ear defenders off, to which his son duly obliged.

"Okay son. It's all over."

"Yeah? Great. That was easier than I thought. Let's go to the shop."

Bernie fought the urge to be sick. He took some solace to notice the red recording light on the video camera was still illuminated. He would put Charlie in the car and go back into the barn to retrieve the camera, once and for all.

Part One
The Setup

Chapter 2

The cold winter months were starting to abate. But the fireplace was still the favoured place to gather around, especially after having just completed nine holes of golf at the Harstville Golf Club they favoured so much. Two red leather chesterfield seats awaited their arrival.

The two gentlemen were not only best friends but they just happened to be the two most powerful men in the United States of America. President Amos Kenderrick and White House Chief of Staff, Jeremy Weinstein.

They settled down to discuss Jeremy's lucky chip shot from the bunker on the seventh and marvel at the way Amos holed a 45 foot putt on the previous hole that had to negotiate two conflicting contours along its route.

"Gentlemen, may I offer you each a glass of brandy?" the waiter enquired.

"Absolutely. We'll take full advantage of your kind offer, thank you. But make sure it's a Hennessy. I'm rather partial to that," Kenderrick said.

Five minutes later, and much to their chagrin, the conversation slipped from lucky golf shots and how beautifully the greens had been tended, back to business affairs, especially the issue of the nation's failings.

Kenderrick started. "In 2020, the population was about 330 million. Look at us now, in 2050. It's 650 million. Back in the early 2020s the yearly increase was about 0.4 percent. That's a little over a million in a year. You don't have to be a genius to realise something has gone seriously wrong since. We've doubled in 30 years. That's impossible."

"Certainly should be impossible. But it's happened."

"Why?" President Kenderrick almost demanded.

"The growth wasn't exponential then. But once an exponential change starts to occur, it goes out of control." Weinstein all but repeated what the government scientists had been telling him.

"Well, we can't afford it. There's not enough food, fuel stocks are running low and people are hating the rationing we have to impose. Congress can't pump any more money into healthcare and as for education, well, that's a joke," Kenderrick said.

"The schools are overrun. They have been for years."

"I need to fix it, Jeremy."

"I'm not sure that's possible, unless you send half of them to Canada and then shut the border. Or Mexico," Weinstein offered.

"Oh boy. Can you imagine how much easier it would be to manage the country if we could turn back time? I'd love to re-start as if it were 2020. Think of the extra money we would have. We could fund just about every project on the drawing board instead of having to write-off so many potentially worthwhile initiatives."

Weinstein mulled over this idea for a while. He hadn't been immune to the cuts either, as some of his own projects had had to fall by the wayside.

For a couple of minutes each man was lost in his own reverie. The pleasant crackling of the fireplace seemed to take over for a while.

"Amos, can I pose a somewhat controversial idea your way?"

"Not until we get that bottle of Hennessy back here," he replied. "I need a top-up."

Moments later, with the waiter having brought to them the remainder of their newly opened bottle, Weinstein was ready to share his idea. He stood up, stretching his calf muscles, wandered around on the plush golf club carpet and stood next to the fireplace, looking back at his old friend.

"What if. And this is a what-if scenario, so purely a theoretical exercise, okay. But what if we reduce the population numbers?" Weinstein offered this for discussion.

"Birth control, close the borders to immigration, and so on. It's all been tried. Gets us nowhere."

"That's an attempt to slow growth. I'm talking about an actual reduction. Don't forget it's a '*What if*' scenario."

"There's no way to do it," the President claimed.

"Let me play with this idea just a little more. I may have a solution. A way to do it. And so, just suppose there actually was an effective way, would you let me take control?"

"What way would that be?"

"With regards the actual method, I'm not going share that with you for now." He decided to try to manipulate a very tractable friend, and laid the trap by saying, "I want to sell you the idea of the advantages at this time. Such as the financial re-boot to the economy, a greater clout on the stock markets. That's worldwide, of course. And there would be less burden on social services and the contribution we make to healthcare, too. I also think I can better control illegal migration. Now, that's got to be worth exploring."

The President replied merely by nodding, thus encouraging his Chief of Staff to continue.

"You can leave the methods up to me," Weinstein said. "Nothing to worry yourself with, in that regard."

"Quite frankly, any way that would achieve it, would be worth exploring, I suppose."

"Any way?" He emphasised the *'Any'* in his question.

"Any. Play with your idea and come back to me."

"It'll mean me having some meetings with senior ministers and scientists." The Chief of Staff was now addressing his President on a professional level.

"If it's scenario-based, take it as far as you can as an exercise but be prepared to pull out, if it isn't feasible."

"I could even clear a massive chunk of the National Debt in just three months, so it will be worth the effort to try."

"As I said, take it as far as you can as an exercise but be prepared to pull out. No good idea gets passed in Congress, anyway."

"Don't bet on it. An idea is dawning," Weinstein said.

"It's something you can do on your own?"

"No, I'm going to need a strong influencer in my team, and I've got just the man in mind."

"Don't tell me you want to work with that slime-ball Attorney General of Maryland."

"You're referring to Robert Gently. And, yes, he's just the man for the job."

Chapter 3

The Federal Building stood at the eastern edge of the city not too far from a private airport into which six dignitaries had been arriving during the early morning hours. A motorcade had been arranged by Homeland Security to bring the six directly to the building and as it arrived was ushered into the secure underground car park. There was a secrecy to the event, from the formal request to attend, the security of the internal flight and a demand that a confidentiality agreement be signed which made direct reference to the country's Official Secrets Act.

A highly polished chart on the entrance foyer wall listed the functions that occurred on each floor, from administrative functions to conference suites, an indication of where the public areas were to be found and which floors had been set aside for specific departments; all clearly listed. Yet floor seven was merely titled *Internal Chambers*. A team of guards stood around the elevator entrance.

A small welcome party politely ushered the group up to the seventh floor.

It was assumed by each of the invitees that the meeting was to talk about the state of the nation. Contributing to this was a population growing faster than the infrastructure could cope. That certainly warranted a discussion. There was also the growing food shortage crisis to discuss, which was getting worse year on year despite all efforts to curtail it. But what could one do when the temperate weather was becoming more tropical with extreme storms, out of season floods and unexpected heatwaves during the growing season? People took to looting for food. Shops and supermarkets became prime targets for gangs and shoplifters. The concept of stealing money from people became less of an incentive than obtaining food, medicines and commodities necessary for everyday demands.

In some areas of society, fuel became its own currency, too. Gas supplies often ran out or were restricted by the oil producers and their supply lines. Gas stations had to deal with supply rationing but rarely received enough to satisfy everybody. People typically combatted this by simply driving less and only essential travel became important. But there were some who used the fuel shortage to their advantage. Selling fuel they had stolen from wherever it was least secure.

The health ministers conveyed their ongoing concern that people took to seeking medical attention from quack doctors or bought medicines that had not been passed by The Medical Association. Hospitals simply could not cope with the sheer number of people who needed treatment, simple operations and routine procedures.

Compounding all of this inability for the country to support their own people was an influx of refugees experiencing similar challenges in their own countries. They crossed land borders (especially from the south), bribed lorry drivers to smuggle them in or arrived into ports in small boats and fishing vessels. To them, the idea of the American Dream prevailed. But those who finally made it into the country soon found out that the dream was no reality at all.

So surely, this meeting was to further discuss solutions. The six dignitaries took their seats at the conference table.

Greeting them in the meeting room was the suave and well-dressed Robert Gently, the current Attorney General of Maryland. Sixty two years old but looking no older than forty five. Sporting slightly longer hair than was currently in style, wearing an expensive Italian suit and silk tie. Failing him in his image however, was the seemingly constant desire to fiddle with his spectacles or he could often be seen checking his suit for dust or fluff and ready to flick it off if he thought he'd found any.

Within 20 minutes of their arrival, the six dignitaries sat around the large oval table in their plush leather conference chairs. Their attention was drawn to a giant wall-mounted plasma screen which displayed the face of the White House Chief of Staff, Jeremy Weinstein, not a sign on his bulbous middle-aged face that gave away the enormity of the forthcoming conference. Though presently a still, frozen image, the message was intentionally paused and set up so they could press the *play button* at the agreed time. Just two minutes to wait until the 10.00 start. They waited in silence. Coffee in small cups had been served. But nobody had touched a drop. They knew this meeting was impromptu, unscheduled, unexpected. But each had been summoned to attend. Their absence would not have been tolerated.

Jeremy Weinstein's previously static face burst into life.

"Ladies and gentlemen, thank you for attending. And please accept my apologies for not being there in person. I hate leaving pre-recorded messages. But on this occasion, I am given little choice. For as you know, in my role as White House Chief of Staff, I continually have presidential matters to attend to at short notice and I have been asked to participate in an overseas global fuel-supply summit which was called at incredibly short notice. This, in itself, could be a disaster if we don't handle it properly but as you all know we have something far more pressing to deal with, too."

"Isn't that the understatement to end them all?" muttered Alvin Rushmoor the rather anaemic looking and somewhat diminutive Deputy Agricultural Minister under his breath and scratching his salt-and-pepper goatee before Weinstein continued.

"As we witness nationwide fuel supply rationing, we witness severe global food supply issues, too. Crops for the last five years have been decimated not only by climate changes, but by the almost indestructible Narvonica Beetle and our scientists are still some way off finding a way to combat their heinous powers. They don't seem to target just one type of crop, indiscriminately decimating whatever takes their fancy.

"In short, we cannot feed our own nation. And that's to say nothing of the demands being put upon our own health service, education, the crime epidemic and more."

Alvin Rushmoor was clearly in full agreement. But as the recording had no natural pauses, there would be no time to discuss until the end.

Weinstein continued on. "So, we have a fuel crisis, a seemingly insurmountable food supply enigma, and no damned solutions. Ladies and gentlemen, over the last couple of years we have had a plethora of fruitless meetings, conferences that have done little more than waste time, disaster action plans that have had no solutions whatsoever and scientists with ideas which should exist only in works of science fiction. I am devastated by the lack of progress we are making in finding solutions."

Tabitha Gretson, a young, well-dressed and also highly respected and knowledgeable Chief Scientific Officer was glad the Chief of Staff was merely on the screen and not actually facing her in person. They had had several meetings over the last few months and she was continually in the firing line when it came to justifying why so much time and indeed funding had been wasted trying to find solutions to the insects' destructive might. The Narvonica Beetle continued to win the battles. But it was a worldwide challenge and with just a few exceptions, she was getting little additional support or advice from other countries' scientists.

The Chief of Staff drew the attendees' attention to a chart of figures that now filled the massive screen.

He said, "I'd like you to consider this please. In 1930 the population of the USA was 123 million. Forty years later, in 1970, the figure grew steadily but gradually to 203 million. Another 40 years on, in 2010 the figure was 329 million. For a short period of time, the rate of increase slowed marginally, but now in 2050, another forty years, we are up at 650 million. The sudden leap in numbers would cripple any economy and damage any nation. We have not been immune, sadly. We simply can't look after them all. Food and fuel. Education and social services. Medicines and welfare."

A sarcastic cough from one of the delegates.

All eyes went to Chrissy Newman, The Senior Health Minister who by now had decided to sip her coffee, though only just managing to get her pudgy fingers into the handle. She had finished her first cup and was considering taking another. "It's true," she said, "no resources." She didn't expect the projected image of Weinstein to hesitate and he duly continued unabated.

"Indeed, we simply cannot feed them all. Our hospitals are full. Refugees arrive and put demands upon us that we cannot meet. Except for people who live in cities or large towns and use public transport, you can barely get around, virtually stuck in your own localised community. Our transport infrastructure was breaking in 2030, by 2035 it was held together by a thread and in 2036 you may recall we had to, with the permission of the then Transport Minister, limit the number of automobiles we manufactured. It was an attempt to reduce the overall number being used and hence draining our dwindling gas supplies. At the time, we denied people the right to travel any further than 20 miles without applying for a permit to do so. But so many people broke this rule that we had to back-track on that decision. I've had many a meeting with Mr. Canetti about what his department can do about this.

And, once again, I've another minister with no answers."

Far from looking embarrassed, the youngest member of the group, Frankie Canetti, the said and most recently appointed Transport Minister, simply muttered out loud, "Too many people in the world, if you ask me." It was apparent from his blasé demeanour that he'd expressed this very view before to numerous people. Robert Gently, chairing the meeting, raised an eyebrow toward Canetti. For he knew what was coming next.

As if prompted by this very viewpoint, Weinstein took up the reins on this theme. "We have to consider how the population growth has not only caused some of the issues, but we now, today, have to have serious conversations about how we can re-gain control of it. I've invited Mr. Robert Gently, Maryland's Attorney General to join the group." Gently took off his glasses and laid them on the table in readiness to take control of the next phase of the discussion. "He will take over the rest of the briefing at this time. I will meet with him in person next week to discuss your conclusions and findings."

But finally, the Chief of Staff's recorded message continued to its conclusion without hesitation. He said, "And so, until then, I wish you the best of luck with your discussion. Adieu."

A collective sigh could be heard as the monitor was switched off and the remaining room lights were put back on.

"Thank you, Sir," Robert Gently said as if Jeremy Weinstein could hear him. "So yes indeed, I'm here to take things to the next level. I'm in rather an awkward position, ladies and gentlemen. For I have no ideas yet on the challenges I am about to ask you to take up. But I invite conclusions and findings from what you've just heard." Gently gestured to the group.

"All of this sounds very cloak and dagger, if you ask me." This was the voice of the sixth attendee, General Edwin Bolwell, a mid-fifties man with a handlebar moustache typically portrayed by the stereo-typical Three-Star General one would see in the starring role in the movies. He was due to retire shortly from active duty but was clearly a General both respected by the Senior Interior Minister as well as a known confidante of the President himself.

Gently now stood to address the group. He replaced his glasses to better see the faces. "The Chief of Staff is concerned by our inability to manage an ever-increasing population. He has tasked us to find solutions," he said.

"Are you talking about increasing resources? Improving services? New sources of funding?"

"No, Chrissy. I know you've been asking for all of those solutions to address the challenges your hospitals have been facing, but as we've already seen, the problems have been exacerbated with time. I believe the Minister is actually talking about population control."

"What exactly do you mean by 'control'?" Chrissy Newman demanded. "Birth control to slow the rate of growth?"

"I believe our esteemed Chief of Staff wishes for us to discuss options to reduce the total figure."

"Birth control will do that. If you stop parents having babies, or restrict them to one child per couple, you're essentially reducing two people to one from one generation to another," she offered.

Rushmoor put his opinion of this idea to the group. "Do please bear in mind, this has been tried before. You can simply look at the endeavours of the Chinese culture of the mid 20th century. They ruled that each family could only have one child. And look what happened. If the child born wasn't a boy, they abandoned the child, or even killed them. Thoroughly unethical."

Robert Gently took a great big gulp of a swallow. "The President's Office wants an actual reduction. A direct and almost immediate reduction. No matter how drastic, he wants to see the population level reduced and much faster, too."

Upon hearing this, it was only General Bolwell who did not look instantaneously disgusted.

"We'll take a fifteen minute recess," said Gently.

Chapter 4

In the privacy of another meeting room on the same floor of the building and with the White House Chief of Staff's virtual presentation still foremost in their minds, Frankie Canetti, Transport Minister and Tabitha Gretson, Chief Scientific Officer, were having a heated debate of their own; bordering on an argument.

Gretson asked, "When you said *'there are too many people in this world if you ask me'*, what exactly did you mean by that?"

"It's a turn of phrase. Not to be taken literally," he replied.

She stated, "But that's where the meeting was heading, clearly. The Chief of Staff has asked us to discuss that very enigma. And find a solution. I think he wants us to look beyond birth control or deportation of illegals."

Canetti went to the window, which from the seventh floor, overlooked the nearby river. Boats and barges headed in both directions, minding their own business. He watched them casually as he mulled over her concern. He had carried his coffee cup from the conference room, but the contents were now undrinkable. There was a water cooler in the corner of the room. He wandered over to it and helped himself to a glass. He took a gulp to quench his thirst.

"I've had dealings with Weinstein before," he said. "He's quite possibly the most self-centred and greedy person I've ever had the displeasure to meet," he added in derisory fashion. "And not for one second do I believe that lie about not being able to make it here today for the reason he gave. Nobody would take him seriously but for the fact he holds his current position."

Tabitha Gretson took a peppermint from her handbag. She offered one to her companion but he shook his head politely.

"You shouldn't openly criticise him, Frankie. He's President Kenderrick's best friend from their college days. They've been close for years. Don't forget, it's the President, himself, that selects his Chief of Staff. If you say a bad word to him about the President, it'll get straight back to the top. And if you're asked to do anything by him, well you'd be well advised to just get on with it. No ifs or buts. No questions. And you do it yesterday. Be very, very, careful around Weinstein, Frankie. I can't overstate that even if I tried."

Canetti nodded in agreement. Gretson continued by stating, "That Gently lizard is no better. So watch out for him, too. They say he's got the head of the National Security Agency under his thumb."

"There's another reprehensible man. It seems we are surrounded by them, nowadays," Frankie Canetti remarked.

Tabitha Gretson carried on talking about the NSA head. "Whether or not Gently controls him too, somehow, I couldn't say for sure, but as this meeting is rife with security and secrecy, he could also be drafted in to make sure we behave, if need be."

Canetti agreed, by saying, "Gently will do anything to get what he wants. He cares more for his résumé than he does the welfare and needs of others."

She said in a matter of fact manner, "His vanity level astounds me, too."

Frankie returned to the key topic. He asked, "So, you think this goes beyond birth control, prompting us to think of more draconian measures than compulsory or enforced contraception or rulemaking regarding family size?"

She merely shrugged in response. A gesture that said, *'Your guess is as good as mine'*. And she supported this by saying, "But there's something fishy going on behind the scenes. You mark my words".

"Momentarily going back to the issue of birth control," he said, "I'm not even married yet. I'll find it equally harrowing if I'm told I can't have a family, just to keep the country's numbers down."

She replied, "This meeting is heading somewhere much more disquieting. Somewhere dark and sinister."

"I'm not sure if you got to see the look on the Army General's face. Bolwell. He positively glowed when he heard the outline of the challenge."

"Tell me what you're thinking," she demanded.

"Well, aside from the birth control idea, assuming that's on the table to some degree at least, I can see a discussion about denying terminally ill patients the care they need in order to cull the infirm, and so on. And General Bolwell will say *'hey, let's draw cards. Oh look, Alabama and Seattle were drawn, so we nuke Alabama and poison Seattle's water system'*. I think he's ready to send in the troops with their artillery into random cities, too."

"And you can tell all of this just by one look," she remarked.

"It's just my opinion, sure. But somehow, I can't shake that thought. And that look of his is going to stick with me for a very long time."

Canetti continued pacing about. It was blatantly obvious he was most frustrated with his own personal situation. Had his predecessor not recently retired, it would have been him sitting at the conference table instead. And he cursed his luck to now realise he'd not been brought in to try to discuss possible solutions to the transport and fuel shortage issues. Oh no. he'd been brought in to have some role in discussing ways to address a somewhat exponential population growth. Not his remit at all, he considered.

"You look most uncomfortable, Frankie," she said.

"Understatement of the year, I'd say." He swallowed hard, running a finger into his collared shirt, trying to loosen his necktie just a little. "I'm not cut out for this crap. This has nothing to do with me or my department."

"How you feel about the whole situation, indeed how you feel about any tiny little bit of it means diddly squat to the powers that be. You want to stand in front of them and say, '*Hey, I don't like this*'? What do you think they'll do just because one person out of 650 million says they're against their plans? You think you've got any sway?"

"But it's our job to think this through, raise objections, and to be the concerning voice of the people," he said. "Checks and balances, I guess you'd call it."

"Bullshit. We've been specifically briefed. We have to find solutions, Frankie. If you take a different approach, you'll be seen as an inconvenience they'll need to deal with. And believe me, they'll deal with you swiftly, quietly, and deny all knowledge you were involved. I wouldn't be surprised if you'll conveniently disappear once and for all. They can't have any sort of whistle-blowing. You won't have any chance to go public."

He looked horrified at the very thought.

She added, "In fact, Frankie, every single thing you ever do again will be monitored. We will be watched morning, noon and night. Your life as you know it has just changed."

"I never signed up for this," he snapped.

"None of us did. So, there's no time to be stupid all of a sudden. Wake up and smell the shit storm that you're part of now."

"Whose side are you on, Tabitha?" But she gave him a look only a true friend could give. Her piercing hazel eyes would have been enough to convey her allegiance on their own, but she explained herself nonetheless, so he was under no misconceptions.

"We are going to have to stick together through this," she said, "and I fear we are both going to have more enemies than friends when people discover the role we had in this."

"Our role in what? I still can't see where this is headed."

"Open your eyes, man. We are being asked to find ways to control the population. To reduce it. Nobody, not a single one of us, is going to leave this building a friend of the people. If there was an election tomorrow, we'd not get many votes. I can tell you."

"Unless."

"Unless what?" she asked.

"Any draconian ideas we eventually come up with get credited to other people. And we express our reservations immediately to all and sundry."

The telephone on the desk rang. Gretson picked it up and after listening for a few moments she turned to Frankie and said. "They're expecting us back in. Apparently, some sandwiches have been sent in from a local deli."

"I'm famished."

"And with regards your idea about denial, let's see how it goes. We need to listen to the ideas the group will come up with and how they actually develop."

With no other strategy formed, they started toward the conference room. Frankie re-tightened his necktie, checked his reflection in one of the glass panels next to the office door and steeled himself for what was coming next.

Chapter 5

Not far from the Municipal Centre in Archville, Iowa, Spencer Dexton walked slowly back from the grocery store with sufficient supplies for the week. Most of the shelves were short of essentials, and some were short of the basics. He had become used to that in recent times. But he selected alternatives and hoped they would be okay. He would wait to see what his girlfriend thought when he got home. The very idea of driving his old grey Volvo the half a mile to the shops would be foolhardy. He simply could not afford to buy gas at the best of times. That was even if he could find it. To waste it on such short journeys made no sense. Like everybody, if he found it available, he bought as much as he could, or was allowed to, and kept it in Jerry-cans under lock and key in his garage.

Besides, a relaxed stroll with his groceries in a small trolley would probably help to keep him in shape.

Having just celebrated his fiftieth birthday, so long as it wasn't too strenuous, he liked to do anything he could to keep in trim. Whether it was looking after the lawn, doing any odd jobs around the house, or a couple of miles of gentle jogging such as heading around the nearby Buttler Park Lake. He was secretly pleased with how time had treated him. His full head of jet black buzz-cut hair seemed as full as ever, his physique still trim, muscles as tight as could be expected for somebody now slightly closer to eighty than twenty and he was pleased to see, every time he looked in the mirror, a set of almost perfectly straight white teeth. It was only his crooked nose that he knew he couldn't do much about. But that was the price to pay for having done so much sport in his youth. A football, hurled at pace, had accidentally contacted with him squarely in the face when he was younger and had wholeheartedly contributed to that aspect of his looks.

Marianne Verlano, his girlfriend, had once jokingly remarked that you could tell how attractive a guy was not by how straight one's nose was but checking to see if his nipples didn't protrude any further out than his belly button.

"Nothing attractive about a pot belly," she had remarked.

Consequently, his 50 sit-ups a day helped to ensure he fell into the right category. But joking aside, and with her being almost eleven years his junior, he considered his physique rather than lack of straight nose was quite possibly one of the things that had initially attracted her to him. That, and the fact that he thoroughly doted on her fourteen-year-old daughter, Jenny, who she had borne from a previous relationship. They had been living as a family for six years now and Jenny was happy to call him her father. Marianne could not be any happier. They had discussed marriage but having been hurt by her former partner, hated the idea of having a piece of paper telling her she was burdened by something called marriage.

Spencer arrived home to his duplex with the groceries, unloaded them from the trolley and asked Marianne to stack them in the cooler, cupboards and wherever else she preferred them to be.

This having been done he walked to the back of the building where his home office was located. It wasn't the brightest room in the house but he preferred a dim environment when he undertook his duties as a Freelance Researcher, as glare from the computer screens prevented him from concentrating. Currently, he was working under contract with one of the smaller TV networks on articles relating to innovative farming practices which Iowan farmers have been experimenting with in an effort to combat the current food shortage challenges.

At the time the fuel crisis began, Spencer managed to negotiate a work-from-home arrangement with the network who was only too happy to oblige. All they wanted was the results of the research, and wherever it took place was of no specific interest or concern.

Today was Saturday, so no work today, he decided. But he had been watching out for an e-mail from a journalist who had been helping him review data from crop yields.

There was no such e-mail in his inbox but his on-line news service was flashing an alert at the side of the screen. He clicked the icon. Five minutes later, after having read the daily articles, he was patently aware the country was in a worse mess than usual. There was not let up in the reporting of demonstrations about fuel and the food shortages he had also been researching for the contract he had with the TV broadcaster.

Once again, he spotted reports about the never-ending arguments about health care you could no longer buy even if you did have a pot of money. The government had taken to contributing partially to peoples' healthcare some years before. But it was little more than a token gesture. So people continued to struggle and the daily newspaper articles continued to convey gloomy news.

He also noticed, within the articles, that crime levels continued their spiralling climb. And he was all too aware that they had been sky-rocketing over the last three years.

Migration into the country was, once again, reaching record levels for the year. And it was only April. Eight months to go to beat that particular record.

There was threat of war in Eastern Europe yet again, too.

Chapter 6

For a number of years, The Homeland Chronicle Newspaper, colloquially known as simply *The Chronicle* by its readers, have run a magazine article amongst its news stories. This is an opportunity for the journalists to mingle with the people, to interview random individuals and families in the Midwest states. The Chief Editor, Constance Brighley, wanted to see the personal touch in her journal. She wanted people to read stories that others shared. Mr and Mrs Missouri could read what challenges or good-news stories Mr and Mrs Arkansas had to share, and as readers, they could say, "Hey, dear, this couple are just like us."

Indeed, when a person or couple got selected, they would tell their friends, neighbours, close family, distant relatives and so on that they were going to figure in the next edition of The Chronicle. It helped sell newspapers. And The Chronicle, having run these articles for several years developed over time a form of accolade, a recognition of the personal touch. Far better to read The Chronicle than the big city dailies that were filled with bad news stories all the time.

However, the latest edition of the *'Chronicle Interviews'* was Edition Seventeen. The theme of this particular edition had chief journalist Martindale 'Marty' O'Toole interview a couple in South Dakota regarding the challenges they faced with regards the food and fuel shortages. The interviews, Editions One to Fourteen, were entitled **The Personal Touch** but as stories came in, Brighley realised the personal nature of these stories spoke of continuing and growing hardship and announced in Edition Fifteen that henceforth the stories would focus on austerity, inviting readers to share with each other stories relating to the challenges being faced, cut-backs people were making or even the good news stories that were often hard to spot. Consequently, the newspaper took to calling this *The Austerity Era*, and its very title made no apology in mirroring the difficulties being faced nationwide.

The Chronicle Interviews-
The Austerity Era- Interview Seventeen

Within the half-page spread the interview was transcribed into, the couple spoke of how they had to take to growing their own vegetables, start keeping chickens and goats on their smallholding, and as for fuel, well, they simply had to ration. They, like everybody else, kept emergency stocks in cans, hidden well away from busybodies and those with prying eyes. They went here and there when they had to, but long gone were the days where you'd take a drive just to get out and about.

As interviewer, Marty O'Toole then asked about healthcare, education and family matters and the couple were only too happy to share their woes. Most of what they said made it to print, but some of the colourful language and direct accusations were best left out, Marty thought.

The interview concluded with the couple expressing hope. In the journal, Marty made sure their parting message was conveyed as the concluding printed interview statement.

"We have every faith in our politicians. They'll find a solution very soon, we are sure."

Chapter 7

The meeting resumed with Attorney General Robert Gently, making sure all attendees were back, seated and ready to resume.

"Ladies and gentlemen, we previously agreed to find solutions to the growing population level, which threatens to grow further out of control if we don't do anything about it," Gently announced.

Frankie Canetti talked over him without asking for permission. "Agreed to discuss, certainly, but the very idea of finding ways to reduce the population is not something I can be comfortable with." He tried to avoid her gaze but noticed Tabitha Gretson gave him one of her looks. One that told him to *'Shut up'* for his own good.

"You undoubtedly understand the remit, Sir," Gently pointed out, "then kindly follow this to the best of your ability." Canetti temporarily condescended to the request.

"So, I think we should record any initial ideas, please. No matter how jaundiced they may seem, no matter how radical."

"Does kidnapping the oldest son from each family qualify?"

"Do I detect a reticence to comply with instructions, Mr Canetti?"

"Of course not," he said. "Simply record it as one of your jaundiced ideas. And you never know, Heaven help us all, it may prove to be more viable than it at first seems to be."

"Jolly good. I shall duly record it." He scribbled some notes on his tablet and this was transcribed by the internal software and instantaneously projected in his selected font onto the screen from which earlier on, Jeremy Weinstein had been addressing them all.

Alvin Rushmoor decided to go next. "I hate to say it and I'd rather the idea was not attributed to myself but there is some merit in denying medical assistance to anybody over a certain age. This would accelerate the reduction of one demographic."

"Or utilise the death penalty for more convicts, perhaps," Chrissy Newman suggested to try to keep the flow of ideas going; but with the specific intention of keeping the topic as far from her Health Department as she could. As Health Minister, she didn't truly care to explore premature death by lack of care for the elderly.

But she wanted to convey her primary concern, so she added, "I cannot believe we are discussing killing people." It was her attempt to come to the help of the elderly and infirm.

Alvin Rushmoor joined in too, by stating, "Nor those unfortunate enough in life to have been drawn into criminal activities."

"Why not?" General Bolwell demanded to know. He added, "Getting rid of criminals has a certain attraction and I bring to you one unalienable truth. If you want to reduce the population, you'll have to get rid of them somehow. And, if this means we have to use words like culling or premature death, then so be it."

Canetti interrupted. "*Culling*? *Culling*? I clearly heard the word *killing* just seconds ago. So please don't hide abominations behind rhetoric, diluted vocabulary or military terms. Do please recognise I'm not at all comfortable with this."

"If this is too much for you, Mr. Canetti I can ask the other ministers if we could find a replacement to fill your role."

Under the table, Tabitha Gretson jammed her heel onto the top of Frankie's foot. He briefly met her gaze and remembered their conversation. "No, I'm here, I'm committed, I'll contribute," but he hoped his face hadn't turned the bright shade of red he was convinced it had become. "I just don't want to go through this without expressing my level of discomfort," he exclaimed.

"None of us are at all comfortable, Frankie," Robert Gently contributed. "But we are sadly obliged to take this as far as we may. And so, General, let's cut to the chase, talk to us about the military option."

Bolwell stood to address the group, scanned their faces and very quickly realised that standing to address this group was thoroughly the wrong approach. He duly sat down again. What worked as a briefing method with other military leaders would not be welcomed here. He shuffled in his chair until he looked more relaxed.

Satisfied they were ready, he commenced by stating, "Though you may be disagreeable with the way I shall explain this, I will not be able to avoid terms like *killing*." He glanced at Canetti and Newman in turn to gauge their reaction. He realised he was being given enough leeway to continue. "I can neither avoid terms like *selective execution*, like *death by military means,* or terms like *intentional culling,* no matter how much that sounds like the word *killing.* I would hate, within the confines of this meeting, to be accused of using the term *murder*, please. Because at this time we are merely discussing theoretical ways of how the military could achieve the stated objective. I stand, no I sit, in front of you to try to demonstrate the more direct methods that could be utilised."

Silence from the rest of the group was short-lived. Alvin Rushmoor wanted to get his point across at this time and took full advantage of the General's momentary hesitation. "General, may I demonstrate the impossibility of ideas I know you're harbouring?" he asked.

"How so?"

"By describing visions I am getting from a scenario that I cannot escape from," he replied.

"Be my guest." He thought he was ready for this. He certainly knew what was coming.

"As best I may describe, here goes," Rushmoor offered. "I see the troops going into town, sitting in the back of troop carriers, guns at the ready, flanked by tanks, leaders barking orders from Jeeps, helicopters hovering overhead. Images you only see in disaster movies. They flood from their trucks and slaughter everybody to get the numbers down." He visibly shuddered. "Horrendous images. I shall have nightmares."

"At this time, I haven't heard any other effective ideas."

"Oh, let's not lose all vestiges of sanity here, General. You can't expect troops to go in guns blazing. Your troops simply won't do it. You'd have mutinies, individuals going walkabout," Rushmoor claimed.

"We use the phrases *desertion* or *missing in action*. And we have steps to make sure it cannot happen."

But Rushmoor was not to be distracted. "Walkabout, desertion, missing in action, I don't see a difference. That's just semantics. I see troops facing little girls playing together in gardens, grandmothers reading the newspaper on their verandas, young boys in football kit at games in the parks, being taken away for slaughter. Troops looking into the eyes of their own relatives sometimes, and simply not willing to pull the trigger. I think *walkabout* is exactly the term I'd use."

He had grabbed the attention of the group and so he continued. "We are asked to discuss options but, ladies and gentlemen, in some obscure way we've come to start discussing mass murder. But there must be a plethora of control options that don't include murder." The General may not have wanted to use the term, but Rushmoor didn't shy away from so doing.

There was clear agreement from most of the attendees with regards wanting to get away from this horror story of a scenario.

General Bolwell retorted, "Yes, murder in whatever guise you prefer it were called. We have to at least discuss the effectiveness of how quickly we can halt and indeed reduce population growth. If ten different methods each achieve part of that, then their collective achievements may have a very comparable effect as what would be gained by reducing numbers by more sinister ways."

Robert Gently interjected purely to pacify a growing unease. He adjusted his glasses and asked, "Ms Newman, are you in a position to explore the medical options?" Gently was known never to call anybody Miss, or Mrs. He theorised he could avoid insulting his female colleagues in this way; though judging by the exasperated look on Chrissy Newman's face, he hadn't avoided that at all.

"There's one thing that springs to mind," she said, "Something we could adapt for our own situation."

"Indulge us," asked Gently.

"Some years ago, we trailed ways to tackle the recreational drugs problem the country faces. We considered spiking a sizeable amount of confiscated cocaine with a deleterious substance. One that would introduce sudden illness, the idea being if it lingered on the streets long enough, people would be discouraged to continue taking it. Who would want to make themselves ill when merely trying to have fun? We thought of doing the same with meth amphetamine, or whatever was the current drug of choice. The aim of this was to turn people against taking drugs before they became hardened addicts, or even just regular recreational users."

"And did this work?" Gently asked.

"Only in theory. The practicalities of doing this weren't on our side as it was an issue of scale. The country is huge, the drug problem too. And there are simply too many people around you'd call *users*. Because our initial plan involved a nationwide rollout and the challenges rather too obvious, we debated trying it at a localised level. As a test bed. But it never got the go-ahead."

"One moment please." Bolwell enquired again, "What's this got to do with population control in the USA?"

"You see, if the theory works but the level of commitment wasn't there, we should explore what we could do if we were fully committed to introduce a drug to control the population by use of a similar regime. Introduce a drug that will control births, one presumes. A form of nationwide contraception. Control the population boom at the earliest possible stage."

Now it was time for the Chief Scientific Officer, Tabitha Gretson to interject.

She said, "Ladies and gentlemen, while Chrissy Newman is offering you an idea, in the hope that we can see the benefits of this style of approach, I need to challenge this and explain why what you've just been listening to may not necessarily be very effective, I'm afraid." She looked across the table to the Health Minister and said, "I'm sorry, Chrissy." She nodded her acceptance of what was to come. Both were scientists, after all.

She took a deep breath and started to explain. "You see, cocaine, cannabis, meth, LSD and so on are drugs people choose to take if they so wish. That they may be spiked is by-the-by. I cannot think of any way to make people take a drug they don't want to or selectively administer it anyway."

"Stick it in the water system."

"Impossible, Robert," she almost snapped at the Attorney General. "Oh, believe me, this has been thought about for quite some time with regards other drugs. Anti-viral drugs, immunisations and so on. But it's not at all practical or safe. Anything added to the water supply would affect everybody and everything. Infants, animals, the eco-system; anyone and everything we would ultimately be trying to protect. A dose that's safe for an adult would be consumed by a child. And, well you can work out the ramifications for yourself when it comes to infants."

"What about at a localised level, to see how it went?" Rushmoor asked. "To see if, indeed, everybody were adversely affected. Run it as a test case. A controlled environment. Introduce it to the water tower of some Smallville or back-country Turkeytown?" He was determined not to have his ideas ignored.

Chrissy Newman said, "Logistical issues. You'd possibly be successful in one town, but how would you get away with going from town to town, doing the same thing?"

General Bolwell had, by this time, lost all patience in proceedings. "I've tried to raise a discussion on troop involvement and I've now just sat here listening to scientists telling us a wonderful story that has no relevance to our remit. We got drawn into discussing something we *can't* do. What a waste of time. And unless we are talking about poisoning the water system, birth control drugs don't meet the objective. We've already agreed that will not sufficiently reduce the numbers."

Few could deny the discussion had not taken the group closer to the objective.

Robert Gently stood. He looked at all of them in turn. Lastly, he caught the attention of General Bolwell and said, "General, could I have a word in private, please?" The General nodded.

"As for the rest of you. Take a break. Let's all have an hour. But please, make no telephone calls whilst in this building. I remind you of the need for continued secrecy at this time."

Chapter 8

The State of Oklahoma is riddled with woodlands and forested areas. Hidden in the depths of part of these and just about as far from any town as you could go sat Wolf Janner's cabin. A tiny place for such a big man. Had he built it himself he'd surely have had higher ceilings and wider doors. The small clearing within which it sat was Wolf's domain. His makeshift shooting range, hard standing for a motorhome and his pickup truck, a 20 year old model adorned with a camouflage paint pattern and bumper stickers both front and back that said, "Guns are for more than just fun". On each bumper he also had a sticker showing the silhouette of a wolf's head, baring its teeth.

He had space for cages for his dogs, a woodshed to keep his winter firewood dry, a generator store and space for outdoor cooking and an adjacent seating area adorned the plot. He also had a separate fuel store where he kept cans of gas he had managed to syphon from strangers' cars over the course of time. He wasn't going to suffer the fuel shortage if he could do something about it.

Inside the cabin there were notably few rooms. There was a small cooking area and sink adjacent to a lounge area which, as furniture, utilised the seats from a dismantled Pontiac Firebird he used to own. There were two bedrooms. One he slept in and the other that was filled with camping equipment, hunting gear, a huge well-stocked gun rack, fishing equipment and a wide chest freezer filled with the spoils of his shooting and fishing trips. This included venison, catfish, and chickens and lambs illegally gathered or rustled from suitably faraway farms. In their original plastic bags he kept vegetables grudgingly bought from grocery stores in towns he would frequent rarely.

He did make a regular trip to his favourite tattoo parlour in a nearby town, however. He got his first tattoo at the age of 14 and now, twenty years later rather enjoyed how his chosen artwork had developed, adding to it from time to time. He had become addicted to the tattooist's needle. He also used the trips to peruse the delights of a very good gun shop where he enjoyed looking at the new weapons that were periodically added to their stock as well as new clothing and accessories. On his latest visit he managed to find some new camo clothing that was just big enough for his 6'7" frame and which also gave him enough space to give his muscles room to flex.

Although Wolf Janner could be called a *loner*, he did have a close circle of friends, but few of which lived nearby. He also had many online followers who watched his hunting videos and his wildly right-wing views on who should, and who should not, live in his beloved state of Oklahoma.

His most watched videos could be found on the Dark Web, however. These particular hunt videos were of a completely different nature altogether. Every two months or so he would invite a group of trusted acquaintances, those with equally dark interests, to meet with him at a secret location for the purposes of a highly illegal hunt.

The most recent of these for them was to Utah's Henry Mountains where Wolf had marked a bison with paint that would show up under ultra-violet light. His hunters had to seek, identify and shoot the specific beast to win the prize. There was no cash incentive. Quite the opposite. There was instead a sizeable entry fee for the participants to "D*onate*' as he was inclined to put it. Nor was there a trophy. What was on offer was the accolade where hunters vied for the privilege of knowing it were they who triumphed. Should the killer wish to secure the beast as a trophy, that would be his or her prerogative. But for fear of being caught the hunters typically dispersed as soon as the kill was acknowledged and the winner officially identified. No specific naming of the winner ever occurred on the dark web blogs, of course.

Unfortunately for Wolf, the last hunt was marred by the kill having been witnessed from a distance by a park ranger and getting everybody away safely and securely, with all tracks covered had been achieved, but only just. There had been a massive search but the ranger had had no idea of the number of people involved nor did he have any idea of the identity of any. The local press became involved, then it went national. There was the expected public outcry that somebody had wilfully killed a bison; a protected species. Social Media went red hot with the story for several days but the mystery prevailed. Consequently, Wolf Janner was satisfied that, ultimately, in the grand scheme of its original intention, his clandestine hunt had been a success; and he made a truck load of money in the process, too.

Now, with beer in hand, Wolf sat on the bench seat from his old Pontiac Firebird warming his toes in front of the fireplace and mulled over what he should plan to do next. He looked up at a picture that hung over the mantlepiece which depicted a bounty hunter handing over a captured fugitive to the authorities.

"Should have shot the swine instead," he said out loud as he lifted his can of Blue Ribbon to the picture as if to offer it a toast.

"I'd have shot him. Better still, I'd have had him hunted."

Chapter 9

Robert Gently grabbed his glasses from the table and ushered the General to follow him. They took the stairs one level down to the sixth floor where a series of empty meeting rooms sat idle. It was clear that Gently intended full privacy with no eavesdroppers or disturbances.

He unplugged the telephone which sat at one end of an oval table from its wall socket.

"Robert?" the General enquired of him, gesturing to the action he'd just taken.

"Old habits," Gently said. "It guarantees no calls and anything with a microphone in it with a wire that leads to a wall simply makes me somewhat uncomfortable, Edwin. May I call you Edwin?"

"I prefer Ed. And sure, in private, you can call me Ed but in front of others I'd prefer you use my title."

"Understood."

They sat in chairs identical to those upstairs, facing each other across the table.

"The meeting is going exactly where I expected it to, Ed."

"Which is where, 'exactly'? It doesn't seem to be achieving anything."

"It is for me," he said surprisingly. "It's both going nowhere and, dare I say it, just where I want it to go." This was met by a puzzled expression on the General's face. But giving no time for the General to quiz him on this, he continued by asking a question. "Ed, did you think we, as a group, would actually come up with a solution to reduce, and drastically reduce at that, the country's population by simply asking them to accept better birth control or conveniently forgetting to care for the elderly?"

"Seems a far-fetched goal to me, certainly."

"And what do you think of the choice of attendees?"

"To discuss population control? Bizarre. I can understand scientists, the Health Minister, sure. But the Agriculture Minister and a relatively junior Transport Minister, that's not right. Why are they there?"

Gently was pleased to explain. "One day, when all this is out and the Press have got their claws into it, who do you think I want to take the blame? You and I?"

"So, let me guess. It's all about having scapegoats. The Agriculture Minister, Alvin Rushmoor is blamed for saying '*I can't feed the*', and the Transport Minister gets the blame for saying '*we've got no fuel or heating oil left*'. The scientists, I presume, will be blamed for saying '*the population is out of control*' and the Health Minister for saying '*how could we be expected to cope with the numbers*'?"

"That's almost exactly what we've discussed already."

"We?"

"Ed, please don't think there hasn't been much discussion at a Presidential level already. And Weinstein's the Chief of Staff. He's the legal mastermind behind this. He's summoned Senators, Congressmen; men and women in senior positions gathered around tables for some time discussing this. Jeremy Weinstein has been chairing all these meetings, in person. We've had different scientists in attendance, too. Weinstein has gathered more lawmakers from their offices than you can count."

"And the military angle? Any reason why I've not been involved thus far?" he asked.

"It's only recently become apparent the extent to which you may be needed."

"Tell me more," Bolwell demanded.

"We need to consider numerical facts, Ed." He removed his glasses, laid them on the table and continued by saying, "The Navy and Air Force will have a role at a later time, but nothing like what the Army will be doing for the whole of the duration. So for the time being we'll consider the Army only. How many people are actively serving in the Army, approximately?"

"530,000, I'd say." General Bolwell replied.

"I assume a proportion of these are support roles, mechanics, caterers, admin functions. So, what percentage of those operate weapons?"

"Not far off half. Give or take."

"Thank you. So, is it fair to presume, we have 265,000 armed personnel in the Army? Give or take, to use your own phrase."

"For the purposes of this discussion, I'm prepared to concede this, yes."

Gently rose from his chair, subconsciously tending to any creases in his Italian suit. He fashioned to simply stretch his legs as if he'd been sitting awkwardly but wanting instead to add a touch of drama to what he proposed to talk about next.

He said, "Ed, I want to present a scenario to you, but I'd like you to avoid taking it as a proposal. Merely treat it as a purely theoretical exercise. Because what I will say is not, I repeat *not*, what we will end up doing."

"Sure."

Robert Gently scribbled some numbers down on a piece of paper, performed a bit of mathematics with them and underlined a total figure.

"Let's just say we ask the armed personnel to kill people, to *cull* the population; allowing myself to use that term without reproach. We know from our earlier meeting upstairs, we have a current population of 650 million people. And let's say, for the sake of argument, we need to reduce this by half. That's the culling of 325 million people. That means that each armed soldier would need to kill 1226 people. Furthermore, if we wanted to drop the numbers to, say 25%, they'd face killing over 1800 each.

"Now, forget the ethics of this", he continued, "I ask you if that is even remotely possible?"

"Ludicrous. Even in a war environment a soldier would only be expected to kill a handful of the enemy. And I'm talking the enemy, Robert. You're bringing into the discussion civilians. Those who have done nothing wrong; who don't deserve it as an enemy would. We'd face the situation Alvin Rushmoor was discussing earlier. Soldiers pointing guns at grandmothers, kids, priests, schoolteachers etcetera. It would never happen. And we truly would be facing desertion, on a mass level."

"Agreed."

"And so, the purpose of this is what?"

"To discuss an alternative idea."

"I'm all ears."

"Do you know how many guns exist in the USA per every 100 people?"

"I'm led to believe it's over 100. About 122."

"That's right. So 122 per every 100 people. 1220 for every 1000, and if you do the math fully, we've something like 793 million firearms sitting in cabinets, glove boxes in cars, tucked into the waistband of people's denim trousers. Essentially enough firearms to arm each and every person in this country. Though that would include kids, I'm talking about those who have the capability to pull a trigger."

"An army of people." The General could see where this was headed. "Let me get this straight. You're suggesting we arm everybody and get them to kill each other?"

Gently, who had sat back down some while ago chose the power of sitting there in silence as his answer.

"Never in a million years could I believe you sat with Senators and Congressmen and came up with this plan."

"It's taken some doing, believe me."

"So, you're being serious?"

"This is a very serious situation we face. And you know, full well, we've no other solutions upstairs." He pointed to the ceiling as a gesture meant to convey the meeting that had still not reached its conclusion on the floor above.

"But how could you possibly pass this through law?"

"In 1787, the Constitution and its Articles was written and signed by George Washington et al. The articles have been amended at least twenty-seven times since. The key term here is *amended* or *creating amendments.* Even the Second Amendment which gives people the right to bear arms was an amendment from the original article. Ipso facto, it can be amended again if we so desire it to be. Amending the Second."

"To say what, precisely?"

"Well, it's a subtle change we propose." He coughed. "You see, the theme of the Amendment says people have the right to possess a firearm to use that for the purposes of self-defence. But the exact wording suggests, and I use the word *suggest* loosely, the country needs a militia and how people are key to contributing to the security of the state."

"That's not what it means."

"Not exactly. But this is where our proposed change comes into play. I'll paraphrase the key change as the exact wording escapes me at present." The General sat patiently. "We change the words, *'Right to self-defence'* to *'Right to exercise and operate to comply with official government instructions.'* Oh, forgive my forgetfulness, it also states, *'Operate within a set of pre-determined rules'*".

"I guess you're expecting people to see this as an invitation to get shooting?"

"Essentially, yes. They become the way by which we can achieve the objective."

"You do realise there are plenty of loonies out there? Ones who'll gladly go gun slinging. They'll shoot anybody on sight, and many of them will probably enjoy it, too. Sickos. They've no idea how what they see in the movies differs to what it means to have the kahunas to go shooting in real life."

"I referred to rules a moment ago."

"These rules you refer to. What exactly are they?"

"We say a firearm may be used against up to, but no more than, two other people."

"Two? Why two? That's very specific."

"I'll be coming on to that shortly, if you don't mind."

Bolwell nodded his approval and twiddled the tips of his handlebar moustache. "Against whom will they be targeting?"

"Believe me, this has been debated more than just about any other part of the proposal."

"And the conclusion is?"

"The rules are a set of controls. You couldn't, for instance, just turn the gun on your own family. You can't just run into a school or shopping mall, all guns blazing. The idea of 'two' as mentioned earlier is to add an element of thought, some level of planning, to control impulse."

He could see General Bolwell nodding in general agreement with this particular idea.

Gently also said, "We've mooted the idea that one would have to select different types of people as their targets. No one person from the same family, no more than one elderly person, both sexes must be included, and so on.

"As much as anything else, if we ensure the killers have to think about who they have selected, this slows them down. It's an attempt to avoid bias."

"You'll never get this passed in law," the General tried to point out.

But Robert Gently seemed to have an answer for everything. Momentarily distracted by a bit of fluff that he found on this sleeve, he subconsciously flicked it to the floor, and replied, "In the courtroom, one should never ask a question you don't already know the answer to. And in the Senate, never make a proposal you know won't be passed. To that end, we already have Senators on board. Weinstein has seen to that."

"How exactly?"

"It was a form of self-preservation."

General Bolwell interjected, "You can't tell me the Supreme Court Justices accepted this."

Gently said, "The nine Supreme Court Justices were handled by Weinstein. He's the Chief of Staff and head honcho lawman in this country. And let's just say that even I was less than impressed at his heavy-handed methods to ensure their acceptance."

"You can't coerce anybody into entering into a legal agreement and uphold its legality, against their will. It's called *Capacity of the Parties*."

Gently countered, "It all depends on who did the coercing and how this was carried out. Suffice to say, we now have a full agreement from the Supreme Court."

"And none of them intend to rescind now they aren't having their arm twisted?"

"As I say, Weinstein is a very powerful man."

"I'm not going to mess with him, that's for sure," General Bolwell exclaimed.

Gently looked at his wristwatch. He'd noticed they had been discussing this for almost forty minutes. Having agreed to meet again with the others an hour after leaving them, he was mindful to wrap up this phase of the discussion in time.

But there was still much to cover.

"I'm intrigued. Tell me more about swaying those pig-headed Senators, Robert."

"Immunity, Ed. Exemption. Or the threat of this being denied them or their families." He had become accustomed to seeing a form of realisation dawn on the faces of his audience. General Bolwell was no different, for he too showed understanding in his facial expressions.

Senators had literally turned pale at the very suggestion they may otherwise not have been exempt from a rule that could have them facing a gun-wielding stranger in the street. One Congressman had to be given medical treatment, convinced, and maybe rightly so, he was having a heart attack. Even the thick-skinned General Bolwell showed momentary discomfort given that his own family could be at risk.

Gently continued explaining, "We've privately discussed this with each and every Senator in the House. They hate the idea, of course, but are resigned to knowing it'll be proposed nonetheless. Do you know how easy it was for us to get them to choose self-preservation, Ed?"

The General showed he clearly could.

Gently added, "They'd sell their own souls to the Devil. I'm certain of it. They folded like a house of cards."

"Explain how this exemption works."

"There are three types of exemption, or immunity. I'll explain the first two, public exemption and private exemption first; and the third type thereafter. Firstly, we will look at private exemption. This is where exemption is granted to key individuals. And their families. The President is exempt, naturally, as would be the First Lady and their two children. We are still debating how wide his family tree gains exemption. Brothers, sisters, cousins, etc. It's a bit complex. How far one would have to go down a family line, and there's an argument that says we are all related to one another if you analyse everybody's family tree in minutiae."

General Bolwell was obviously following this and so Gently continued.

"Exemption has to be given to you, let's say, because of your military role not only here in this development, but because of your former service to the country. And your wife, too. But at some point, we may not include your sister, your niece and so on."

At this, the General tried to say something, but Gently would not let him talk.

"Surgeons, judges, district attorneys, public-facing police personnel and similar roles would gain a form of exemption. Senators who are willing to agree, to be on our side, will be added, too. But not those who oppose it."

"You sly son-of-a-bitch."

"Hence the subtle arm twisting. However, here's the cruncher. If we grant exemption, we have to deny exemption too."

"Deny?"

"Oh sure, we have to demonstrate we don't grant this form of immunity for frivolous or shallow reasons. Doing a good deed, being a great schoolteacher or running a charity doesn't gain immunity. And the Senators are all too aware of that little bombshell. It's a self-preservation thing. If we can be sure of just one little thing, it's obvious the Senators are a self-centred bunch of misfits, they truly are. The result of which is they're almost all on our side. It was like taking candy from a baby.

"Public immunity next," he announced. "Firstly, I'll explain age as this matters to qualify for immunity. The discussion has been contested regarding maximum age and I think the consensus will be not to have a threshold for maximum age but trying to decide the youngest age has met with a good deal of internal hostility, understandably. Presently, there is a discussion, not finalised yet, on including boys as young as ten, or girls from thirteen upwards to participate."

"Ten years old? My goodness...," but he was interrupted again.

Gently stated, "But let's discuss those who will be expected to participate. Though it may help work toward the population reduction objective quicker if they go on shooting forever, which we cannot possibly have happen for obvious reasons, if somebody has killed two others, we will deem him or her to have reached the capacity level. And they gain immunity from being killed themselves. We've a plan to ask the scientists to develop some sort of electronic tagging system people who have made their kills can use. It'll indicate when people have gained an immunity."

"But if somebody shoots one of these people by mistake?" asked Bolwell.

"Got that covered. That will be deemed to be illegal and the normal repercussions remain in place."

"By repercussions, I can only presume you mean some form of imprisonment?" Gently answered this with a raised eyebrow and disparaging look.

Bolwell was taken aback. "Oh, holy smokes, you mean execution." Clearly he did. But General Bolwell regained his cool and instead he asked, "How will people get their tags?"

"Killings will have to be supported with evidence. Video footage, for instance, or if witnessed by an exempt party. Photographic evidence may be accepted. We'll thrash out the details in due course. The tags will be issued by authorised people based at multiple locations within each State. Some will be in major cities, others in the larger towns, perhaps at banks. Security of this system will need to be of paramount importance to us."

"You've thought of everything already, so it seems. You've got a plan, you've got the law on your side somehow; you've got a team of scapegoats unknowingly about to take the blame in the eyes of the press and public. Do you have a timeline for this? And how are you going to announce it?"

"In terms of a timeline, it'll be in place within eight months from now. The public will get about three months' notice. And what they'll do in that time is anybody's guess. We've already tried to analyse their behaviour. We've concluded there will be a run on guns and ammo, a stockpiling of food and water by those who will think that hiding away would work."

"Will it?"

"Ultimately, no," Robert Gently exclaimed, "We can categorically state the data shows that hiding away simply prolongs the period of time this will all last."

"I know some who will try. I've come across some yellow-bellied cowards in my army days, I can tell you."

"We'll see."

Gently subconsciously took a look around, to make sure the door was still closed and they were still talking in private.

He continued, "Only time will tell what anybody actually does. Nonetheless, we have to forewarn the public of the change to the Second Amendment so they can decide for themselves how it will affect them. In terms of announcement, no. We have no specific plan at this precise time, although it's being worked upon."

"Just one more thing, Robert. What's my role in this, am I to be a scapegoat, too?"

"Your place within this, which brings with it the third type of immunity to you, your team and anybody involved in the role, will be the role of enforcement, as well as tag security and perhaps issuing them too."

Chapter 10

In 2036, the United States, facing an ever-growing transport dilemma, needed to take radical action. Domestic fuel supply was drying up and efforts to find new oil fields were not being successful. Middle east supply was being withheld by their own countries who were starting to realise the obvious issue if they gave all their own fuel to other countries. Especially, the gas-guzzling Americans.

The POTUS of the day, President Hofferson, exercised an Executive Order to introduce a new form of law, calling this a National Citizens Compliance Order (NCCO). In essence, this decrees that anything the government decides should go in an order such as this must be complied with by every USA citizen. No exceptions.

Within this particular NCCO, he decreed that in any family, there could only be one fuel-consuming automobile.

There was, of course, a public outcry. There were demonstrations. People initially refused to give up the second car, arguing that, '*I work in that direction, and my wife takes the kids to school the other way. We need both cars*', or '*My second car is a classic Buick, I should be allowed to keep to this for casual use*', or 'I'm *self-employed, my van is used most of the time, but at weekends I want to take the family places*'; valid arguments, one and all, but ignored by Hofferson and the Supreme Court.

There was also a massive march through the streets of Detroit by the anti-oil do-gooders. They were delighted at the news. The march did not last long as physical violence ensued and the police disbanded their march with help from army personnel.

But the concept of the National Citizens Compliance Order (NCCO) was born. Though exercised for the first time in 2036, it was not exercised again until 14 years later. Now, in 2050, a second issue of it was about to occur.

Chapter 11

Understandably, when what was to become known as *The Announcement* was made, nobody took it seriously initially. Nobody wanted to believe it. Nobody could. Most people thought it a sick practical joke made in some dingy attic by some computer hackers who had created a form of Artificial Intelligence video. But it looked and sounded so real and was being presented as a National Citizens Compliance Order.

The citizens hated the term almost as much as they hated the concept, and so it became known simply as the NCCO or a National Order.

Here was the Speaker of the House of Representatives standing next to the Vice President, in his role of President of the Senate; two people who rarely got on either in public or in private. Yet here were both. Working as one. They took their turns explaining certain aspects of the National Order.

Indeed, *The Announcement* was presented with gravitas and a sombreness that conveyed just about everything that the dystopian nation had become. And, what's more, it seemed to take place from the Oval Office, after which time both men left, flanked by their individual entourages of military personnel and climbed into two Navy helicopters which took off from the White House grounds carrying each to their own chosen destination. This was witnessed by many.

Yet there were so many confusing terms and phrases being used by both men. Ones which raised obvious questions.

"...*freedom to use any kept weapons or firearms*..." Did this mean you could shoot without needing cause to do so?

"...*objective to use arms twice successfully*..." What constitutes success, what am I being asked to do, exactly?

"...*impunity after use*..." Would I avoid punishment?

"...*mandatory achievement of the objective*..." What would be a punishment if one chose not to comply?

"...*a successful Amendment of the Second*..." Surely, by this, they've inferred the Second Amendment has been changed.

"...*freedom to use*..." That's a repeat message, surely?

"...*so may God go with you at this difficult time*..." How dare they insult us by suggesting this is acceptable in the eyes of the Good Lord?

"...*the timeframe is to be eleven weeks from now that action should commence*..." Are we supposed to be ready in just eleven weeks, and when will it all be over?

In the absence of any ability to quiz either man about this new National Order and with just about every State Senator or Congressman being suddenly unavailable for comment, verifying what had been conveyed became of utmost importance. The urgency to do so trumped all other activities.

Analysts pored over the film footage and soon realised the footage was real. A conclusion not solely based upon what they studied, but by the actions that would transpire afterwards and the speed at which they would ultimately occur. Nobody could have anticipated the efficacy and voracity of what the government and army would do next.

The Press went ballistic, attempting to find somebody to talk with. A multitude of unsuccessful phone calls, government offices were forcibly entered, favours were offered or called in, they even attempted to barricade the White House gates until answers were forthcoming, but they were no match for the security services who quickly moved them along.

Church leaders assured their parishioners that this was all some form of sick or macabre mistake that would be cleared up soon. Little did they know at this time that was ultimately not to be the case.

Eventually, the Press were promised, by way of a series of telephone calls, that they would have access to "T*hose in authority*' in due course. Yet in the days that followed, the Press were simply informed in the form of a stream of e-mailed documents of the necessary facts, details, schedules, objectives, rules and controls that they were to broadcast verbatim to their audiences.

In essence, they were all required to convey these rules:

- Adults of 18 years and over must kill two people.
- Kills must be different sexes and different ages by at least 10 years.
- Children- boys 10+ and girls 13+ must kill one person.

- Boys younger than 10 and girls younger than 13 are immune from being killed.
- Video or photographic evidence must be obtained.
- Comply with the above to gain immunity.
- Failure to comply with this NCCO will result in the strictest punishment.

The Press's ongoing attempts to quiz the decision-makers were continually met with a standard response.

One that demanded, "Convey what we tell you at this time, word for word, and in due course you will have the opportunity to take part in further discussions and interviews." As it transpired, the opportunity for said discussions and interviews did not materialise.

Chapter 12

At much the same time that *The Announcement* was being made, Spencer Dexton, Marianne and Jenny were driving from Iowa to Steerwagon Falls, Oklahoma, a journey due South of their home, to visit Marianne's aging parents, Bruce and Irene Verlano. In the past they would make the journey every month, but as obtaining fuel started to become difficult the trips became less frequent; every two to three months. As the problem exacerbated this became even less frequent. This trip was special.

They intended spending a long weekend there to help them celebrate their 40th wedding anniversary. All journeys were a difficult decision to make due to the transport challenges. Spencer hoped to find fuel on the way. It may be rationed, but there should be some, he thought. But, just to be safe, he carried a large Jerry can and Marianne's father assured them he had plenty of supply in containers he kept in his garage, for their eventual return journey.

Spencer and Marianne were oblivious to *The Announcement* being made at the time it came out. They were literally on the road in a car with a poor quality radio which he rarely, if ever, switched on. Besides, even if he had heard the news at home, they would have travelled to Marianne's parents anyway. That would have been his number one priority. To get the family together, to be with them, to deal with this all together. Furthermore, he was not a gun owner and had he been one, he would not have taken it with him on such a trip in any case.

Upon arrival in Oklahoma, at Bruce and Irene's bungalow, they were warmly welcomed and Jenny was about as excited as she could be and received two years' worth of hugs and kisses as it had been a long time since she last saw her grandparents.

During the afternoon, Irene was noticeably upset about something and was clearly keeping something to herself. She had agreed with Bruce that there would be a certain way and time to explain something they knew about which, quite obviously, neither Spencer not Marianne knew anything about. They planned to wait until later.

Yet before the opportunity arose, at one point during the day, Marianne asked her mother what was wrong.

She said, "Mum, you're not yourself today."

"There's something we have to talk to you about, darling. But your father will explain later," Irene told her daughter.

"What is it? I have to know."

"Not now, darling. We are going to wait until Jenny has gone to bed. It's adult stuff and she may get upset." She was clearly understating something of great import, but it was also clear that she would say no more about it now.

Chapter 13

The Announcement caused a panic. Not only in what it meant to people and what they had to do, but there was a defined time frame by which people had to prepare. Eleven weeks had been announced, after which all hell would break loose. That would not be long at all, not nearly enough.

In the early days, there was a lot of speculation, discussion, debate, doubt, false bravado and despair.

Moreso, there was an ongoing hope that something must be wrong. Perhaps there was a national misunderstanding of what the government meant to do or say.

Everybody was glued to their TV sets with the hope, with an expectation almost, that somebody would come on and say: "Sorry, ladies and gentlemen, the announcement of a National Order was a government exercise to see how people would respond in a disaster scenario." But this was neither a scenario nor was it something the government wanted to discuss.

That was until the Press broke through the seemingly impenetrable wall of government silence.

In a bar in downtown Raleigh, North Carolina, a member of the press, Jasper Conningbridge, was having a drink and snacks with some friends and across the room he recognised the unmistakeable Attorney General of Maryland, Robert Gently, sitting at a table with somebody he did not recognise. He excused himself for a few minutes with his friends and sidled over to an empty table within earshot.

Gently was seemingly very agitated.

"Robert, you have to relax," his companion encouraged.

"How the fuck can I relax when that idiot Canetti is still on the scene?"

"Canetti being who, exactly?"

"He's the fuckwit who came up with this whole scheme. And he's only some junior transport minister. Moaning about how people are using too much fuel which the country's running dry of."

"You mean the mastermind behind the new National Order and its *Announcement*, is nothing more than some junior transport minister?"

"T*he Objective* part of the National Order, yes. The whole plan to get people to kill each other, yeah. That's a hundred percent Canetti. Apparently, he thought up the whole scheme as part of a wager with some friends of his."

Gently's companion looked on aghast, as the remainder of the story was laid out.

"*The Announcement* is simply that, an announcement and a manner to convey the message." He kept his voice down, but Conningbridge, even with his back to the two, was able to take in every word.

"One sick son of a bitch, he sounds like to me."

"That's not the half of it," stated Gently, in as genuine a tone as he could muster.

"There's more?"

"Oh, boy, yeah." Gently, as he was prone to doing, flicked an invisible bit of fluff from the sleeve of his designer jacket. "He refuses to talk with anybody now his idea's being put in place. He claims he has had nothing to do with it, but I know secretly he's laughing inside."

"And where is he now?"

"Gone into hiding somewhere near Pittsburgh, I think."

"Why Pittsburgh?"

"That's where he lives. Two blocks from the theatre, in his big fancy Colonial house with his pathetic little red Mazda sitting on the drive."

"You look so agitated. Can I get you another drink?"

"No. But thanks. I just think I need some fresh air. I think I'll head home."

He stood, shook the non-existent creases from his slacks and headed toward the exit.

Though he didn't make it obvious, he checked Conningbridge's reflection in the tall window next to the exit door. It was obvious Conningbridge had taken in every word.

He left the bar, pulling his jacket around him. The door swung closed by itself. As he rounded the corner of the street, he allowed himself one great big smile which nobody saw.

Part Two
The Emotional Rollercoaster

Chapter 14

Chief Editor, Constance Brighley, of The Homeland Chronicle was still managing to run her publication during the early days following *The Announcement*. The stress of it all made her feel at least 10 years older than the thirty-eight years she had already seen. She even thought she had noticed the first vestiges of grey hair coming through her long-flowing strawberry-blonde hair. She initially doubted there would be either the need for her low-level reporting nor a market for a publication that would normally concentrate on community matters with no importance other than at a local level. But feedback she received from her readers encouraged her to continue regardless. For the time being at least.

With some effort and careful persuasion, she managed to get most of her reporters to regularly give her something she could use. Something to share with her readers. Nonetheless, the printed paper, like its stories therein, was predictably thin on substance.

Yet somehow, the publication with its regular articles, advertisements, product reviews, sports stories and other familiar features manged to run for just a short time during the period people were making their preparations until the killings started. At that moment in time and, unsurprisingly without any formal notice to the readers, The Chronicle suspended its issue and distribution.

The time it was out of print would pass painfully slowly but the day would nonetheless come when it's rebirth could be celebrated.

Though the killing atrocities would shortly commence, a few months later, Constance would eventually run a supplementary edition, comprising of just a couple of pages. Its intention was to do little more than announce its impending return. If one had the ability to look into the future she would eventually be spotted distributing enough copies to get the word around that she was back in business. She would target some of her larger known outlets in the Midwest states. She would one day be seen personally dropping them off at distribution centres, key news vendors, and eventually gain agreement from a chain of superstores that allowed her to place copies in all of their stores. They, too, were there for the people, so they would later claim, and be delighted to offer an additional service for the benefit of the communities they served.

Further in the future, word would soon spread, and her newspaper start to flourish once again, albeit by a smaller base of readers. Sadly, many of her former clients will have been prematurely taken by the NCCO atrocities. But, as she would find out, people would want to know what was going on now that they had somehow survived. They looked forward to sharing their stories.

Though she could not have envisaged it any earlier, a decision she eventually took to making was to rename the interview editions. The **Austerity Era** would become a misnomer as would the previously adopted interview numbering system which had to start afresh. The new interviews would commence with '**Interview One**' under the new banner '**Post-Disaster Era**'.

One such interview that would be published after the killing spree had concluded is previewed below.

The Chronicle Interviews-
Post-Disaster Era- Interview One

"I have with me here, Bradley from Fort Dodge, near Des Moines, Iowa. Good morning, Bradley."

"Hi Marty, great to have you here with me. Welcome to Fort Dodge."

"A pleasure to be here, Bradley."

"Hey, just "Brad", okay?"

"Fine by me, Brad." Martindale O'Toole smiled his big toothy grin at his latest interviewee. "Are you ready to begin?"

"Ready and rearin' to go. We are talking about the early days, I believe, the days before all the shit happened, yeah?"

"Yes, that's right."

"And I'm the first, you say?" asked the interviewee.

"The first of many, Brad. We intend to conduct lots of little chats with people just like you. Build up a great picture. Like an inquest, you could say. I enjoy meeting people who have survived the many weeks of that awful ordeal, those of us who struggled through the relentless turmoil, who witnessed atrocities none of us were prepared to face and who continue to live with the hardships that continue today, of course. But today, we're going to discuss just what you and your family thought just after you heard about *The Announcement*."

"I understand."

"I have to extend my sympathies to you, Brad, for you and I both lost members of our families in the shocking events that followed, so I think you're being very brave to have me here with you. I hope you'll cope with this horrid reminder of how things were."

"Marty, I'm simply going to have to move on with my life. And your newspaper will help me. I'm sure of it."

"Let's hope so."

"How do I start, Marty?"

"I'm going to have to ask you to concentrate solely on the days after *The Announcement*. Even though I know much about your full story, it's how the newspaper is going to publish our collective memoirs. Lots of short stories from lots of different people. So, let's start with what could be the hardest question of all to answer. What was your initial response to hearing the government saying we have to go out killing other people?"

"A joke. It had to be a joke, and a sick one at that."

"That was a common response."

"My wife and I, bless her, were in a shopping mall. With friends," he said. "We heard this on the big screen T.V. that had been set up outside a big electrical appliance store. Went over to see what was goin' on. Thought it was some sci-fi show. You know, the ones with that supernatural stories guy telling stories you had to guess if they were true or false."

"There's quite a few shows like that," Marty claimed.

"Well, a great big crowd had gathered by then. And then this scientist or government guy in a suit and tie started telling us what they called *The Rules*. 'Rules', like it was something we had to do. Compulsory shit. Oh, excuse my language."

"Not to worry, Brad, I edit the interviews before print. You can say what you want and how you want to say it, in front of me," he stated.

"I carried on believing it was fake until they said you had to kill two people if you're over 18 years old and if you're 10 to 18, you only had to kill one. 13 for girls. And no maximum age, either. Like it didn't matter if you were 90 or more."

"This surprised everybody."

Brad continued. "As people heard this there was some clamourin' goin' on, I can tell 'ya. Swearing, cussing, shouting. You know. Denial. Some guy told the store keeper he was a sick dude by running a recording onto the screen just to draw attention to his shop. But it soon became apparent, he had nothing to do with it."

"So, what did you think or do next?"

Brad said, "I was dumb-struck. Had nothing to say. I even thought all the blood had left my body. I was cold, clammy. Sweating at the same time. Then there was a conversation going on between two guys near me about them both having 13-year-old girls. What were they supposed to do?"

"That was the biggest surprise to me, too, I guess, Brad. Asking kids to participate, as well." But Marty didn't want to interrupt Bradley too much, so encouraged him to carry on.

"10 and 13 respectively. Couldn't believe it. My kids are a bit more grown up. 19 and 21. And stupidly, I didn't think of them at all for a few minutes while these two guys were sayin' this and sayin' that. Claiming they'll argue, appeal or do nothing; refuse to play along."

"But from what you're telling me, this suggests people were soon accepting it as real, though. Not a story at all, anymore," said Marty.

"Oh, there was plenty of denial, but people soon started talking like it was real. '*What if*' this and '*what if*' that. People were on their phones. Everywhere you fucking looked. Hollerin' into their phones. Super loud, like. Oh, I'm sorry, I swore."

"No problem."

"And still the biggest question was '*why?*'"

"Thanks for the insight into the initial response, Brad. So, what were people saying about the 'why' part of it all?"

"Well, that scientist guy in the suit told us why. He said there were simply too many people and it had to change. But killing people?"

"Crazy, huh?" O'Toole muttered as a prompt.

"So, I got to thinking we should just send back all the immigrants. The Army could surely round them all up into great big camps in Texas, New Mexico, Arizona or California and get them back over the border. If you can't prove you're American, get out. Reduce the population that way. Best way I can think of. There's got to be five million from Europe and Africa, too. I'm guessing, of course. And countless more South Americans, as well. And what about them?"

"But Brad, we know the Americans tried to tell the Mexicans this."

"And the Mexican people, themselves, realised the safest place was back where they came from. I watched plenty of them on the T.V. trying to get back south. Cross the border to escape USA while they could and the there was much confusion when they couldn't."

"Why not?"

"Well, the Mexicans closed their own doors. They said they had no space for them anymore. I mean, how sick is that?"

"You're referring to a border closure?" the interviewer asked.

"Damn right I am. The Mexes shut the crossings and said, '*No way José, you can't come back now you is there*'." Brad tried to mimic a Mexican accent.

"So what did the USA do next, any ideas?"

"Only what you hear from other people."

"I'd like to hear what you heard, Brad."

"Oh, this and that about the USA stopping all aid to Mexico if they didn't re-open the border. I think there was a threat that our army would simply transport them across the Rio Grande in army waggons, or boats, or whatever."

"I think I'll have to avoid adding this into your interview when I write it up for The Chronicle, Brad, but it's interesting to hear what you heard and thought nonetheless. So, thank you."

"No problem."

"Let's get back to you and your own story."

"Uh huh," he nodded.

"And at what time in all of this did you start thinking that you'd be having to do it, too?" asked Marty.

"A lot damn later than you'd have thought. I simply can't say why that didn't cross my mind much earlier than it did. Perhaps it was a denial thing. Or perhaps I was still hopin' it was all a big hoax."

"When it dawned on you that it was for real?"

"I've got a gun- That was my first thought. I've got a cellar with a big lock- That was my second."

"And your family?"

"My two boys don't live at home anymore. The youngest, Karson, lives close and, boy, can he handle himself. So can my wife; she's not to be messed with, or so I thought." Marty knew she had been killed in the NCCO atrocities and thought Bradley may stall at this point and struggle to carry on. But he need not have worried. "I was more worried for the oldest, Liam. He's not a tough cookie. Oh, man, he's a wet blanket!"

"So, in the days that followed, what did you tell them?"

"Didn't get the chance. Karson told *me* what we needed to do. At first, I disagreed, but what he was telling me made so much sense, really."

"What was that, exactly?" asked Marty.

"He told me to befriend my neighbour, get his trust. And as soon as we are told to start the killing by our government, get Mum to go round there with my Glock and make her two kills, get her '*Two-person*' target. And Karson said I had to go next door the other way and do the same."

"Brutal."

"It's not as if we'd make enemies. No retribution."

"But, even so, Brad. That's barbaric."

"Is it? Why should I wander the streets looking for somebody who deserves it? What would I look for? Somebody with a tattoo that says, '*I was a former mass murderer*' or a guy with a tee-shirt printed with the message, '*I molest children in my spare time*'?"

"So, there was no hesitation on what you had to do?"

"Not much, no. Except later on I realised my plan had a slight flaw. We found out I had to pick a younger person and an older person, a guy or a boy and a woman or a girl. We were told *The Rules* made us choose different types of people and no kids under 13. Well, any 10-year-old looks like any 15-year-old to me, so I decided to avoid picking a real youngster. In case I got it wrong and I got punished."

"So, what about your oldest boy? Liam?"

"Karson agreed, Liam's a wimp. I tried to have a conversation with him about what we could do to get him involved. We agreed Liam would never hold a gun. He'd probably shoot himself or break his face with the recoil as he squinted along the sights just to see if he was shooting straight. Karson suggested he gets some poison and simply slip it into two people's drinks somewhere. That'll get him his two kills without having to lift a gun."

"And all these thoughts were ones you had early on after hearing *The Announcement*?"

"I guess, yeah. Cos *The Rules* were included in *The Announcement*."

"Yes, I suppose they were," Brad said.

"And finally, Brad, what were your thoughts on this including girls of as young as 13?"

"Thinking of that hurt. Still does, all this time later. Even now that it's all over. I was reminded of those two guys at the mall. In all the conversations I've had since, all the guesses go towards the idea that if we took girls just before their child-bearing age, that helps keep the population down for part of the future."

"So you think there was something to do with preventing new births?"

"Ask the doctors, Marty. I can't say for sure. And I'm not even sure it would delay anything all that much. My version of the maths says that if you remove a five year age group, it'll delay growth by five years. 'Ain't that right? I dunno."

"I'm no mathematician nor scientist either, so couldn't possibly comment." Marty replied.

"I can't imagine what it would be like for a parent to see his 13 year old girl killed by a complete stranger on the street."

And in the first time in his journalism career, Martindale 'Marty' O'Toole, had to wipe a tear away that had fallen onto his own writing pad.

———————————

Though The Homeland Chronicle would ultimately fire itself back into life, with interviews such as this, that would be several weeks in the future. As things currently stood, the killings had yet to start.

Chapter 15

Wolf Janner sat on a makeshift wooden bench at the top of the stoop to his cabin. Sitting opposite him, each on an old beer crate, were two of his friends. At the foot of the stairs heat from coals scattered inside an old oil drum was barbecuing a couple of wild rabbits, the occasional ember dancing its way just above the wire mesh on which the rabbits sizzled.

"That was a poor day's hunt today, Wolf," remarked Steevo; real name Steve Baxter. "Was hoping we could have nabbed us a deer."

"It goes like that, sometimes, Steevo," his younger brother Wex; real name Wexley, suggested.

"We've got beer. We've got food. Just shut up 'ya moaning," Wolf laughed.

Steevo enquired of him, "So, what do you reckon on this killing stuff? It's like an order that says *'go out shooting, you won't get in trouble'*. Can't believe it!"

"I think all my birthdays have come at once."

"Wolf?"

"We kill our two easy. Right?"

"Suppose so," Steevo responded.

Wolf continued. "First, I'm going after Mitch Spooter at the auto body shop. Having the cheek to want to charge me $290 for a job that would take him an hour. And I'm shaping to take out my old school teacher. Mrs Willis. She made me feel like shit when I was her student. Every fucking day. *You'll never amount to anything, you'll never grow up, you'll never achieve anything, you'll be a drop out',"* he mimicked her in the most patronising tone he could muster.

"She still around?" Steevo asked.

"Yep. Saw her last time I was in town. Bitch saw me, crossed the pavement just to avoid me. She don't live on that side of the street. Did it on purpose."

"And that'll make your birthday special?"

"You misunderstand. You see, once we've all got our kills, we sell hunts to them rich city slicker types and people who can't get their kills. Those who don't know who's still a valid target. And those who want the sport of it. And people who always wanted to do a hunt but never got started. We teach 'em."

"I see."

"We set up people hunts. We research people we can kill and we set 'em up as the target. We sell the hunt to our followers."

"Suppose we kill somebody we shouldn't?" asked Wex.

"We walk away. Hide like we always do after a kill. Talk on the dark web. Announce the winner later on."

"But it'll be a guy, not a buffalo or a deer like normal."

"Don't care one little bit. There's going to be enough killing going on for the authorities to deal with. They won't spot what we are doing. No chance. Oh, this is going to be so much fun."

Chapter 16

It was, by now, very late into the evening and Bruce and Irene Verlano asked Marianne and Spencer to join them at the dining table as they had to talk. Marianne already knew something was amiss but did not yet know what. Bruce had changed from his corduroy slacks and white button-down shirt and now wore a more casual lumberjack shirt and denim jeans.

Irene was still in her floral knee-length dress. But she had tied her grey hair back into a ponytail.

Bruce said, "There's no way to sugar-coat this, my darlings, so I'm just going to give you the basics and then we'll turn the television on, as it's on every station all the time."

"What? Has there been a disaster, we've declared war, we've..." Spencer started to ask.

Bruce interrupted him, and said, "Time to just listen, son."

"Okay. Sorry."

"Oh, boy. Where to start?" but he realised he was stuttering. '*I'm too old for this*', he mused. "Right, it's like this. The government have gone start raving crazy. They've lost control. They truly have. I just can't believe it. Not sure what's going to happen."

Irene interrupted him. "Sweetheart, you're doing the fandango. You're 69, not 20. Slow down and just tell them."

Bruce took a gulp of water from a tumbler. "They want us to go out killing people. They tell us there's too many of us in the country and they can't cope with us all. They say we have to cut the numbers. By killing each other. It beggars belief. They're also changing the Second Amendment to say you're free to use your guns, so go do it."

Spencer tried to interrupt. He didn't get far before Bruce held up his hand, palm facing him, in a gesture that said '*Stop*'. "They say there's too many people, there's next to no food, no fuel, welfare has crashed, we're inundated with migrants, transport links have all but failed, and other stuff they say they can't deal with."

"That's just bad management. They'll get voted out. An emergency election and get a regime in that will take over and manage things."

"No, son. This is a multi-party arrangement," he said. "They announced it yesterday. Surprised you didn't catch it on the radio as you drove down from Iowa."

"We don't listen to the radio, Daddy," Marianne offered.

Spencer exclaimed, "There must be some mistake, Bruce. Irene, he must be getting this all wrong." He looked in her direction and she was full of tears, and by now unable to speak.

Bruce continued. "This sounds like a mistake. Most folks are calling it a sick joke which will surely be explained. But what's on television doesn't come close to an explanation or apology, or whatever you want it to be."

"Turn the T.V. on. I need to see for myself," Spencer said and Marianne nodded in agreement.

For the next two hours they watched reports, interviews, or newsroom guests sharing their opinions and concerns. They watched reporters clamouring at the doors of locked government offices while being filmed doing so by confused cameramen. Celebrities were even drafted into the studios to try to pacify watchers. ABC, Fox News, CBS and CNN now all, for once, shared footage and agreed opinions. By flicking through all of the channels they even accessed overseas broadcasts to see what they were reporting; but their lack of direct access to information merely offered a watered-down version of the situation and was rife with speculation rather than substance. But the long and the short of the situation suggested Bruce Verlano was absolutely correct. America had finally gone mad.

Marianne snuck upstairs to the room Jenny was in to see if she was asleep and was relieved to see that she was. The long journey had tired her out and she seemed comfortable and quiet. Marianne would also have been tucked up in bed by now, but the very idea of getting any sleep having heard this harrowing news was beyond consideration. She closed the panel door making as little sound as possible so as not to disturb her daughter as she left the room, tip-toeing away as silently as she could. There was fresh coffee waiting for her by the time she got back downstairs.

"What does it mean for us?" Irene asked the two men.

"I've no idea," Bruce stated. "Spencer?"

"At the moment my mind is fried. I can't think straight. I try to think of *this*, and my brain goes somewhere else. I try to think of *that*, and I'm then suddenly lost in another thought altogether. So, let's tackle this whole beast one step at a time. Okay?"

"Starting where?"

"By considering the whole gamut of our options, with no detail at this time."

"We run away. Hide," Marianne was quick to suggest.

"I fear this is what most people will try to do. Where would we go, anyway?" Bruce enquired.

"Canada. Great Britain, or anywhere else in Europe. As far from here as possible," she said.

"I'm going to guess we won't be welcome. And how many people will be booking flights, boats etc? I seriously think escape is going to be a closed door. I'm not even sure if there's anywhere in the USA that'll be remote enough, either. A place that would be suitably isolated from other people. And if we stray far from anywhere safe and familiar we are exposing ourselves to danger."

"Danger?" his daughter asked.

"People will consider us as a target, too. If we have to kill each other, I'm a target for someone. You are, too. So is Jenny." At this, Marianne let out a scream.

Somehow in the confusion she hadn't thought of her daughter as a potential target for some killing spree.

There was movement from upstairs. Moments later Jenny appeared at the top of the stairs and called down. "What was that? It woke me up."

"Sorry darling, we had the television on far too loud. Go back to bed."

"But..."

"Don't worry. It was nothing. Just a terrible movie on the television. We've turned it off now. Go back to bed." Partly with a reluctance but also with a glazed look, Jenny went back to her room.

"C'mon let's get back to planning," Spencer prompted.

"Hang on a minute," Bruce demanded. "Hiding away is not the worst idea in the world. We've got a sort of underground cellar or bunker at the back of the garage. It would make a great shelter. We can't access it from the house though, but it's got an entrance half-way down the side of the back yard. By the old Sycamore tree. Almost hidden in the shrubs. I think it was an old storm shelter. The door is like one of those tornado shelter doors. Like a great big sloping hatch."

"How big is it, down there?" Spencer asked.

"About 12 foot square. It's got proper steps that take us down. There's garden tools, boxes of old books, empty plastic drums and just junk in there. There are some shelves, but they could come out easily. From what I remember, it's not at all damp or rotten; though

I haven't been down there in a long time. We could make a proper shelter out of it."

"Electricity? Water? Cooking facilities? Toilet?"

"None of that. But I've got plenty of car and truck batteries in my lockup. I'll charge them up and we can get lighting. We'll store water for as long as we can. And food. We can go back to the house at night, in the dark to use the bathroom."

"That's not a crazy idea, I figure. But how long could you hold out?"

"You say 'you', Spencer. Don't you mean 'we'?" Marianne had a puzzled expression on her face.

"I've been thinking of that whilst your Dad was telling us about the shelter. On the television, they were talking of gaining immunity by making the kills. One of us is going to have to be immune. To be above ground, to get supplies. To keep the house secure. To search for food if it's made available."

"And that'll be you?"

"Who else?" Spencer asked.

Bruce interjected. "Hang on, son. If there's going to be the need for a protector, to look after the family, my hat's in the ring for that one." Irene put a hand on her husband's arm, her long painted fingernails resting on his wrist as if to say 'you're my hero', but at the same time saying 'just calm down, dear'.

"But doesn't this get us down to the nub of the problem?" Spencer asked.

"Which is what?"

"We don't have to discuss hiding if we are prepared to do the killing they want." Spencer said it out loud, because he knew they had to start talking about it sometime. Perhaps now was as good a time as any.

"Are you stark raving crazy?" Marianne asked vociferously.

"Not yet. But give me time with this and I'll probably turn into some crazed lunatic by the end of it all. I'm only trying to get us to discuss all options. Hiding is one. Doing this abominable deed is another. We've got to talk about it. Like it or not."

"Why should we actually discuss killing people? We are surely going to wake up tomorrow and find out it's all that big mistake it has to be. They'll issue an apology on ABC. I just know it," Marianne almost pleaded.

"Doesn't look like it's going to be. So, let's talk about the killing option. We have to even if we don't want to."

"Do we have to talk about it?" Irene asked as she got up from the table to go into the kitchen and get a tablet for a headache that had been creeping up on her and had now hit her full on.

Bruce started the talk, and stated, "I've got a shotgun and a Beretta hand gun. Plenty of ammo. Bought it to defend ourselves. Looks like it'll have another job."

"Having the guns is one thing, but we've got to ask ourselves if we can use them," Irene remarked.

"In self-defence, no problem," Bruce suggested, followed by a pregnant pause. "Never thought about having to use it any other way for any other reason."

"Could you walk up to a stranger and simply point it and shoot?" Spencer decided to ask him.

"I guess that's exactly what I'd have to do."

"But could you?"

"Son, if I knew that would get me in a position to look after Irene, Marianne and Jenny, I'd simply have to."

"Try to imagine walking up to a guy in the street. He turns to face you and you ask, just as an example let's say. "*Hey, sir, do you have change for a dollar?*", and as he's distracted and puts his hand in his pocket you've got just enough time to draw a weapon, point it at his face and pull the trigger. Could you do it?"

"What about you, Irene? Marianne? Could you?" He regretted asking this the moment the words came out of his mouth.

"Steady on, son. Let's just us two be the ones who discuss this right at this time," Bruce said and Spencer encouraged him to continue. "Maybe I'd avoid eye contact. Walk up slowly behind someone. Shoot him without looking at him."

"I guess it's another way of doing it. Or you could stab him in the neck. Hit him over the head with a big lump of iron. A baseball bat. Push somebody out of a tall window. Run..."

"Please Spencer. Can't we talk about something else?" Irene looked apoplectic with distress.

"I'm so sorry. But there's something else we haven't discussed with regards the killing."

"Which is what?" Bruce asked.

"Proof we did it. I saw on the news report one of the commentators said you have to take proof. Evidence you did it. Take it to the authorities to get your immunity ticket. So what do we do? Wear a body camera when we shoot the guy? Film ourselves swinging a baseball bat round some guy's skull?" The vision of doing this was clearly upsetting to all.

Bruce took a stand. "I could do it. I'll do what it takes. I know you'd do the same, Spencer. But what about the girls? What about Jenny, she's over 13? They say she has to kill one person to get her own immunity."

Marianne wrapped her knuckles on the table to grab the attention. "Now listen here, you two alpha males. I'll let Jenny kill me if it assures her future. My daughter's far more precious than I am to myself."

Prompted by this very idea, Irene interrupted her. "Darling, I'm 79 years old. I've had a wonderful life and I'm sure I've not much of it left. Seriously. If one of us is going to let her do that, it'll be me."

Bruce looked across at her in horror. But Irene was not to be stopped. "She can't wander down the street with a gun, looking for a stranger to shoot. What's wrong with you two? No, she can take me instead."

Marianne was about to say something else but Spencer got there first. "If you think it right for Jenny to live the rest of her life with the thought and memory that she killed her own mother or grandmother, you've got another think coming. Can you imagine the psychological mess she'd be in?"

They looked on, aghast at this realisation.

"We need some rest and we'll talk more later. We're making ourselves ill with worry and confusion. I say we get off this topic and think of other options. A fresh start in the morning. What say you, Bruce?"

"That gets my vote, too."

Four hours later, at the crack of dawn, Spencer wandered into the kitchen, having had nothing but a few minutes of broken sleep, to get himself a coffee.

He realised the jug was half full of hot coffee but there was nobody about who would have made it. He guessed Irene had made it and taken a cup back up to her bedroom. As he started pouring himself a cup, he saw movement out in the back yard and spotted Bruce wandering about.

He was still dressed in the very same lumberjack shirt and denims he had had on the evening before. He guessed he hadn't slept much either. He had probably just crashed into one of the green recliners in the living room rather than go up to bed. This morning he was lugging plastic tubs out of the shelter he had previously mentioned. Spencer put on some shoes and ventured outside.

"Hey there, fella," he called. Bruce turned at the sound and waved a greeting. "So what are you up to?"

"If I was going to show you the shelter, I wanted it as empty as I could get it."

"What time did you start?

"About 30 minutes ago."

"In the dark?" asked Spencer.

"I've got a flashlight. And it's pretty light now. Though I do still need it down those steps. It's black as night."

"What have you moved so far?"

"A dozen of these barrels. Which, by the way, we can store water in once they are washed out. Some of the shelves are out, too." Spencer spotted the barrels in the doorway of the open garage. The shelves were all broken up now and were little more than a pile of splintered planks and would never be used as shelves again, it was clear to see.

"What do you need a hand with next?"

During the next hour, the two men had emptied out the shelter.

All that was left were some rags, a couple of old newspapers which had tumbled out of one of the boxes as they were carried up the narrow staircase and a patch of decaying sawdust that had once been in a sack but, the sack having split sometime in the past, had spilled over the floor. With a shovel, a broom and some garbage sacks, and with one man holding the flashlight while the other went to work, the two soon had the room as clear as it could be.

"Is there an air vent shaft?" Spencer enquired.

"There sure used to be."

"Where is it?" Spencer asked. Bruce pointed the beam of light to the corner of the ceiling where a web-covered vent grille could be spotted in the shadows. There was certainly no light coming through it from above ground, thus suggesting it was blocked.

Spencer asked, "I guess it's some sort of tube. How far up does it go?"

"It's only a couple of feet underground to the top of the ceiling."

"Have you got a metal rod? A good stiff one?" In answering the question, Bruce confirmed he had. Two minutes later he had it in his hands and between them they had managed to force it through whatever it was that had blocked the tube to the fresh air above. With a few thrusts and twists, the rod had helped completely clear the last of the blockage.

"We need an extension cord next, Bruce. Let's run it from the garage, feed it down the tube and get some power and light into here. You may have to cut the plug off as it wont fit. Just feed the cable and I'll re-fit the plug after."

"Splendid idea."

By the time the ladies of the house had risen from their equally restless sleep, the two men had converted a dark but dry shelter into something resembling a cosy hideaway. They had managed to find two folding garden chairs and an inspection lamp which they had managed to hang onto a long screw that was already in the wall, now serving as a hook.

"This is bigger than you said it was, Bruce," Spencer remarked.

"Probably because it was always full of clutter. You never get to appreciate the size of anything like this until it's empty."

"I reckon it's about 18 by 18. Plenty of room for us all."

"So, we follow the shelter idea? Hide away for as long as possible?"

"Yes, for the girls. But not for us two. We are going to have to seriously think about going along with this National Order. The NCCO. We have to be able to get about and do what we need to, to protect the family and provide for them."

"How long do you think they'll have to hide away for?"

"As a complete guess, I'd say a year."

"I was hoping for less," Bruce commented.

"Hope for the best and plan for the worst."

"We have to tell Jenny something, Spencer."

"She already knows. Last time I was above ground, I spotted her in the kitchen with Irene and Marianne. They were in a three-way hug and there were a lot of tears going on."

"Heaven help us, son."

"I think Heaven's had to hide away, too."

"What next?" Bruce asked.

"You may think I'm stupid, but I'm going to put my running shoes on and go out jogging."

"You what? At a time like this?"

"Steady on. It's part of a plan. I jog regularly. I've got the kit, the proper running shoes and one of those fancy watches. Anyone who looks at me will think I'm a proper runner; in training for something. I'm not going out to keep fit, this time. I'm going to do a full reconnaissance of the area. See what there is. See what's going on. See how other people are acting. Get an idea of the lay of the land and what, if anything, I could get my hands on for us if we need it."

"Steal, you mean?" asked Bruce.

"Bruce, there's going to be a lot of stealing happening soon, believe me. So, in the meantime, take a good look around the grounds and gather what you may need. Essential stuff only. Don't worry about nice useless stuff like garden furniture, your sit-on-mower etcetera. Just important survival stuff, okay? And you do as good a job as you can to secure and hide it. And while I'm out, I'll have my earpiece in for my phone and I'm going to make some calls to a couple of guys I've been working with recently. Journalists. I'm determined to find out what I can."

"Clever boy, Now I know what my daughter sees in you."

They shared an uncomfortable chuckle, but it was a very welcome respite to the doom and gloom that had started to inflict its disease upon the family.

"It's a quiet town we live in, Spencer. There won't be much trouble even when all the shit hits the fan. Not an area where gangs are going to roam."

"Let's hope not!"

"And it's not as if there are any Redneck loonies out there intending to kill indiscriminately."

Chapter 17

"Ms Gretson. It's Robert Gently calling." Tabitha Gretson listened to his voice coming over the speaker. "Is this line secure, please?"

"The line's secure, Mr Gently, but I just have to switch off the speaker so my secretary can't hear us. Where are you calling from?"

"Not at all far from where you are. I'm in Tupelo for the next few days and I'm hoping we may meet in person. I can travel to St. Louis if necessary, though somewhere in between would work well for me. Share the travel. A couple of hours each, I estimate."

Gretson knew that if the Attorney General of Maryland *suggested* something, you'd do well to go along with it; so, she didn't interrupt him.

He said, "I've a sensitive scientific topic to discuss. An opportunity for you and your department to get your teeth into."

"And this is suited to my position as Chief Scientific Officer, in what way, Sir?"

"That's what I wish to discuss with you. Two specific projects for your specific area of expertise. It's rather more official than something we may do by telephone."

"Then may I perhaps suggest a formal meeting in my office where we can take minutes of the meeting, access our office computer if needed, easy access to other team members, especially if it's an opportunity for my department." She attempted to do anything to avoid a clandestine meeting with who she believed to be one of the most dangerous men on the planet.

"Absolutely no need for that, Ms Gretson. There will be plenty of opportunity for department briefings later on. But in the first instance, it'll be just you, me, a coffee and a chance for both of us to get out of these stuffy buildings. What say you?"

They agreed to meet for a light lunch the next day at an Interstate Diner called O'Cleary's on I-55. During the trip there, Gretson mulled over what this could be, trying to link it to what had previously taken place. She managed to take in the scenery, often seeing woodland or open expanses, farmers toiling on their land and pretty townships that she'd have liked to have stopped in had she had the chance. But not today.

O'Cleary's was a tidy diner with plenty of customer parking to the side. Once this would have been a hive of activity, catering for many a day traveller or long distance lorry drivers wanting to take a break and enjoy Aaron O'Cleary's world-famous Roast Chilli Pot. It had to be world famous, because the giant 10x20 billboard on the roof said so. Upon sitting down at a corner table, a waitress approached Tabitha Gretson.

"I guess you're here to try our world-famous cuisine. You saw the sign, I hope?"

"Great sign."

"I have to ask, you see. He," she pointed toward the rear of the diner, "expects me to ask everybody. So how about our chilli?"

"Any other time, I'd say yes. But today I'm meeting a friend, and when he gets here I'll order a tuna melt if you've got tuna."

"That's not as easy to get hold of nowadays as it used to be. But I'm pretty sure we've tuna at the moment. Shall I hold off that melt until your friend arrives?"

"Please."

"In the meantime, a coffee?"

"With creamer. Thanks." With the waitress gone, Tabitha Gretson sat doodling on a pad for a while to keep herself occupied. She figured if Gently saw her with an electronic tablet he'd have her remove it. So she had left hers locked in her car. The coffee arrived at about the same time Gently did.

"Mr Gently," she called out as he approached, hand extended in readiness to shake hers.

"Perhaps we can suspend the formalities today and stick to first names, Tabitha. I'd not want anybody to get suspicious."

"Who's anybody? Haven't you noticed we're the only ones in here?"

"There's a couple with a kid or two who are just parking their car. They'll be in here shortly, no doubt. There's a lorry coming in now, too, as we speak. Those drivers love gossiping to one other."

Sure enough, she had just heard the rumble of a parking articulated lorry and the sound of crunching tyres as it came to a stop.

She said, "First names it is, then. Here comes the waitress with my coffee. I didn't order for you."

"A black coffee for me," he asked the waitress and after a bit of indecision on the part of her newly arrived gentleman guest, she walked away with an order for a tuna melt and one for an egg salad.

"Quaint place." He exclaimed. "These red plastic chairs and booths and black and white checkerboard floor tiles remind me of those very old movies where the boy meets the girl in a booth with his biker friends at the counter, slurping on sodas."

"Or standing around the juke box deciding how many times to put the same song on the turntable. Elvis's latest Number One on repeat play!"

"My favourite was the Bee Gees. Or the…"

"We aren't here to reminisce, Robert. I really don't care much to discuss old pop groups. I know you're here for something. So have the decency to call it as it is." She decided to take this tack in an effort to say *'don't you try to railroad me, so treat me with respect'*, and from his demeanour it was apparent he was all too aware of this.

"Cut to the chase?"

"Cut to the chase." She mimicked in agreement.

"I'll not bore you with going over old ground. People are going to die. Lots of them. We need to know who they are as soon as we can, after it happens."

"Let's talk scenarios."

"Go on," he encouraged her.

"Bob Smith shoots John Brown in a village in middle Nebraska. Bob's a retired guy and John's a farm hand. Neither is a town dignitary, they are both ordinary people, right?"

"Sure."

"You want us, the authorities, to know about John Brown's death as soon as possible after the event. Is that what you're saying?"

"In a nutshell, yes," he replied.

"And Bob Smith can't just rock up to the Town hall and say: '*I killed John Brown*' and have anyone believe him."

"This is what I'm saying, yes. So, I need you to come up with an idea that offers a burden of proof."

"Like film footage," Tabitha suggested.

"Or photos."

"Film footage is pretty undeniable. Photos would have to be 100% bona fide. Could be tricky if they are grainy, but cameras are getting better all the time."

"How would we verify them?" he asked. "You're the scientist."

"That, Sir, is easier than you think. We've been working with the Crime Unit for a number of years on something I know will work."

"I'm all ears. But sssh and hang on for a moment or two, here come our meals."

Tabitha thanked the waitress politely who was wise enough to realise this was a private meeting and she promised herself she'd not come and disturb these two business-people any more than necessary. Clearly, they were planning a big company buy-out, a banking deal, a merger or suchlike. Stuff that didn't interest her at all. Little did she know that one of the two was more than instrumental in putting in place something that would ultimately claim her life just a few weeks from now.

Gretson resumed from where she had paused moments before.

"Facial recognition has come a long way. Further than most people think. You could give me a photo of someone you know, let's say your own family member, so long as they were alive until at least ten years ago, and I'm prepared to proclaim I'll identify them just about every time. We can't promise accuracy any better than 70% for people who died over 10 years ago. For anybody alive today, I'll get it right 98% or more."

"The other 2%, are what?" Gently asked.

"Probably people who have never been to a town, and so have never been in the line of a street camera. We used to call those 'CCTV'. Or they may never have been inside a shop which has CCTV, which is very rare nowadays. Those who don't have a driving licence, or who have lied to authorities about their own credentials may be a bit tricky, too."

"And immigrants who have only just arrived, for instance. I don't think your system would work for them, Tabitha."

"Undeniably. Collectively, they'll all contribute to the 2%."

"We need everybody to be identifiable."

"Impossible, in my opinion, but 98% of 650 million is 637 million. I can identify your photo in less than 3 seconds with our facial recognition software. Isn't that the best you'll get?"

"I think, perhaps, you're right. When could you have that in place?"

"Huh?" she was taken aback. She didn't expect a request to initiate it.

"I need that system in place in a matter of a couple of weeks, max. I need to be able to bring you fifty random photos. No, better still, fifty movie clips, or a mix of both and have you confirm their identities. As a test."

"You'll bring me clips of missing felons, those who have been working undercover, long lost kids, people who have been missing for decades, etcetera, knowing you. You're a snake, Robert and you never play fair." She almost regretted calling him this, reminding herself not to say out loud everything that she secretly thought of the guy.

"No. Absolutely not. It'll be a range of recently taken clips and pics of everyday folk. Sure, I'll give you a low resolution photo or two, or a video clip where the face may be visible for just a second or two. I may add a photo of some hillbilly back-woods redneck who I don't think even knows how to spell the word 'Internet'. I can't give you mug shots from police lineups, of course."

"I think you'll be surprised. We were running similar tests twenty years ago. Not me, you understand, but my predecessors, and they were hitting a score of 80%. Nowadays it's a virtually guaranteed success."

"Here's the second part of that particular challenge. I need to have that recognition software accessible by computers in any location across the USA. As soon as possible. I want to be able to go into a town in Utah, for instance, and say "Here's a picture of a dead body, identify him", and the guy on the computer will scan it, process it and come out with an answer within your three second timeframe."

"That's not a problem. But '*any*' location?"

"Public office, I'm thinking. Like a courthouse, police station, town hall, and so on. Maybe even a library, a university bursar's office."

"Oh, that's okay. For one moment, I thought you meant in homes. On people's tablets and phones, etcetera." To this, Robert Gently was shaking his head.

During the conversation, their snacks were finished, they ordered coffee top ups and they managed to keep their talk sufficiently confidential. The family that had arrived earlier had sat at the opposite end of the diner and were just in the process of settling their tab and heading on their way. The waitress busied herself with clearing away their dishes.

"Whatever you need to get it in place, you've got it. Cash, resources, personnel, access to laboratories. I'll even coordinate your needs with military assistance if it comes to it. But please get it done. Like yesterday," and Tabitha recognised the demand for the official order it was.

"You said there was something else. A second project," she said with some trepidation, which she hoped her voice didn't betray.

"We need some sort of mechanism, or tagging system, to identify, at a glance, those who are exempt or immune from being killed. Like you and I, like the chosen law enforcement officers, like judges who are exempt from the killing, the senators, congressmen and women. Then there's another category of person who needs the same. Those who have made their kills, who gain immunity by their actions."

"At a glance? Not on a computer?"

He said, "It has to be obvious. If you're on the street and someone doesn't know you're immune, you could get shot. I'm sure you don't want that to happen."

"Of course."

Gently pointed two fingers at her, mimicking the action of pointing a pistol. "So John Dillinger number 2, or GrandMa Baker, who are out with their guns looking to kill, need to know if somebody is exempt. Immune. At a glance."

"Hmm. Something visual. Something's coming to mind. A bracelet with lights. Let me just play with this idea for a minute or two."

Gently twizzled his glasses between his fingers. He brushed back his long and well-coiffured hair. He had time to check his suit hadn't collected crumbs from the meal. He even glanced down at his shoes to see if they had escaped the parking lot dust.

She resumed, and said, "Continuing with a bracelet idea, because I can't think of much else, we could have something that would be fitted by somebody in authority. One that could only be fitted or removed mechanically, with the right tool."

"Can we have two types? One for dignitaries who are exempt, for instance. And another type for those who gain an immunity by making their kills?" He asked.

"Colour-coded is easiest. Like Red and Green."

"Some people are colour blind between red and green. I read that, somewhere."

"That wouldn't matter. They could see a bracelet. Both colours are exempt, so they wouldn't need to know if the bracelet was red or green. Just that the person was wearing a bracelet."

"Good point. What other features would you recommend?" he asked.

"They would have to have some sort of special LED lights that flash in a particular manner, or similar, so they can't be forged by somebody simply bending a bit of green plastic around their wrists."

"Is that possible?"

"In principal, yes. But in practicality, I'm not so sure!"

"Why?" he enquired.

'Scale. They can be made. That's easy. But you want millions of them and distributed all over the country."

"Forget the distribution. Your job will be design and manufacture. Bulk supply," he announced.

"We don't tend to manufacture things. That would get contracted out. We favour research, development, finding scientific solutions for problems, facilitating things for others to action. You could say we work more on the vision side of strategy than the action element of it."

"Well, this time Tabitha, you get to do it all. Except the distribution. And make sure they can't be forged or replicated. They have to be unique."

"We don't have the resources," she said.

"As I mentioned before, and I'll say it again. Whatever you need, just ask. If you want to commandeer factories and their equipment, just ask. If you want a team of people, you simply tell me how many, and they'll be sitting on the doorstep of your factory the very next day."

"We may be too busy. We've got your facial recognition software project to manage, too."

"Not acceptable. You claim the A.I. facial recognition stuff is just about ready to roll out, therefore you can concentrate on your red and green bracelets. Put your main effort into this. Start now. Because I need them now. Or yesterday. Last week, even. You get the idea."

"Let me make a call straight away. Because I think I need to make sure all the right people are at my office first thing in the morning. The more notice that they have, the better the chance they'll be there first thing."

"Do it where walls don't have ears. The waitress keeps hovering like she wants us to finish off and go home, or something."

"Keep her happy and order another coffee. Get me a diet cola. I'll be 10 minutes. Outside. Once I get the ball rolling and my team on the road, back from their separate laboratories, we'll be here talking for a while longer. There's a few details I'll need to thrash out with you."

Gently waited until she had gone. Then got on his own phone. He dialled a number. Started talking quietly. "She's outside now."

"I can see her," the voice said.

"What's she doing? Have you got a clear angle?"

"She's just on her phone. Pacing up and down a bit. Some arm waving going on, too. It's like she's describing something really big."

"Yes, I think she is, Claude. Anyway, just get those photos I need. Make sure you capture her face as clear as you can. And be sure it's obvious where she is, too, so make sure one of the diner name signs is in the same view, too."

"It would be easier if I finished the job here. It's very secluded. No witnesses."

"Doing it whilst I'm in the building next to her? You're kidding, I hope. Besides, she has a very important job to do for the next few weeks. Until then, she's not to be touched."

Claude said, "You still haven't explained what this is all about."

"All in good time. But for the time being, as I've told you already, I want her followed and monitored only. She's not to be harmed. But you'll be back behind the sights of your beloved Remington M24 soon."

Claude ended the call, without even a '*goodbye*', but that was his regular terse manner, Gently reminded himself.

He had time to make another call.

"Ed, it's Robert Gently."

General Edwin Bolwell was somewhat surprised to hear the voice of Maryland's Attorney General.

"Good morning, Robert. What can I do for you?"

"We need to meet. I've a massive logistics and security challenge to discuss with you. We need to meet. Where are you?"

"Houston, in my home state of Texas. God's country."

"I'll take a helicopter to Barksdale Air-Force base. How does tomorrow morning at 0800 hours sound to you?"

"Sounds like you've made a decision and you just expect me to agree."

"See you then." He terminated the call before Bolwell could argue.

Chapter 18

The next few weeks were a period of panic, rash decisions and frantic planning. The options to avoid being forced to participate in what would be by far the most macabre and horrific era in the history of the nation were being shut down one by one.

The airports were closed to all but anybody who already had a visa to visit other countries. Those who were allowed to leave did so in a hurry. Embassies were inundated with visa requests but turned people away because having a post-dated agreement would serve no purpose.

The ports came to a complete standstill. The National Coastguard Service were issued with the simple instruction to return all shipping to its port of departure. Fishing vessels claiming to be going out for their business were required to log a journey plan with the Port authorities before departure. They were issued with tracking devices they were obliged to take with them. Tampering with said devices would be dealt with harshly. Thereafter, they were carefully monitored and if any attempt was made to stray far from their recorded route, the Coastguard was more than inclined to step in and intercept. Worldwide, ships due to arrive were instructed to stay berthed at port or turn about en-route if they could do so safely and with enough fuel to return to their port of origin.

Those who owned private jets were to find their aircraft confiscated or, in some instances, removed by Airforce personnel altogether. Permissions to leave were denied across the board. Attempts to do so without permission were quashed by the authorities and reports came in of several aircraft who somehow made it to take off but forcibly made to land shortly thereafter.

Mexico and Canada closed their borders and both witnessed attempts by people to cross illegally. Periodically, fighting occurred at borders and troops took control as best they could. Some managed to escape across the Canadian border in the remotest of locations in North Dakota and Montana in particular. The Canadian authorities attempted to deal with this dilemma as best they could and were soon ably assisted by people living in those regions. Those who slipped the net were swiftly met with hostility by Canadian citizens who wanted nothing of the Americans in their territory if they could help it. For many fleeing Americans, it seemed more dangerous to cross the border than it was to gain immunity by way of complying with the rules of the NCCO.

Gun shops all but sold out of stock within days. The government having relaxed the 30-day cooling-off period fuelled the panic. People not only purchased guns for themselves but even bought extras when a theory did the rounds that essentially said *'buy guns so others can't have any'*. Ammunition stocks didn't last any longer, either.

The Verlanos and Spencer Dexton in Oklahoma were, by now, well into their planning to barricade themselves into their own home, oblivious to the knowledge that so many other families were in the process of doing the exact same thing. It was a popular strategy. The use of a basement, if one's home had one was by far the most favoured option. Houses that had no basement soon found their windows boarded up from the inside. Some folks even bricked up their front doors, deciding that access in and out of a secluded rear door was easier to secure and defend. But therein lay a different dilemma. Unless you had food to last what would seem like forever, how long could one survive? Nobody knew how long this awful situation would last. Some speculated a spike in initial killings which would trail off quickly and plateau after about a month. It may take a long time indeed before numbers came down to target levels; not that anybody knew what the government's target was. How long supplies would last was open to speculation. And when you came out would the rules of The NCCO still be in force? You would still be a player, a target. Barricading yourself into your home was potentially counterproductive. And simply running from the cities and towns to rural areas was no guarantee of safety as no house in America was any safer than another.

While shock and denial were rife, there was a reality that dictated:

Whatever you are going to do, do it with full commitment.

Some wise street prophet had even graffitied this message on the wall of a mid-town courthouse in psychedelic rainbow coloured paints and it was a saying that caught on. A photograph of the wall-art had gone viral.

Inner city response was the most significant. Those who abhorred gangs and their lifestyle realised they, too, would soon be pulled kicking and screaming into a similar lifestyle.

People gathered in new groups, forming unlikely partnerships. To pool resources and to plan actions they could collectively take in order to defend one another. Proponents of a safety in numbers philosophy. These groups were to become known as the Green Gangs.

Those with any modicum of experience in gangland warfare knew one had to look after yourself first and foremost. Looking after others was of secondary importance. The chances of anybody from a Green Gang surviving very long on the streets was considered to be very low, indeed.

Those determined to avoid violence, those with devout religious beliefs and anybody who realised their chances of long-term survival were little more than zero left the cities as early as they could, convinced they would find relative safety in the quieter parts of the country. As time would tell, only a limited amount of success would be achieved by this course of action.

In all instances, there were riots, looting of foods and essential supplies. In much the same was as Bruce Verlano had been doing, people tried guarding their belongings, but properties were regularly broken into, possessions stolen, vehicles taken, guns sought and removed where possible and many lives were lost in civil unrest even before *The Objective* could be formally pursued.

The USA, for some time classed as being in turmoil, had exceeded its own low point. Though the Police were not powerless, they were outnumbered, understaffed, had insufficient resources and, to top it all off, not all of the individual officers were to be granted immunity. Clarification had been sought as to who would, and who would not be granted immunity, but details were sketchy. Many officers erred on the side of caution, and walked away from their law enforcement jobs to look after their family members who, they knew, would not have been granted any exemption. It was better to try to take care of family than to respond to a call that says Joe Redneck just had his truck stolen, or Mary Schoolmarm had just had her heating oil tank drained by a hooded gang.

Consequently, the philosophy of look after number one, spread like a disease.

Some of the more inspired people saw a way out of this turmoil by seeking to gain immunity under the rule dictating:

> Anybody signing up to, and whose applications to join are successful, a formal position as Controlling Officer (aka Enforcer) will gain immunity.

Few who applied for such a post recognised the diabolical sting in the tail that would beset them at a later time.

The Army increased their presence on the outskirts of cities and major towns all over the country. At this time, they did little more than take over vacant industrial or commercial properties and sites, using these as makeshift army bases. In some areas, they set up new camps with portacabins, tents, communication trucks and high security access. In all instances, communication with them by any member of the public, press or unrecognised officials was strictly forbidden. They maintained a thoroughly silent presence.

But they were there to stay, and the population knew this, which would not bode well for the days ahead. Seeing the army on the street was more than most could bear.

The dystopian nation further sank to its knees.

Chapter 19

The Chronicle Interviews-
Post-Disaster Era- Interview Two

The interviewer, Marty O'Toole had set up his recording equipment on the stoop of Bob and Katie's humble little home. The Mayburys had been very welcoming and had laid on cool drinks and some light snacks. Such a nice way to start an interview on such a sensitive situation.

The late summer sunshine, though starting to ebb away this late in the afternoon, was both welcoming and refreshing to have after the long and cold, inhumane spring the nation had endured. This late summer heralded a time of rebuilding and The Chronicle wanted to interview many families to share their stories, no matter how hard or harrowing they were, with their readers.

"Thank you for agreeing to talk with us," he started.

"Well, you're The Chronicle. Best newspaper in the state."

"That's very kind of you. Would you rather be out here in the fresh air or inside?" he asked, mindful of some annoying noises going on around the neighbourhood. The couple agreed the noises were distracting; the re-building of a broken wall, perhaps, or somebody knocking an old one down. It was hard to tell for sure. They moved indoors and sat around a round table which had a Gingham tablecloth draped across its surface.

"It may be summer out there, but I feel the cold nowadays. It's got to be an age thing, I guess," Bob Maybury exclaimed, taking off his green quilted gilet and hanging it next to his wife's coat on one of the hooks by the back door. He politely asked their guest if he'd like another drink, but he declined with thanks.

"Before we get started, I just want to check that you're okay if I record the conversation. I can't just take notes on a pad of paper as I'll miss some of the things you'll want to tell me."

"Of course that's fine, dear," Katie said.

"And as we've also discussed before, we won't be publishing your full story from start to finish, your edition will be one of the first of the series, so we'll concentrate on the early days."

"Yes, we fully understand. It's the second in this series, isn't it?"

"Yes, it is indeed, and I bet if I tried to publish your full story, we'd fill the whole newspaper from start to finish." He chuckled, and the Mayburys laughed along.

"My word, dear," Katie Maybury said, "it's been such a long time since I've had laughter in this house. It's been such a sad time."

"I need to set the scene for the readers, Bob and Katie. As you can imagine, when people read these interviews, they want to imagine what the house looks like and even create a mental picture of both of you, too."

Bob asked, "How are you going to do that?"

"I'll start the column by saying something like: I've been kindly invited into Bob and Katie's lovely home. Bob and Katie have been married for... 10, 20, years?"

"26". Bob volunteered. Marty gave him a thumbs up gesture.

"...Bob and Katie have been married for 26 years, though neither looks old enough to have been married any more than five years..." the couple blushed at the compliment "...and live in a suburb of Jonesboro in Arkansas in a beautiful house with a red front door that looks down on a well-tended front lawn with a rose bed on each side on their path. I'm sat in their perfect little kitchen-diner where there are pictures on the wall of their lovely family."

Bob and Katie Maybury smiled uncomfortably at the brief introduction but a sadness prevailed after Marty had mentioned the pictures.

Marty carried on. "I extend my sympathy to the lovely couple as one of the pictures shows the lovely, smiling face of their teenage son, Lester, may he rest in peace. And I'm blessed to have the privilege of hearing from the very brave couple, Bob and Katie regarding how fine a young man he was and how he came to lose his life at the hands of an unknown culprit."

Bob smiled that awkward smile that said, "I guessed that was coming".

"Is that okay for an intro? Can't hide some of the truths, I'm sorry to say." They didn't seem to object so Marty kept the interview momentum going with a direct question. "How old was Lester when he passed?"

"He was 15."

"And the readers would like to know something about him. What was he into?"

"He loved his computer games. Perhaps a bit too much. We wanted him to be sporty. You know, get out and play baseball. Basketball. Hockey. Anything, really. He was so fit and playful when he was younger but once he turned 13, and we bought him that GameBoxStation thingy, he lost interest in going out as much. We've only ourselves to blame, I suppose."

"That's a dilemma for all parents, Bob. Not sure if any kid doesn't get distracted by those computers."

Katie had her turn. "Anyway, he liked his fashion, too. He was lanky and slender. Looked great in Levis. And he loved his designer gear. Not that we could afford much of it. But he treasured his Cobsport wristwatch and his Trekaplus trainers. He said all the girls liked his style. Maybe they were right. Maybe he was just a bit of a dreamer." Bob was nodding at the last statement.

"We need to get onto the story of what happened to him, sadly. Once the NCCO had come into effect."

"Well, one day, he decided he was going to go into the town to the mall where he figured it was relatively safe and get a new battery for one of his gadgets. Don't know which one. He had a few. Can't have been one of those modern rechargeable ones, I guess."

"Is it far away? The mall."

"By car, two minutes. Not that we took the car out much, of course. So little fuel at that time. Bicycles were popular at the time. You could do that trip in about five minutes. Ten minutes walk if you didn't hang about."

"How would Lester have gone?" Marty asked.

"We told him if he had to break *Priority One* he better be as fast as he could and take his bicycle."

"Priority One?"

"We had our own rules. Number One was '*Don't go outside but if you have to, don't get spotted*'. Priority Two was, '*Do everything quickly*' and Number Three was, '*Trust nobody, even if you know who they are*'. We had other priorities but we taught the kids, even the youngest, Ellie who's only 7, that if they lived by those three priorities, they would be safe. We didn't like the word *rule*. Thought *priority* would make them sound more important."

"So, what happened to Lester?" the interviewer asked.

"They found his bicycle bent and twisted at the side of the road. A couple in a house nearby said they saw everything. First, they saw him coming down the street, cycling on the sidewalk. We had often talked to him about that, thinking it may be safest. But this dirty grey van was following him. It mounted the sidewalk and drove right at him. He had no chance. He was thrown thirty feet. Landed in some guy's front yard. A guy in a black hoodie and mask got out of the van, took a few photos of him as quickly as possible, got back into the van and sped away. Didn't check to see if he was still breathing. No care at all. The word callous comes to mind. The couple who witnessed it said the licence plate was covered in that wide black tape you use in your garage for DIY jobs."

"I'm so sorry." Marty tried to offer a sympathetic response, but in truth, he already knew this story, and hoped his sympathy came across as genuinely as he meant it to be.

"We heard about it by telephone. The couple who saw it asked around, starting with their neighbours.

One woman said she thought it was Lester but couldn't be sure. Said she knew him from seeing him at school when she used to collect her own kids. She found out his name from another neighbour who knew who we were. We got a call later in the day."

"And what did you do? It's dangerous out there."

"When it's your own kid, you ignore any danger, Marty."

"Yeah, I know."

"So, we got in the car," Bob said, "and drove to where he was. We crumpled when we saw him. Devastated. He was all broken. Dried blood everywhere. Knew he was dead immediately. Anyway, we got him on the back seat of our car. Took him home. We tried calling the police to ask if they knew what happened. But there were no reports. Apparently nobody ever reports the killings. That's a sad and sorry state of affairs. One of the worst parts of it for some, because many people never know what has happened to their loved ones. I mean, can you imagine being at home one day, and saying '*see you later*' to one of your kids who wants to do something outside, and that's the last you ever know about them? At least we found Lester."

"What happened next?"

"We buried him here," Bob said. "We dug a big hole in the back garden. We found a bible and went through it to find a passage we could read. We found a few of his favourite things and wrapped them in a towel and placed them next to him in the hole. Covered him in a sheet. We couldn't find a coffin, of course, they just don't have any anywhere. I had nothing I could use to make a box. So he just laid there. After we were finished saying what we could, we put the dirt back on top of him."

"I'm so sorry."

"And you know what? I said to Katie *"that dirt is heavy, so let's lay it on him slowly and carefully so we don't hurt him"*. So, we put the dirt in by the handful. Didn't use a spade. We also planted a cherry tree with him, next to his heart, so it'll grow with his goodness as he releases it. Can't do that if he was in a coffin."

"That's very commendable," Marty O'Toole offered. "I bet you stand by the tree and talk to him."

"All the time. Ellie does too. And what scares me most is she seems to understand fully. She loved her big brother, so much it hurts even more than words can say."

"You're being so brave."

"You want to come outside, see the tree and say a few words?" Katie asked.

"More than anything else I've done in a long time."

They took a break from the interview and went outdoors. The rear garden was as well tended as the front, if not more so. Some of the flowers were still in bloom, the lawn was well cut, there were no weeds in the beds and O'Toole immediately saw the young cherry tree sapling he expected. It sat on a plot that was surrounded by a low bright white picket fence. Clearly it was the site of where Lester Maybury rested forever more.

"Beautiful," he remarked.

"We think so too, don't we darling?" Katie suggested to Bob.

"It looks like the best plot to me, and we can see him from most rooms at the rear. Do you want to take photos, Marty?"

"Sadly, they don't let me put pictures in my part of the newspaper. I only get text in my column inches. Oh, sorry, that's just the term we use for the space my stories go into. One day, when we are as big as the Washington Post or the New York Times, I'll insist on them allowing me space for photos." This was met with a chuckle or two. "But if you don't mind, I'd love to take a picture on my smartphone for my own memento of a lovely family and wonderful summer's day."

"Of course you may." He duly obliged, taking two photographs of the plot and then demanding he got a photo of the couple standing in front of the makeshift headstone and the sapling.

"We've still got some things to chat about for the interview if that's okay. Shall we go back inside?"

"I'm making coffee, this time. Would you like some?" he was asked, to which he agreed.

When all were sat back comfortably, he recommenced the questions. "How did you eventually hear that the NCCO had come to an end?"

"Same as everybody else to start with, I suppose. Somebody went running down the street a-shouting and a-hollering. Didn't know what all the commotion was. Thought somebody else had been shot. Figured it was a livid and bereaved parent or suchlike. But it wasn't, of course. So we switched the radio on in here and the television on in the living room. We figured one of them would have some details. An explanation. A confirmation."

Katie added, "It was that lovely lady on the KXB..., KXC..., oh, I can't remember its name, but the news channel that serves the area."

"Can you recall the actual first statement you heard? It would make for a great part of the interview."

Bob replied, "Don't remember what I heard, but one of those flash banners, you know, the one that scrolls across the bottom of the screen kept flashing across with the words "M*adness Has Ended*' and that said it all."

"What's the first thing you did after that?"

"Well, we tried contacting friends. And some of our relations on the West Coast. But all the lines were busy, stuffed up with people calling each other, I hasten to think."

"So we just went outside to talk with Lester."

"That's a great thing to do," Marty said.

Bob continued by saying, "The next day we planned to go to find supplies. Anything fresh. We hadn't been anywhere for some time but we decided to stay indoors for another day or two until we could be pretty certain everybody had got the news. Didn't want any gun slinging lunatic trying to have just one more pop whilst he was still allowed."

"But we had our green bracelets on, Bob. I told you we'd be safe."

"I wanted one last day, honey. Better to be safe than sorry."

Marty asked a new question. "Do you mind me asking the details of how you gained your immunity, how you earned your bracelets. Oh, I'm sorry about the word '*earned*', so inappropriate."

Katie looked toward her husband who nodded for her to proclaim. "We vowed never to talk about that to anybody, Marty. It was an experience I never want to re-live ever again. Even in a conversation."

"I respect your privacy on the matter. What happened in the early days once you were free to roam in safety?"

"We queued up at the Municipal Centre where, we heard, they had a machine for removing these bracelets. They were as bad a memory as the deed itself," Bob said.

Katie said, "Then we went to visit people we haven't seen in ages. Local friends. And of course we had to see who had survived, and find out who hadn't."

"So, that was a happy time, seeing old friends."

"Not to start with, no!"

"How so?"

Bob started telling the story. "We went for a walk down Kingland Street and there were two houses completely raised to the ground by fire and several that were either boarded up or fully open to nature. No doors, no windows. Ruins."

Katie wanted to tell some of the story, too. "Most of those ones were houses belonging to people we didn't know. But then we saw the Norton House. Lovely family. It was desolate. Mostly destroyed, and there was graffiti on the side. Some sick bastard had painted the words "DEAD. I KILLED "EM" on the front wall in big yellow paint. Words were three foot tall. And their car was a burned out shell, too."

"Like some sort of vengeance killing, it was. But that family was a good family. Didn't deserve any of that."

"Did you manage to get any supplies?" Marty asked. He realised getting them away from another sad and harrowing aspect of the story was advisable.

"Eventually," Bob said. "There wasn't much available for many days. It's not as if the supply lorries were quick to respond. I have no idea how much farming was going on during all the bad times, so we had no idea if there was wheat for bread, fruit, dairy. And all the other stuff they produce for us. We did manage to find some canned foods, thankfully."

"Yes,' Katie joined in, "not much to start with but somehow things picked back up again several days later."

"And fuel?" Marty then asked.

"We simply didn't want any right then. So we waited a couple of weeks before looking. And, remarkably, we managed to get some much easier than we had anticipated."

"What else can you recall of those early days?" he asked Bob.

"The Army. They arrived and went from house to house. Clearing up stuff. Removing anything dangerous. Isolating gas supplies in abandoned homes. And forever carrying black bags out on stretchers. Y'know, body bags."

Katie remarked, "And within just a couple of days, the stench had gone. The horrid putrid smell that had lingered in the air. A stench you could almost taste. Gone, just like that."

Marty held back the urge to gag at the memory. One he had experienced for himself. Time to move on, he thought. "Can I just ask you for one more thing so I can finish the interview in a fun way?"

"Of course. What would you like to know?"

"I want the readers to finish reading your story with a funny memory of Lester. Have you got anything that will leave them with a smile on their faces when they get to the end of the story?"

"Oh boy. So many stories like that. Which to choose?"

Chapter 20

Jasper Conningbridge looked at the map, once again, in some vain hope that where he lived in Wilmington, North Carolina and where he knew Canetti was in Pittsburgh were somehow nearer one another than the last time he looked. He cursed his luck that yesterday he was being told where Frankie Canetti was, instigator of arguably the world's most abhorrent idea, and today he was slowly realising that he would not personally have the chance to visit him to demand an interview.

Fortunately, his broadcaster KXHB, had reporters across much of the country, and having spoken to his Executive Officer, Archie Hewlen, during a long telephone call, they had decided that Jo Lechie lived not too far away. That's if you considered Fort Wayne in Indiana to be close. It was still some distance, but the Editor was prepared to authorise her travel expense.

"Organise a conference call for this afternoon," Hewlen instructed him. "We'll give her a full briefing."

When it came in, Jo Lechie answered the telephone in her study. A converted dining room that she and her young family didn't use for its intended purpose. They favoured sitting together to eat in the annexe next to the kitchen area. Her study was the quietest room in the house and she neither got interrupted very much, nor did she disturb her husband and kids from there, either.

They called her to explain that Frankie Canetti, Acting Senior Transport Minister, was apparently the man who devised the scheme behind the National Citizens Compliance Order, and she should find out exactly where he lived in Pittsburgh and trouble him, no "*hound him*" to quote Hewlen directly, into answering for himself. Lechie recognised this for the opportunity it was and readily agreed.

Conningbridge spent some time telling her what he witnessed in the restaurant in Raleigh just the night before. She thanked him profusely for the opportunity. As soon as they ended the call, she got her own map out to study the route.

However, she was not prepared to simply drive to Pittsburgh and drive about looking for a red Mazda somewhere near a theatre in Pittsburgh. Even if she tried, if a red Mazda was all she had to go on, she may turn up at the wrong house. There could be several red Mazdas in the vicinity. Or she may drive past his house when the car wasn't on the driveway, perhaps at a store. She needed more detail. After mulling this over for some time, she recalled a guy who collaborated with her as a researcher some time before. Spencer Dexton.

She looked at the wall clock in her study. Not too late to call him. She found his cell phone number from her contacts list and gave him a call.

"Good evening, Spencer, it's Jo Lechie."

"Lovely to hear from you, Jo. What can I do for you?"

"I need an address for a government minister in Pittsburgh," she stated.

"Home or business address?"

"Home."

"Tricky. But not impossible. Any clues, such as general area. Even knowing which town will be a good start."

She told him what she knew and after chatting for a while he made a confession.

"Jo, I'm at my girlfriend's parents' house in Oklahoma. Nowhere near my own office. And after the news regarding the National Order we've just received, it looks like we will be staying here for some time. To support the family."

"Does that mean you won't be able to help?"

"It will mean a delay, but I should still be able to access my system remotely. Just give me everything you know about him," he said.

Four hours later, just before retiring for the night, Spencer telephoned Jo back with the information she expected, and more. Name, address, length of time he had lived there, vehicle he drives including licence plate number, and he even forwarded to her a picture of the building.

"How on Earth did you manage to get all of that?" she asked him. "You're the best researcher I've ever had the pleasure of dealing with."

"Ask no questions and I shall tell you no lies," he said, playfully.

"I haven't heard that saying in a very long time."

"Like you, I have to protect my sources, Jo."

"Well, a big thank you from me to whoever should get the credit. You included."

"Believe me, I get as much satisfaction from doing the research as my clients do at getting their info. And the more challenging, the more fun it is for me."

"Glad to hear it."

"Any chance you telling what this is all about? It is not every day I have to find the address of a government minister."

"Sorry, Spencer. Not right now but one day I may tell you all about it. Over beer and pizza."

"I'll hold you to that!"

Armed with an address for Frankie Canetti, a car full of gasoline and a full Jerry can in case she had trouble finding a filling station with a supply ration, she was almost ready to make the journey to Pittsburgh.

She estimated it would normally prove to be a long journey from Fort Wayne, but she decided to travel overnight. On the one hand she wanted to try to catch Canetti first thing in the morning; and on the other hand, she feared she may otherwise be stuck in traffic if people were trying to escape the cities, migrating to quieter or more isolated places across the state, also seeking safety. Overnight travel would be less harrowing.

As it turned out, she saw more traffic going in the opposite direction to where she was headed.

"They're leaving the cities, for sure," she said to herself. "It'll be pretty hectic by daybreak, at this rate." Talking to herself, as she was prone to do on long journeys, helped focus her mind, keep her alert and think problems through.

She arrived at Canetti's address at just after 6 O'clock in the morning. It would be a little too early to start banging on his door, so decided to drive around a bit to look for an early morning breakfast stop. There was a small diner only about half a mile away from his house. She settled into a window seat with a pot of tea and a bagel, nibbling the latter very slowly as she made notes on her writing pad. She wanted to be sure she knew what questions to ask him and silently practiced them while enjoying her drink.

At 7 O'clock she could wait no longer and went to his house. If she knocked hard enough, he'd have to answer the door. "And I don't care about the neighbours," she almost said out loud.

As she walked up his garden path, the front door opened to her arrival.

"Good morning," a mild-mannered gentleman greeted her.

"I'm looking for Frankie Canetti."

"That's me. And you are?" His care-free demeanour took her aback. She figured he would be far more difficult to find, approach and talk to. Especially in the light of what governmental evil he had been up to.

"My name is Jo Lechie," she said. "KXHB News."

"I don't tend to give interviews dressed in a bath robe and bedroom slippers, madam. I'll be at my office at about 9 O'clock. I'm sure my office could find a slot in my diary for you. Maybe even for later today."

As taken aback as she was, Jo wasn't about to go soft on him. "Sir, seeing that you've devised a heinous abomination for the people of the USA to partake in, I don't want to be fobbed off with having to make..."

"Heinous? Wait a minute, Mrs. Lechie. You throw words like *'heinous'* and *'I have devised'*, and this confuses me somewhat."

"What's confusing? The country is about to have to comply with a National Order that says *'hey, enjoy the way we've adapted the Second Amendment'*, and *'you must get out there, fully armed, and kill each other.'* Doesn't get any more damning than that." She laid it out as clearly as she could.

"And you think this is my directive, because?" he started asking her. Then stopped. "Look, you better come inside. My neighbours will wonder what all the commotion is, at this early hour of the day."

She hesitated.

"I'm guessing you've been on the road some time and could do with a coffee." She shook her head, but he carried on regardless. "Well, I certainly could. And some clothes!"

The invitation to come inside set her on edge. She knew the dangers of being inside a strange house, especially when dealing with a hostile or sensitive situation. But he seemed about as threatening as a cosy jacket on a cold day. She accepted, tentatively, but decided to be ready to bolt the moment he went on the offensive or tried attacking her.

Within half an hour, she realised she was in no danger, for the both of them spoke honestly to each other about what each understood to be the situation.

Some questions had not been asked, however. Ones she was keen to get answers to. And ones he wanted to know, too. He started.

"Let me get this straight. One of your colleagues, Conningbridge, was in a restaurant or bar and heard Robert Gently claim all of this was my idea?"

"In a nutshell, yes," she admitted.

"But Gently's dinner companion is unknown, though, so we have no witness to back this up. Is that right?"

"That's right, too."

"I can tell you, straight away, I had nothing to do with inventing this atrocity or deciding it should go ahead. Quite the opposite. I can wholeheartedly state I was probably as against this NCCO as it is possible to be. It sounds to me that you've got the wrong end of the stick, or your source has mis-interpreted what he heard."

"I'm developing another theory, Mr. Canetti."

"Which is?" Canetti asked.

"Gently's setting you up. He doesn't want to take the wrap for something if he can help it. I'd imagine it would be bad for his political future. After all, who would vote for him when he's trying to worm his way in to the Oval Office?"

"That deserves some consideration. I can't believe he wou... Correction, I *do* believe that's the type of thing he would do. What a scumbag. So he puts me front and centre to mop up anything that goes wrong."

Jo Lechie said, "It seems like it to me."

"And the press are going to hound me for answers, especially because no other government official is prepared to say anything?"

"No."

"No?" Canetti asked.

"Aside form Conningbridge and our Editor, I'm the only person who knows about the claim being made of you by Gently. But I think Conningbridge was also set up. Used. Gently wants to turn the press against you. To deflect attention from himself."

"And I think maybe Weinstein is playing a much more active part in this, too."

"Jeremy Weinstein? Oh, you're referring to the Chief of Staff," she said.

"Yes."

"You have to tell me why he would have anything to do with it."

"I'll explain if we can strike a deal."

"Such as what?" she asked.

"I'll tell you more about what happened in those meetings, if you promise to help me keep my name clean or defend me from other reporters."

"Your name isn't being slandered yet. I suspect we are the only press organisation who Gently has set upon you. I think he expected Conningbridge to tell everybody; all the media, by selling his story. But Gently's plan didn't pay off. Because Conningbridge kept it in-house. Though I fear it will only be time before Gently does something similar. To another press guy."

"I wonder why he picked Conningbridge, specifically," Canetti said.

"I doubt we'll ever know. Maybe picking that Pulitzer Prize guy who's always running stories in all the big-name papers was too obvious. Maybe he thought a less well-known journalist would have more ambition. And a loose mouth."

"So you think he'll try the same thing again," echoing Lechie's concern.

"Yes I do. I think he'll do exactly the same thing. But next time he'll do it in multiple places. To be sure it works. In fact, we can't be certain he hasn't already done it more than once. Though I suspected we were the only press organisation to be picked upon, it could be that Conningbridge wasn't the only one to have this happen to him at much the same time."

"Great. I'll just sit on the stoop and wait for an army of reporters to come along."

"So, let's deal," Jo demanded, "you tell me everything that happened in those meetings, I'll keep your name out of our broadcasts, and I'll help you expose Gently."

"How?"

"I've a researcher friend who has skills and contacts. I think he'll be up for helping out. But you'll have to travel to meet him in Oklahoma. He's not going to be able to leave where he is for the foreseeable future."

"Set up a meeting, Jo. I've got to leave this house, anyway. Immediately. If what you say may happen actually does, I'll never escape the deluge from you press people. So set up a meeting though I'll quite possibly be in Washington when you do. Got plenty to do there."

She replied, "I'll set it up in due course, but it won't be immediately. I'll be in touch."

Chapter 21

The weeks between the day of the *Announcement* and Day One of the action phase of the NCCO being in place flew by.

The people of America did what they could, from stockpiling food and fuel, to securing themselves and their homes as best they could and planning their own security. Whilst a high proportion of people suitably weaponised themselves, some continued to refuse to believe they would be called upon to kill others to protect themselves. They doubled down their efforts to blend into the background. To become invisible.

One mathematician attempted to prove that for every 500 people who went out killing each other, just 118 would survive. Scaled up to the whole population, 153 million people would survive and 497 million would die. Presenting the madness was done so in such a way as to try to make the politicians alter their game plan.

"Stop the madness," they were told, or "Reduce the target if you can't put a halt to it". Such compromises were proffered, as was, "Change the rules before you regret your own decisions". But alas, all these protestations fell on deaf ears.

Later on, the same mathematician also proved that if you started with 500 people and they killed in a particular sequence, just one person would survive. Though valid and technically correct, the odds of that specific scenario coming to pass were miniscule and so did nothing to help the pleas.

Those who did not intend to hide or isolate polished their guns and made sure their ammunition was to hand. Others sharpened their knives or collected what they would need to make their kills in their intended ways.

Some would ultimately kill indiscriminately with utter randomness in their actions, some would be opportunistic by taking advantage of situations that would come their way and others were stone cold in their emotions, giving very careful forethought to *who* they would attack and *where*; and with regards the issue of *when*, they envisaged being able to carry this out in the early days. Get it done, get the immunity, become instantly safe, move on and watch everybody else panic.

The authorities were being asked to mobilise in ways they hadn't had to ever before. One such area was with regards the process and administration aspects of the NCCO. Tabitha Gretson's software had been uploaded to computers at key locations and the army had successfully distributed several million green immunity bracelets to the same locations; the first batches having only just been sent to them from the manufacturers, working around the clock to hit the seemingly impossible manufacturing targets suddenly imposed upon them.

Furthermore, at each of these locations, a Lead Enforcement Officer, whether this was a mayor, justice of the court, a sheriff, or other person of local importance, was appointed and trained in how to deal with the enforcement role. Enforcement support teams were also employed and trained.

Those who were collectively called '*Enforcers*' were issued with, and had to display at all times, their red exemption bracelets. These were identical to the green immunity bracelets except for their colour and the colour of the LED lights that flashed around the band. Once fitted, they could not be removed without the necessary tool.

The Army deployed across the country and, in typical military style which proved their efficiency, had set up camps all over the country. Personnel had been briefed as to what was expected of them and they simply stayed put, waiting for the proverbial starting gun to fire.

Spencer Dexton and the Verlanos were pleased with their preparations, and simply waited as did so many others.

Frankie Canetti put himself in what he called a position of '*full dedication to my role*', a fancy term meaning '*I'm living in my office and not leaving it for the foreseeable future*'. He found a way to convert an adjoining office into a makeshift living area, complete with a reasonably comfortable camp bed and hanging space for the clothes he managed to pack in time before his escape from Pittsburgh. Fortunately, his government building intended to continue to serve as it had been even when the atrocities were due to start and so he had access to a cafeteria and a fitness suite in the basement with shower cubicles and changing areas. A pretty comfortable place to be, by all accounts. He had no issues with personal safety as he had been awarded a red exemption bracelet, which had been fitted to his left wrist by an army serviceman of some rank, or other.

Toward the end of the weeks building up to Day One, during the days Spencer had been assisting the Velanos, Jo Lechie started working with him on finding ways to prove the collusion of Jeremy Weinstein and Robert Gently. They were after evidence. Cast iron proof Gently and/or Weinstein was to blame for the current mess and the hell that was expected to follow.

A break-through would come in this regard when Spencer managed to highlight Gently's involvement, even if Weinstein's was still being investigated.

Spencer had approached, via a video call, the owner of the restaurant in Raleigh where Conningbridge had overheard Gently. He enquired if the restaurant took and, better still, kept CCTV footage of their guests' comings and goings. He was delighted when told that they did, indeed, take footage. And, yes, copies of footage were still safely archived. They kept six months-worth before it was over-written by their recording equipment.

Although initially the owner said he couldn't release the footage as it was private and confidential, Spencer persuaded him it was linked to a crime associated with the setting up of the National Order and, as the owner was dead-set against *The Objective*, subsequently agreed to forward a copy of the necessary piece of footage to Spencer.

Subsequently, Jo sent the clip to her own laboratory, who had their own version of facial recognition software on a computer. In the blink of an eye, the name of Gently's mysterious dinner guest had been finally identified.

She informed Dexton who then tracked him down and obtained and confirmed the necessary credentials. Name, address, the vehicle he owned and a photograph. He sent them across to Lechie as soon as he had them.

In a form of returning a favour, Jo Lechie offered Jasper Conningbridge the opportunity to track down and question the man in the hope he would confirm Gently's claim that it was Canetti who was to blame.

Conningbridge agreed excitedly. It transpired that the man, himself, was innocent of collusion but angry that Gently had used him as some sort of pawn in a deadly game. He didn't take kindly to this realisation and openly volunteered to share with Conningbridge everything he knew and could tell him.

By the end of the meeting, Conningbridge had been able to record enough details and produce a makeshift affidavit that mirrored what Gently had said to him.

Though this might not stand up in a court of law, it would be more than enough to confront Gently with a watertight accusation, which would be the plan of attack at a later time.

The six weeks build up to Day One had flown by. Everybody had busied themselves in their own chosen way. Yet, for most people, the stress of the very last day made it feel like it went on forever.

Chapter 22

The Chronicle Interviews-
Post-Disaster Era- Interview Three

The heat in the city centre was oppressive. A storm was about to hit Illinois, that was for sure. You could feel it in the air. The TV weather service was not what it used to be before the killings, but they made a pretty good effort to offer the viewers something. Today's weather girl said the storm was brewing and as it does, one should expect the thunder and lightning to come soon. But "so*on*" didn't stop the humidity climbing as it did right then.

Jabari Adebayo nervously paced up and down in his apartment's corridor. He had changed his shirt twice already, both having been soaked in perspiration.

"This damned heat," he said to his girlfriend, Ionie, "it's driving me insane."

She replied. "It's not so much this heat, babe, you're sweating like that because you're nervous. Did you have to agree to an interview with a newspaper guy? Can't say I care too much about having a stranger in here. You know how people give me the creeps nowadays."

"I've got things to say, honey. Been waiting for this chance for weeks, since he agreed to see me. Things people have got to know about. Gotta clear the air and clear my conscience."

"And this'll help to get rid of your ghosts?" As she asked him, Ionie sincerely hoped it would. Jabari had not slept well in weeks. He had never talked out loud in his sleep before the atrocities but nowadays he never slept fitfully. She often heard him muttering in his sleep, regularly discovered the quilt had been kicked off the end of the bed and sometimes she heard him calling out for his mother. It was most unsettling.

"Something has to exorcise these ghosts of mine. I'm not a religious person anymore. God knows I used to be. But him and me 'ain't talkin' right now. This is going to put things a little more right than they are."

"But talking with a complete stranger? And a news man at that? Not sure I approve," she said to him.

Ionie needn't have worried about creepy people arriving that morning, for from the moment Martindale O'Toole turned up at the apartment door she felt instantly at ease with his gentle manner and broad smile. His appearance was comforting too. For rather than choose a stuffy suit and tie in this weather he chose to turn up in shorts, pumps and a Cubs tee shirt.

"I hope you don't mind me being too casual," he asked her. "And I so hope you're a Cubs fan. I do have a White Sox shirt in my bag and could always change." She did not know he had painstakingly found out that the two were regular Wrigley Field attendees, home to the Cubs, and the ploy to turn up suitably attired and armed with the White Sox joke carefully worked out in advance.

"Jabari's inside. Come on in. He's so nervous, Mr. O'Toole."

"Please, it's just Marty. Or Martindale if you want to be formal or if you want to call me what my Mother does if I'm naughty. So, are you an Adebayo, too?"

"No. I'm a Welles. Jabari's family kept having boys, so the name Adebayo survived. I'm plain old Ionie Welles. Third generation New Jersey girl. Family's roots are somewhere from the deep south, but I'd be hard pressed to research them, now."

"We've got a girl at The Chronicle who'd be more than happy to help you research, Ionie."

"Can't admit that I'm all that interested. I'm convinced there's a link to Trinidad somewhere a million years ago, but I'm not the kind of girl that cares much to know. But thanks for the offer."

"Hey, what are you two talking about?" Jabari called from further in the apartment.

"We're just chatting, babe." And with that they all gathered in the living area, the windows wide open and a ceiling fan doing nothing more than to stir already hot air about.

"Jabari. It's so good to meet you," Marty started off.

"Can't tell you how long I've been looking forward to this," he replied.

"Works both ways, Jabari. I didn't get Immune Status like you did by becoming an Enforcer, so I've no idea about things from your perspective. And I dare say, 99% of our readers weren't Enforcers, either, and so it's vitally important that they know what it was like."

"Worse than you even know, Marty. Worse."

"But most people would think having immunity would be a highly desirable thing."

"Didn't think it through, did I? And they wouldn't have thought it through either before applying. Wish I'd never done it."

"And you're going to tell me all about it. Let's start with the application process. How did you even get to know where to start?"

Jabari momentarily stood up. Having been hunkered forward in his chair, his shirt had well and truly stuck to his back. He excused himself temporarily and came back in wearing yet another fresh tee shirt. Plain white.

He started to explain. "I work, or rather I used to work, at the Community Centre most days. Helping old folks or just keeping them company for short spells of time. I was often handing out sandwiches to homeless folks. We had some sort of soup on the go most days. And never a shortage of folks who was grateful to us for our community spirit. The City didn't help much but we had a couple of rich benefactors who were always donating money. So very kind of them. And they wanted to remain anonymous. And hey, whilst the cash is coming in, we're not going to upset them, so we respected their privacy. Oh, I'm sorry, I'm diversifying a bit too much, I guess."

"Perhaps just a little. But I'm fascinated, Jabari, as it helps set the scene, and gives me and ultimately our readers a great impression of who you are. A kind person."

"Kind? You may not think so, soon."

"Working at the Community Centre helped the application how?"

"Some staff from the local courthouse came around. With a policeman in tow. Y'know, like an escort. Security. Apparently, they were quietly asking around if there was anybody who wanted to apply for this Enforcer role. They were avoiding asking absolutely everybody as they'd be inundated by applications. They asked Reverend Tichley, here at the Centre. He said he couldn't possibly have anything to do with the enforcing of killing folks. Made some comments about Medieval Europe. *Barbarians* was a word he used a lot those days. Said the word "*Jihad*" a lot, and "*Nazi*", too. But I don't know much about all of that history stuff."

"They asked you?"

"No, the Reverend suggested they talk with me. Claimed he did so because I was the next most responsible person here. Except Miriam. She was helping out too. But she did all the food cooking and cleaning up. He said she was *'Grade 10 indispensable'*. He called her that a lot. It made them laugh. I guess it was a private joke they shared."

"Nice lady?" the interviewer asked.

"Miriam was the greatest. She wouldn't say "*Boo*" to a goose. Loved everybody. Never even trod on a spider if she found one. She'd carry it outside. She was only supposed to work three hours a day, Monday to Friday; but she seemed to be there just about every minute of every day. I loved Miriam like she was my Mum."

"So you applied, instead?"

"Only once I'd talked with Ionie."

Prompted by hearing her name, she joined in. "He told me there was a way out of having to do this killing.

Said we could get immunity if he took a position as Enforcer."

"You say '*we*', but my understanding is that Enforcers only got immunity for themselves," Marty exclaimed.

"And you're absolutely right, so it happens. But they didn't tell us that at first. Made me think I was getting a golden ticket. You know. Protection for me and my family. They were lying, of course. There was a lot of lying going about those days. Government officials telling us this and that. None of it true. The press telling us shit. Sorry, Marty, no offence intended."

"None taken. We published what little we knew. Had to somehow fill in the gaps. In the absence of actual facts and the inability to find the right people to talk with we had to speculate more often that we wanted, ideally."

Sirens wailed in the street below. Some minor event happening downtown, probably. But the sound of the siren had clearly unsettled Jabari who was now visibly shaking at hearing the noise.

"Babe, it's nothing."

"I know. Can't help myself. Honey, get some cold drinks out, would you please?" She gladly got up and collected some bottles of pop. In all the food shortages going on, somehow those infernal drinks companies managed to churn out those awful sugary drinks. Having a brief rest allowed Jabari to calm down enough to continue with the interview.

"So you applied and were accepted, I take it."

"It was quicker than you think. Next thing I knew, it was about four days later, these two army guys turned up at the Centre. Said I had passed the application and told me they were taking me for some training."

"You got to go home first and collect stuff, I guess. Feed your dog if you had one. Hug the kids?"

"No. You see, the questions on the application asked about all of that. When I got to this training centre it turns out they had only accepted applications from people who were all the same. No kids. No pets. Them that wasn't caring for elderly or disabled folks. People with no real ties."

"He couldn't even tell me," Ionie sobbed, "I mean, we weren't living together then, just girlfriend and boyfriend. I got to hear in a letter that got posted through my door."

"You still have the letter?" he enquired.

"Not anymore. It was one of those bad memories folks like us wanted to get rid of. Kept it until I saw Jabari again. Then I didn't want it. Didn't need it. Got rid of it."

"I bet you remember what it said."

"It was a plain old form with standard text which everybody got the same. But two boxes were filled in by pen. The name of the person and an emergency phone number. So, it said something like: "Jabari Adebayo has agreed to assist the USA government by conducting his civic duty to become Objective Enforcer. He now resides in one of our application centres..."

"*Approved* centres." Jabari corrected her.

"Yeah, that's right... *approved* centres. He will not be returning to his registered home address for the foreseeable future." At hearing this, Marty looked horrified. It was some form of enforced incarceration. "Should you have any emergency situations, please call 555... something-or-other."

"Which, I assume you did."

"Always an answer service. But it said, and I quote-"Please leave a message no longer than 15 seconds long including a return telephone number". And, yes, before you ask, I did do that. Several times. I never got a reply ever. Not once," she despaired.

"Jabari, where was this training centre?"

"I didn't recognise where they took us. But if I had to guess, based upon some of the things that happened later, I'd say it was somewhere between Quincy, Illinois and Kirksville, Missouri. It was a small place. I think it was an abandoned farm."

"How long were you there for?"

"About three days. Then we got moved by a bus to the Enforcement Centre. I asked when I could contact Ionie. To check she got her immunity. I was told, as did the other folks that family members didn't get immunity. Oh, the arguments and protests that happened amongst us and the army guys was unreal. But it soon became apparent it was a lie we were told, and those we were complaining to had been lied to, themselves. About all sorts of stuff. Essentially, we were all in it together. Right up to our necks in some sort of shit. We just had to carry on with our new jobs as best we could."

"That must have been very difficult to do," Marty said, trying to empathise.

"I'd have stayed at home to protect her, if I had known. I'd never have applied." Ionie squeezed his hand. Jabari knew the difficulties she had gone through for herself over the next few months, but she had refused to formally contribute to the interview. Consequently, her turmoil remained a private matter between the two and would not find itself written up onto the pages of some newspaper or other.

"Where was this enforcement centre?"

"I'd rather not say. Sorry. There's folks who live in that area who'd gladly come looking for me. After what happened there."

"Fair enough, but we need to tell the readers of The Chronicle that phase of the story, Jabari."

"It all started off okay. We helped the army control the incoming supply of the green bracelets. Even though we knew they had already been counted, we were asked to do a double-check. So we counted them yet again to make sure they were all there. The numbers always tallied."

Marty listened intently as Jabari told his story. He did not interrupt.

Jabari said, "We were shown how to access a database. It was just a tiny computer screen. Linked to the mainframe, I suppose. I'm no computer geek so I don't know how it all works. But we were shown how to access anybody's name. Everybody could be found on this. Even yours, Marty, had I wanted to. It was a bit of fun at first. We found our own names. Then I searched for my uncle Alvin. The guy next to me found his sister and did a search on one of his uncles. Only, he didn't tell us first that this guy had been dead for three years."

Jabari stopped to have a brief rest. The humidity was high, his clothes stuck to him, but he was parched. He gulped more soda pop.

"And?" Marty wanted to know what happened.

"The computer flashed the word '*Deceased*' on the screen. It knew. Then this guy in charge gave us a short list of names. Had three people on it. He asked us to watch carefully. First, he typed one name in. This woman's details came up on the screen. He entered a code number. Like AV123GF, can't remember exactly. Doesn't matter. But the screen said, "*Access granted to...* and showed his name... *select action option*". He selected '*D*' and the label '*Deceased*" was applied to this woman's record."

"Simple as that?"

"Simple as that. Then he said he had two more to do. He called this 'The process of managing *The Death List.*' He then asked for volunteers to have a go. I didn't see much harm in this, even if the term '*Death List*' doesn't sound all that appealing. So I went next. He checked his hand-held device and gave me a code number."

"Like that AV number you said a minute ago?"

"Yeah. Mine started 'GY'. Not going to tell you the rest. We each had one. Were told to "*remember it, or else...*", and believe me, we did."

"Or else what?"

"Luckily, we never got to find out. But it wouldn't have been good. Anyway, I took the chair and did what he had done. Another elderly woman's details came up. I went through the process, selected 'D' and the same message appeared. After that another of us, Maxine, did the same. It was a young child. Maybe four years old. Maxine hesitated as soon as she saw this kid on the screen. We were all told we'd have to do men and women, boys, girls, convicts, nurses, celebrities, disabled people; you name it."

"But you just had to process data and change records?"

"That was just the easy stuff. And what we were asked to do in the early days only."

"Jabari, I can't thank you enough for what you're telling me. But I'm not sure how much space I'll have in the paper for this whole interview, so although I know it's difficult, I need to ask you to share with me the worst parts of the role of Enforcer."

Jabari told Ionie to get him a drink. "A real one this time please, honey. A double."

O'Toole braced himself for the shit to hit the fan.

"Marty, I took on the role because becoming an Enforcer meant I didn't have to go out shooting my friends, my neighbours, a shop worker, the local fireman. You know?"

"It must have been a popular reason."

"So I could live with my conscience. Be at peace as best I could. But I ended up killing twenty five or more in the process of doing this role."

"What?" O'Toole asked incredulously.

"Killed at least twenty five. You heard me right."

"How the blazes...?" The question trailed off, as he didn't know how to ask it properly.

"The clue is in the word 'Enforcer'. The first time I realised that is when we were asked, after minimal training I hasten to add, to accept into what we were told was a holding cell, a guy who we found out later had killed an old guy and a young girl in an attempt for him to gain his exemption. It turns out, the kid girl was only 12 years old. Too young to be deemed an acceptable subject. We were told to decide if the facts matched the claim, by investigating details on that database I spoke of earlier. They emphasised the concept of "facts only". Not opinions. Never extenuating circumstances. Just what facts we were handed. And sure enough, the girl's details came up. 12 years old. Fact confirmed."

"What happened next?"

"We had to update his details on that database. But obviously we didn't pick 'D' when the screen said, *'select action option'*, we selected 'N'- which stood for *'Non-Compliant'*."

"I've heard that term before. I think my own boss used it once in the Editorial Office," he said, and added "I can't recall where I first heard it though. I beg your pardon, I'm interrupting you, Jabari."

"I then learned the computer sent some form of electronic message to the army officer in attendance that day and they carted him away. And every time they did this it was with a siren unnecessarily blaring away from the truck. Two days later we saw his name on the *Death List*. I vomited all over the floor, there and then. I had sent him to his death. I was judge, jury and fucking executioner. I'm sorry."

"Completely forgiven, Jabari. You cuss as much as you want. And there were twenty five of these?"

"Easy to count at first, but eventually you lost count. Hard to remember them all when you did your best to try to switch your brain off to what was happening.

Though you didn't remember them all, you remembered the stories, the circumstances. You just couldn't forget the stories, the reasons behind why you decided what you did. And every damned night you lay in bed asking yourself if you interpreted the facts right. Did I miss something? Did I just send a woman, or man to their death because I mis-read a fact or two. It gnawed at you like a cancer."

"Would you mind so much telling another, just for the readers you understand?"

"Grudgingly. But one that comes to mind is an elderly woman. Poisoned her husband and his brother with Arsenic. Rules say no two people of the same demographic. Well, I had to refuse. I couldn't send her off to the army to be killed. Not in my nature to allow that. Not an old woman in her eighties."

"What did they do?"

"Threatened me. Said if I didn't do what I signed up to do, I'd be seen as a non-compliant."

"Non-compliant again. Hmph. And you'd end up where?"

"On the fucking Death List. I ask you! What a shit-storm of a place I had found myself in. And no way out."

"There must have been some escape route. Within the rules, surely?" he asked.

"One of the Enforcers, Patricia, tried. She asked to see somebody in charge. Would not do anything until she did. And you can figure what happened next. Though I didn't see her name on the list, one of the other Enforcers had to process her details on that database just a few days later. And clear as day it was marked 'D' next to her face on the screen like anybody else."

"You're kidding." Marty did not expect this, at all.

"Wish I was," Jabari said. "But nothing was funny in life anymore. I feel lucky though that it wasn't me that saw her name. But instead, I see ghosts of the faces I had to look into. One day it may be a guy who had killed too many when a stray bullet got a ricochet. Next day argumentative people who simply refused to kill others; and I wish I could have taken their side, but the concept of "facts" trumped everything we decided. I see the ghost of a librarian who faked the killing of two people who were already dead so as to spare another two innocent people. Her face will haunt me forever. Think about it- I sent them all, and others, to their own deaths."

"I can see why you have sleepless nights."

"And now I see their faces again on computer screens that swim in my dreams and nightmares. Still images that animate. I see them pleading with me not to push the 'D' button. I try to push another key. And the keyboard has fifty or more 'D' buttons. I can't find another button and my fingers have a mind of their own. I can't force my hand away from the keyboard. Then 'Click', it's too late, I depress the key."

The remainder of Marty's time at Jabari and Ionie's apartment was spent trying to chat about other things. The Cubs. Wrigley Field. Their impending wedding. Their plans to have a great big family. And Jabari just wanted to get back to working at the Community Centre, as he had so much to offer.

And he had to take the place of Miriam, who had been bludgeoned to death by a homeless man who wanted more than just a bowl of soup that night.

Chapter 23

Long before Jabari Adebayo and Ionie Wells would be interviewed my Martindale O'Toole, America entered the darkest days in its peoples' history. The first day of the National Citizens Compliance Order had finally arrived.

People across America started to follow their course of action. Independent observers, if onlooking from afar, would have seen most actions fall into one of two categories. Fight or Flight.

In terms of flight, this involved different levels of isolation, hiding in basements, boarding up doors and windows and hiding in homes, getting as far away from other people as possible or grouping together with a safety-in-numbers philosophy. Whichever form of flight these groups of people took, they hoped and prayed that something would happen to overturn this demonic decision or bring the era to an end as soon as possible.

In terms of those who were willing to embrace the directive and fight, independent observers would have to have used the term "chaotic" to define what started happening. If it wasn't so tragic, one may have even called the early days farcical. This was borne out in specific examples of utter stupidity on the part of some who were determined to gain their immunity as soon as possible. One such example was witnessed on the streets of Denver where a man in his late twenties, who had clearly watched too may wild west shows or films, had dressed himself up in a cowboy outfit, had put on a two-gun holster, and strode down the middle of the street in his Cuban-heeled cowboy boots, intent on saying something like "I'm *the fastest draw in town, how about trying your luck*", but, exposed to just about anybody watching. Within just 10 seconds of being on the street displaying his bravado, somebody shot him in the back of his neck from just 20 feet away, sneaking out from round the back of a courtyard wall. Kill Number One for a 40-year old woman using her husband's carbine. She and husband retrieved the body as quickly as possible to take the necessary photograph and promptly got themselves to the local municipal centre to register the kill.

It was in the cities where killing happened fastest. Knife attacks were commonplace as gun ownership was less common than it was in the more rural locations. However, gun crime featured second on the list of killing method. Attacks with blunt instruments came third. But the range of methods chosen were wide and varied, and one resourceful man even managed to gain his two kills by electrocuting two people at once.

The city was not a safe place to be. Those who had to venture out for food or supplies gambled with their very lives.

In rural areas, gun-related killings were top of the list, with knife crime being fifth most common. Other chosen methods were those which would be described as crudely physical.

In the woodland domain of Wolf Janner, he and his closest friends, Steevo and Wexley Baxter couldn't wait to get their kills.

As intended, Wolf took the life of Mitch Spooter and a customer of his at the same time, a lady who was only at the auto body shop to collect her father's hatchback car.

Steevo Baxter killed an elderly gentleman who had had the misfortune of being visible through his front window, and the gentleman's neighbour had been screaming so loud having witnessed the killing that Steevo decided to shut her up forever. His brother had reminded him to take something that would take photos when he went out hunting as he would need to prove his kills. Some sort of bodycam, a smart phone or even a conventional camera.

Wexley dispatched Mrs Wills, the former teacher, on Wolf's behalf, as Wolf had already had his two. Wexley recalled Wolf's intention to see to her and so duly obliged. His second kill was a young boy of eleven who was determined to go rollerblading along the street as it was his favourite thing to do. His parents made an effort to run down the street to stop him when they realised he had snuck out, and seeing the murder of their own son was understandably devastating.

By the end of the first day, the callousness of Wolf Janner and his closest companions had achieved what they intended. By mid-day on the second day, each was sporting a new green immunity bracelet, clipped onto their wrists and with its pulsating light flashing away, which helped other people see the wearer had achieved immunity.

Whether one was pre-disposed to fleeing or fighting, nobody could anticipate how sickening the first few days were. And because there was no real let-up, this feeling not only lingered but got worse over time. Those who claimed they were 'man enough to deal with this' were sometimes those who suffered most. Nobody was strong enough not to be affected in some way.

Periodically, the army arrived in the area to help collect bodies and they sometimes unloaded boxes of basic food stuffs at the municipal centres, town halls or school campus offices.

Chapter 24

The Chronicle Interviews-
Post-Disaster Era- Interview Four

The Homeland Chronicle Editorial Office authorised Martindale O'Toole to conduct an interview with an anonymous member of the armed services. They intended to find out how challenging or harrowing it would have been for a serviceman in those dark days. One who may have been asked to conduct themselves in ways otherwise considered to be somewhat beyond what the readers understood the role to entail.

It took their team of researchers several weeks of searching for such a person. Very few wanted to talk. Some were scared of the ramifications of being found out, should that happen. One wanted money, and lots of it. But The Chronicle neither had the budget nor the inclination to be held financially liable for information they would glean from such an interview. Ideally, they wanted somebody, whether a serviceman or woman, to try to convey the personal side of their story. Thankfully, having searched for a very long time, they found somebody who was prepared to compromise. A female army Private who was prepared to offer just a basic insight. Constance Brighley, Chief Editor told O'Toole, she was the best he was going to get.

The day of the meeting had arrived. Marty O'Toole carried his leather briefcase to the park bench where he met a sheepish looking woman in her mid-thirties, wrapped up in a nubuck bomber jacket and sporting a Cardinals beanie hat, trying to keep as warm as possible on this very cold, bleak morning. The woman was wearing nothing at all that said she was ex-army. She wanted to make it look like she was just an ordinary person out for a bit of fresh air. Marty wasn't looking for an army type. He was simply looking for somebody who didn't really want to be there. From a distance, as he approached, he knew he was heading to the right person. She simply looked out of place.

"Good morning, O'Toole," she called out as she saw the newspaper man arrive.

"Hey, it's Marty, okay and good morning to you too, erm, er..."

"You can call me Ellis. Not my real name of course."

"First name or last name?"

"Don't matter none, does it. I'm going to call you O'Toole. So go figure."

The two had agreed to meet for the interview but the nature of this one bucked the trend. Instead of taking pride in the discussion as most interviewees did, this lady didn't want to be interviewed unless full anonymity could be assured. The Homeland Chronical had duly obliged, for fear of losing the opportunity.

"Well, I really appreciate you agreeing to meet, Ellis, and though I'd rather be in a warm coffee shop or a diner with you, I appreciate your desire for full confidentiality."

"We won't get overheard here and nobody's going to recognise me, 'cos I'm a million miles from home, so it's all good."

"May I ask where home is? Just the state or county, not your actual address."

"Let's just say Birmingham, shall we, O'Toole?"

"Alabama. So, I'm guessing what you did was quite a lot of coast watch or patrols."

"Coast and port patrol. City control. Bracelet distribution, issue and security. Township clean-ups. Burials. And being at that damned horrible detention centre they made us manage from week to week."

"I've never been in the army, Ellis, but I've several friends who had, many years ago. And all I can say is those I've spoken to recently have all agreed they had it easy compared to what your intake recently went through."

"I guess you want for me to describe what we did there."

"Our readers are going to want to know."

"No, they are most certainly *not* going to *want* to know. But if you choose to tell them in your paper, then that's your choice."

"Shall we start there?" he asked of her.

Ellis looked about. She couldn't shake old habits. She wanted to make sure they were alone. Secret stuff to discuss. Until it was in print.

"That damned detention centre is where we took people who didn't comply. Enforcers who stole bracelets. People who refused to partake. People who killed too many others. People who killed the wrong types..."

"Wrong types?" he enquired.

"The rules. If you killed two guys, you broke the rules. One of each was the rules. If you killed a kid younger than 10, you got a one way trip to the detention centre."

"This happened?"

"Sure. Too often. All thirteen year old kids had to kill. Sick rule. Sick. But he, or she, wasn't likely to pull a gun on a 30 year old mature guy who knew how to defend himself. So, the kids tended to kill other kids. But some of them got it wrong."

"Wrong?"

"I remember taking a kid to the detention centre who stabbed a 9-year old."

"Stabbed?"

"Turns out, many of the teenagers felt it best to do that. Guns was not their thing, mostly."

"And you took the kid, where, exactly?"

"Tupelo detention centre. Mississippi."

"What happened to them?"

"You know, full well, what happened to non-compliants!"

"I have to hear it from you for the interview."

"I'm army. I'm strong. Or so I thought. But we both know the detention centres are execution camps."

"I'm so sorry."

"And the non-compliants tended to be them kids, or elderly folk who weren't at peace with their beliefs. Those who may simply have made a mistake in how they interpreted the rules. Or mis-interpreted them at any rate."

"Who did the killing and how did it happen?"

"Not me. That's for damned sure. But here's the shit-ass-truth of it all. Some guys joined the army because they are mentally fucked up. They'd kill for the fun of it. Women, kids, you name it. And I betcha that each of these centres had psychos like we had at Tupelo who couldn't wait to try out this gun or that." She shuddered at the memory. "We had a guy who compared how effective one gun was at killing people over another weapon. He awarded them marks out of ten. And all this time, the bodies were just piling up."

"Piling up?"

"Figuratively speaking. Sure. Our job, or one of them, was to dig those great big pits everybody knows exists and we took the bodies and buried them there."

"How many at a time?"

"It was like those Nazi World War 2 documentary clips you see. We were taking about a hundred or more per pit and had to be sure each one was tagged, and their names tallied against the printouts we were given. That way there was accountability as to who ended up where."

"This must have been very distressing."

"Well, 'ain't that the understatement of the year, O'Toole. One army recruit simply failed to carry out his orders. Three days later I saw his name on one of those fucking lists. Can you believe it?"

"I somehow wish I didn't."

"And you want to write all this up in your newspaper column? There's something wrong with you, O' Toole."

"Sadly, I have to do this, Ellis. The full story would have gaps. But it's going to take me a long time to edit the story so the reader can cope with what you're telling me. I'm going to be as sympathetic as I can."

"What else do you want to know. I don't care much to rekindle these memories too often."

"I understand."

"What about what happened in the towns and cities?"

"In the early days, we arrested people, and we collected the dead. Smelly. Stinking. Putrid."

"Let me get back to the arresting. Tell me more."

"We were told if people weren't complying, we were to gather them up and arrest them."

"To take them to the detention centres?"

"No. Well, not so we thought. You see, we weren't told what was going on in the early times. We had no idea these people were invariably going to their deaths. We were simply told we were taking them in so they would sit in front of a magistrate or judge to explain why they were non-compliant."

"Sounds like you were duped," he said.

"Well and truly. We were lied to. Told we were just doing a bit of policing. I figure... Well, we all figured, we weren't told the full truth so as to ensure we did what they wanted. How many of us would have froze? Refused? Gone AWOL, if we were told the truth to start with?"

"Oh, I see," O'Toole stated.

"Yeah, they educated us slowly. And when we could be trusted to do our jobs, we were put to work in the detention centres. Fuck, that was a sick place."

"Let's do ourselves a favour and talk of other stuff you did. Bracelet security, you said."

"Green ones only. The red ones were already issued to the exempt folk a long time before."

"Yes, I suppose they were allocated at the very start," Marty O'Toole surmised.

"Those green bracelets were sent to the air force bases all over the country from wherever they were made. Nobody knew where they came from. Do you, O'Toole?"

"No. I've no idea who made them and exactly where."

"That's how the army wanted it. As much secrecy and security as possible. Anyway, we took armoured trucks to the bases and collected a couple of hundred or a couple of thousand at a time. Each batch was sealed in these high-security boxes and taken to where the localised army bases were. I remember taking a batch to Charlotte in North Carolina from Elgin."

"Elgin Air Force Base, Florida?"

"Of course. Well, those were kept under 24-hour surveillance on our camp. I sometimes got night watch. The local mayor would come over with a requisition order to collect, say, 12 bracelets which were to be issued to folks who had made their killings. The mayor was always accompanied by two to four army personnel so as to ensure they were issued to the right town folk. We also made sure they were fixed properly round their wrists and initiated electronically with this "Signal-sender' thing. Those people used to scurry off as quick as they could and probably hide in their basements if I had to guess."

"Some folks were shot for their bracelets, ya' know."

"What's the point in that? If you made your killings, you got your own bracelet legally."

"Maybe I guess they think you can kill one, steal the bracelet, wear it and not do the second kill."

"I'm led to believe you couldn't get the bracelets off."

"Not a snowball's chance in hell of getting them off without the tool the government made for the job."

"I remember it well. When they finally took mine off, it was a bizarre contraption."

"So, who did you kill, O'Toole? You want my story, but I want some of yours."

"I'm sorry, Ellis. You want confidentiality with what you're telling me. I want a bit of the same for my own story, right?"

"Right." She understood.

"So, what else did you have to do in the towns and cities?"

"Well, I told you before, we had to cart the dead away. And we had to try to disinfect some places. Death is one thing. Then there's the stench, pestilence, disease. Animals who don't have owners anymore trying to eat some of the bodies that were simply left in the streets or in doorways. On dark staircases. Sat motionless in their own cosy chairs in their own cosy houses. Every couple of days we had to wear these white full-body clinical outfits, with breathing tanks on our backs. Oxygen. We used those industrial-type spraying machines to fumigate the areas and spread detergent."

"How did you collect the bodies? And how did you access buildings safely?" O'Toole asked.

"That wasn't easy at times, but we worked in teams, had plenty of trucks and made regular visits."

"Didn't people take them away just after they were found? Like relatives or family members?" he enquired.

"Most people were scared to get onto the streets. Or even to cross a street to the other side. Even if they had them green bracelets on, showing clearly and fully lit up."

"I can empathise with their fears."

"Was everybody taken away? All bodies?"

"Families wanted to bury their own. I did, too. But one day I discovered my own brother was killed. I don't know by whom, of course. We never find out. But I wanted to bury him in the family plot. Simply wasn't allowed."

"Surely, they'd allow for that, Ellis."

"The army generals and decision makers said the numbers we were recovering did not allow for religious services to take place. And for hygiene reasons, the dead had to be handled almost clinically. Another sick episode in the story of our crippled country."

"Ellis, I normally conclude interviews by thanking my companions for their time and sharing the good and the bad with me. For you, it must have been doubly difficult and so I mean this with extra sincerity when I say, *'Thank you'* and I'm also going to tell you, you're the bravest person I can ever remember meeting."

"I'd say it was a pleasure. But it wasn't. I hated recalling this."

"I know." The two parted with a warm handshake.

Chapter 25

The Verlanos were not coping particularly well with having to hide away and live in such a relatively small and enclosed space as their cellar. They very soon nicknamed it the Dungeon. But it served as a safe place to be, especially at night, when they often heard, from somewhere in the distance, a muffled gun shot.

There were other sounds they didn't like, too. On one occasion they heard an explosion. On another, something they never got to identify but it sounded like something big, heavy and metallic falling down.

Most disconcertingly, just three days into the ordeal, they thought they heard somebody in the house in the early hours of the night. But taking a careful inspection in the morning, Bruce and Spencer found nothing untoward.

The family took turns in standing guard when anybody wanted to use the bathroom in the house, which they limited themselves to so doing only during daylight hours. They promised themselves only basic meals, ones that could be cooked quickly, thus also limiting the amount of time they would be in the house.

Periodically, Spencer needed on-line access to do his researching, and this was only available inside the house.

The very act of leaving the safety of the cellar to go into the house to help Jo find this Canetti guy and other matters, was thwart with danger. Not only to himself but to the others, too, for he may be distracted by his work and unaware of anything that was going on elsewhere on the grounds. There was certainly no signal down in the Dungeon. Consequently, if working from indoors, he was doubly careful and forever listening for any suspicious noises.

Luckily, the Verlanos became used to the lock-in regime and within a few days started to regain a vestige of hope for the future. If they could get through the first couple of weeks, surely the stress would reduce and the pressure on their lifestyle ebb away, too.

Supplies lasted fairly well, all things considered, their planning had gone well.

But one of the only things they hadn't accounted for was just how cold it got down in the Dungeon at night. It was becoming obvious, all too quickly, that they would need to rig up some form of heating. But try as he may, to think what he may have in the garage to help, Bruce admitted there was nothing appropriate.

"I'll head into Steerwagon Falls centre and see what I can find," Spencer suggested.

"I could ask the neighbours," Bruce offered.

"You'll simply be admitting we don't stay in the house at night to people who are essentially strangers. And potential enemies, too, dare I say it."

"Oh, I see your point."

"I'll take the car and be as quick as possible."

"I don't think that's safe, honey," Marianne cautioned him. "You'll be a sitting duck in town."

"I'll drive about when I get close to the town centre and seek out a really quiet place to leave the car. Then

I'll sneak the rest of the way into town using alleyways or suchlike."

He left later that morning.

The trip took him just six minutes. The only vehicle he saw on the road was a big truck with camouflage paint and a bumper sticker that read:

Guns are for more than just fun

There was also a bumper sticker of a wolf's head. The redneck driving it gave him a full and proper stare as they passed but he hardly slowed down, clearly having business elsewhere.

For the next hour or so, he went to some of the stores, but realising most were closed, he took to knocking on back doors to get the proprietors' attention. He finally found a portable oil heater for sale.

The owner spoke to him through a partially open overhead window. "You post the cash through the letterbox, Sonny, and the heater will be by the back door when you go back round there. I'm not opening the door to nobody." The old shopkeeper stated as clearly as he could.

"That's understood, Sir. And thank you for helping," he replied.

Spencer retuned only a matter of two hours after he had left. And as soon as he got back to the property it was obvious to him that something was wrong. The first thing he noticed was somewhat innocuous. There was a garment of some sort lying on the ground by the corner of the house. He tried to gauge if it looked like it had simply blown there in the wind, but not only was it in a sheltered part of the driveway, it wasn't particularly windy, either.

As he got closer to the house, he caught sight of the access section of the garage door which was partly open and next to that were some flowerpots on the floor. He was hoping it was just a stray dog having found its way in somehow and caused the mess accidentally. But then he saw a bright orange glove on the floor. It was certainly not one of Bruce's. And there was broken glass on the floor, too, from the window that led from the garage into the kitchen.

Fearful that somebody must be in the house, he took a piece of pipe from the garage, brandished it above his head and edged gingerly to the house door. There were no sounds coming from inside. But he opened the door with caution, nonetheless. Still no sound. He decided to try scaring whoever may be there by shouting Bruce and Irene's names. As loudly as he could. It would also serve as notice to them, probably in the Dungeon, their cellar, so long as they could hear him that he was back. He could now both protect them and scare away any intruders.

There was neither any sound from the house, nor from Bruce calling back to him. As stealthily as he could, he went from room to room, checking each as he went and within less than a minute concluded the house was empty. The others would be so relieved.

Lastly, before going outside, he checked the kitchen for further evidence of the break-in and sure enough, most of the food supplies were gone. That proved to him it was just speculative looters. No real harm, but an annoying inconvenience, nonetheless.

"Bruce. Irene. Marianne," he resumed shouting as he went back outside toward the garden. "Jenny. Bruce. Ire...". He stopped in his tracks. The storm door they used to secure the Dungeon was not only open but now thrust aside and twisted on its hinges. Clearly it had been forced open from the outside.

Convinced the thieves must have long since departed, he rushed unhesitatingly down the stairs, where the glow from the lamp below was casting its shadows on the floor. But there was something else he could see, too, even when only halfway down the steps. Somebody on the ground. It was Marianne. He stumbled down the last steps, having lost his footing. The steps were slippery.

As he regained his balance his heart sank. Boom. His life, his loves, his dreams and his reasons for joy all lay on the floor, motionless. Marianne lay face down with a knife in her back. Unmoving. Jenny was alongside. As lifeless as a rag doll. Bruce also lay on the floor. Face down, but his head was turned slightly to the left. His hands were tied together behind his back with some form of power flex. He had a hole in his temple. A gunshot, surely, but there was a bloody screwdriver lying next to him. The thought that this may have been the murder weapon was very chilling indeed.

Screaming at the top of his voice, now, Spencer was distraught. But having not seen any obvious wounds on Jenny's tiny body, he desperately hoped she may just be unconscious, so he shook her carefully to see if she responded. But alas, she too was dead.

He dropped to his knees and his screaming had taken on the form of some sort of wild animal and at some point in his turmoil he had vomited profusely, but was unaware of having done so.

What seemed like forever later, he then realised Irene was not there. He checked in the shadows behind two water butts. He looked under the only camp bed where there may have been hiding space, but no. She was not here. Fearful for her safety, and more than just a bit hopeful she was only hurt and had tried to get upstairs to get help, he raced up the steps. When reaching the garden he shouted her name continually, at the top of his voice. Screaming until he was hoarse.

She was nowhere to be found in the back garden. He looked everywhere. He went back into the house. Had he forgotten to look anywhere? He continued shouting her name.

After a few moments, he could hear distant shouting. From across the street.

"Mister. Mister. Man in house opposite. Mister," the voice was calling, trying desperately to get his attention. He looked across the street and the house owner directly opposite was waving to get his attention. "Woman here. Woman here," he could hear.

Without a care for his own safety, he sprinted across the road. The man was gesturing for him to go to the side of the house. Sure enough, Irene was there but she also lay prone on the ground. A gunshot wound was clearly evident. It had taken her life.

Spencer, his soul shaken to its core, took several minutes to gather his thoughts. The man and his wife cared nothing for their own safety. They realised this man was a broken man. Not one who has gone out of his way to make a kill. They were safe from him. Of that, they were confident.

Their names were Dixon and Claire Brown. They introduced themselves, sat him in a chair so he didn't fall down if he fainted and gave him some water. Claire also offered him a bowl of soapy water and a cloth to help him clean up some of the vomit that she noticed he had on his hands, forearms and knees.

A while later, his heart rate finally slowing, they managed to get him to speak coherently and tell them what had happened. Spencer confessed he didn't know. He had merely followed a trail of destruction and murder. The Browns were devastated to hear one of the victims was such a young girl. Barely old enough to fall into the category of a viable target for those who sought their killings.

But seemingly, Spencer wanted to know more about Irene than the other three for at least, here, he had two witnesses. Back home, the three were dead and nobody he could quiz about it; but here, there were some clues.

"What did you see, Dixon?" he almost pleaded. Hoping for a full version of events.

"Sadly, not everything. We both heard a commotion and looked out of the window. We saw two figures rush out of your house there."

"There were three of them," Claire tried to contribute to the story.

"Yeah, three but only two of them were being chased by Irene. She was pointing that shotgun you found her with at these two."

"What did they look like?" Spencer quickly asked.

"They had those hooded tops on. Dark green ones. So, I didn't see their faces clearly. I'd have said they were teenagers. Or early twenties. Their hoodies had some sort of logo on the front. I think maybe I saw the words *'tree specialist'* but I can't be sure, Spencer."

"I saw the word *'tree'*, too. Nothing else," Claire added.

"What happened to Irene? She was chasing them, you say. Did she catch them?"

"She reached our driveway. I think she was already hurt. She wasn't running well. Limping like she was injured."

"She is in her seventies," Spencer said, "I doubt she could run anywhere."

"Oh, believe me, she was giving a good chase. Until that kid come along."

"Kid?" he asked.

Claire finished the story. She said, "Irene reached our driveway, and we could hear those two lads trying to climb a fence, maybe to get away. Irene was shouting *"stop"* all the while. But this other kid suddenly appeared. The third one. He can't have been more than 12 or 13. He had a shotgun. He shot Irene. Not the two older boys."

Chapter 26

Spencer walked back to the Verlano house in a daze. His head was full of questions.

"Why did they pick us?" / *"Why were they so determined they even broke the cellar's security hatch rather than be deterred by it and go somewhere else?"* / *"Why didn't Bruce get to defend the family with the shotgun?"* / *"How did Irene originally survive the initial attack?"*

These were just a few of the many more that would plague him for days.

The question that was foremost on his mind, however, was *"What shall I do with their bodies?"*

Although they would be safe in the cellar, they couldn't stay there. He made some effort to call an undertaker, but nobody was willing to help. He called the police and got a similar response. Eventually, he decided to bring the bodies up to the garage where he lay them alongside Irene's which he had lovingly carried back from across the street. He truly dreaded seeing them there, next time he ventured into the garage and knew they could not stay there for long, either. He decided he would prepare a family plot in the back garden. Burying them all together seemed the most appropriate course of action.

Over the next day and a half, he dug a hole wide enough for them all, but could only manage to get down about three feet. He simply did not have the motivation or strength to dig a fuller grave. As he took each spadeful of soil out of the hole, the tears ran from his eyes, the salt from the tears stinging continually.

Dixon and Claire kept a watchful eye out for him as he worked, periodically bringing him water or simple snacks; for which he was grateful. In conversation they speculated on who could have done this. Dixon told him he had been trying to find any on-line advertisements where he may recognise the '*tree specialist*' logo or lettering. But he was being unsuccessful. Spencer thanked him nonetheless for trying.

Once his adopted family had been laid to rest, with Spencer having done his best to say a few prayers, he ventured down into the cellar to retrieve anything useful. He was looking for batteries, torches, fuel cans, or leftover tools. He stacked them in the garage then man-handled the broken door back over the cellar. He threaded the padlock back through the latch plate, clicked it closed against its ratchet and vowed never to go back down those stairs ever again. He had made the decision to live in the house from now and not hide away. He would make sure the windows were secure and the door properly locked at all times, but he would stay in the house at all times of the day and night. Sometime in the future he would travel back to Iowa but he still had things to do here in Oklahoma.

Continually nagging him was a desire to know if the tree specialist logo would be something people in Steerwagon Falls town centre would recognise.

He knew he had no right to seek retribution, those boys had simply complied with the rules of the National Order. But they picked on four completely vulnerable and almost completely defenceless people. *Cowards*, he'd call them each time he thought of them. *Cowards*. But despite knowing he had no right to seek retribution, that's precisely what he was intending to do. He made a vow. For Jenny mostly, as she was so young, so demure. She wouldn't even harm a spider or fly. He would do it for Marianne. He loved her so much and he wanted to honour her. And Bruce and Irene, people so special, they would probably say to Spencer, if they could talk right now, *"Just forgive, Spencer, just forgive."* But he couldn't, and so his vow was for them, too.

The store where he got the oil heater from just a couple of days ago would be a good place to start, he thought. They sold garden equipment and there was a very good chance that a tree specialist would need that shop for some of their supplies. They may well be known by the shop keeper.

Exercising as much caution as he could when he drove, he went back into town and parked in the same place he had previously chosen. Over the next couple of hours, wandering from place to place, he asked about. He chose anywhere that was occupied. Such as the stores who fought for scraps of business, the courthouse, a tattoo parlour which vigilantly remained open, and he met somebody at the library who was only there to check the place was still secure while it remained closed. He spoke to as many caretakers or proprietors as possible. He conveyed the same message to them all.

I am trying to contact some young men who run a tree specialist company. They could be local, or work in the general area. Their company colours are dark green, judging by the colour of their hooded tops they wear. If you know of them, please contact me on this number... 555-1773 or drop a note through the door of my house... 106, Independence Lane. Thank you.

Though nobody knew of such a company right away, they would ask about and let him know if anything came up.

When he got back to the house, he contacted Jo Lechie and told her what had happened. He just needed a shoulder to cry on and he knew Jo to be a good listener. She had an idea and promised to find out which local newspaper publisher covered that area and said she would contact them in case they know of any tree specialist companies that may perhaps advertise with them.

The next day, Jo rang him back up and warned him to think twice about what he was trying to do. "If you try to seek revenge, you're going to get shot. I just know it. You'll ask the wrong person, and they'll be friends of the tree specialists who'll simply come looking for you. And they know where you live."

"What would you do?"

"Two things. Firstly, if I were you, I'd ask your favourite KXHB news reporter, that's me by the way," she could hear him chuckling in the background, "to admit she has a team of '*Tekkies*' sitting around the studio who are continually browsing things that happen on the internet. She could ask if they can search for anything posted, let's say on social media, by two young men in your area who may have anything to do with tree specialism."

"You do?"

"You're a researcher, Spencer. You know we do. And they know how to surf the Dark Web, too, so you'd be surprised what those guys discover on our behalf."

"And what's the second thing?"

"I would get in touch with the government guys who started all this abomination off and give them a piece of my mind."

"Wonderful idea. Only nobody knows who he or they are, Jo."

"Wrong, Spencer. I know exactly who those guys are. And, in a round-about way, so do you. You just have to ask Frankie Canetti."

"That guy in Pittsburgh I got you the address for. Why would he talk to me?" he enquired.

"Because you both want the same thing, essentially. You both want the head of the snake. I'll ring Frankie tomorrow and see if he'll meet with you."

"Is he still in Pittsburgh?" Spencer asked.

"No. He's holed up in Washington again at the moment. At his government department's main offices. Hiding away from the press."

"Too far. I'll be travelling back to East Iowa in a few days. Will he be anywhere on the road soon, even back in Pittsburgh?"

"I'll look into it and see if I can set something up. It may take a few days, so just hang around down there until sometime next week and I'll coordinate something."

"Thank you."

"You're welcome," she said.

Spencer settled back into the house for a few days and waited patiently. He was in no rush to leave as he had spread word around the town about the tree specialists and wanted to see if that led anywhere.

The storekeeper where the fire was purchased was good to his word. He asked all of the customers who bought things through the door (cash through the letter box, please).

The security guard at the courthouse asked about for him. He asked several cops who continually came and went.

The library caretaker spread the word as promised.

At the tattoo parlour, the owner mentioned this to one of his customers. Wolf Janner. Who found this very interesting indeed. In fact, he realised, right away, what this Spencer person was trying to do.

"I love people who fight back," he said to himself. "Far more interesting than dumb animals lacking the right type of fighting spirit."

Chapter 27

The Chronicle Interviews-
Post-Disaster Era- Interview Five

Martindale O'Toole was unavailable to conduct the interview of Sheriff Canley. Besides being unavailable, Canley didn't want O'Toole involved anyway. He demanded to be interviewed by the Chief Editor instead.

He was heard to have said over the phone when being asked for an interview "If you want my time, I want to talk with whoever's in charge."

Constance Brighley was happy to oblige.

They were due to meet shortly, at his office in Consetta County, Georgia. Just before she pushed through the door, she checked her image in the reflection of the glass. She chose to tie her medium-length red hair back in a ponytail fashion and checked it still looked suitably conservative. She enhanced the look with a tweed jacket she had thoughtfully selected from her wardrobe.

Upon meeting him, they shook hands firmly. He guided her past the reception area into the business-end of the office. She was impressed to see a well organised space comprising of five desks, various filing cabinets, whiteboards on the wall adorned with handwritten notes held there with button-shaped magnets, sticky labels and photos of two low-level undesirables; one of which she noted had the letters DUI underneath his image and the other the word

BAIL. There were neat charts pinned to a board on the wall opposite.

"Sir, I'm honoured that you've been able to find time to see me."

"Madam, I've plenty of time nowadays. I took instant retirement as soon as I knew I could and when it was safe to do so."

"Safe to do so?" she asked him.

"I'm referring to those atrocities and the period of time immediately thereafter."

He then counted off each of his examples on the fingers of his hands as he spoke.

"I didn't want any ramifications. I intended to tie up any loose ends. Complete any specific paperwork. Pass back any equipment. Mail any paperwork they wanted from me. Delete any unnecessary communications from being linked to me. Save any files they wanted or ones the next Sherrif may have needed. Say a polite but final goodbye to those who deserved it." He then gestured to the tidiness of the office space all around him as if to say "Look, it's all organised already."

"That's eight good reasons," Constance said having counted the number of fingers he had held up. "So you really have had enough. But you don't look any older than your early 50s. Isn't that a bit too early to retire?"

"Lady, after what I had to go through, age doesn't matter. Oh, I won't retire from work. But I'm leaving Consetta County next week. Got myself a venture out in California which has nothing to do with policing or seeing dead bodies."

"You'll be saying goodbye to friends here?"

"You don't have friends after what I was made to do. You have acquaintances in position, no less, no more. You have people around you who hate you less than the next person. You just hope those around you aren't holding back some deep rooted grudge, packing a piece and just itching to use it. And this lack of friends applies to me, more than anybody else I know."

"In what way?"

"Oh, it's the things I had to do, Ma'am."

"Well, that's what I'm here for. To hear your story, Sheriff."

"Where do you want to begin?" he asked.

"I think we begun about fifteen minutes ago. You've told me so much already."

"I guess I have, at that, too. But what next?"

"Because I really don't know what you went through, how about you sorta' list the main things you had to do and them we'll concentrate on them one after another?"

"Sounds like a plan." He scratched his stubbly chin in thought. "Not sure which to start with. But let's do the obvious first. Just a list, huh?"

"Yes, to start, just try to recall the main things, one after the other and I'll jot them down like a list."

"I had to verify kills on this database thing. I sometimes had to collect bodies and bring them to the morgue. I had to hand out those green immunity bracelets when people qualified and keep the ones we had in stock perfectly secure. I had to take *non-compliants* to the detention centres. Somehow, I had to minimise regular crime, which rose massively as soon as *The Announcement* was made. Also somehow, I had to get my hands on a slice of Missy Beaumont's apple pie from the diner as often as I could. Oh boy you should try that pie. It's…"

"…It's going in the newspaper, Sheriff as part of your story. It truly is. But at the moment I'm still listing the yukky stuff."

"Let's see. I had to keep the peace around here during the build-up to Day One, too. I'm not sure if people called it Day One round the whole country. But around here, the first day of the killing is known as Day One."

"I've heard that term. Not sure it was an official label. But it was used a lot. What sort of things did you have to deal with on this build-up phase?"

"Protests. Enquiries. Requests for protection, which of course I couldn't give. Looting. Some minor riots, which folks quickly realised would achieve nothing, so they fizzed out of their own accord. But maybe the worst of it was the need to quash religious rallies. Ma'am, I'm a religious sort. I supported my local church and had nothing against other denominations. But I was told, in no uncertain terms, that religious rallies were to deemed unlawful, had to be discouraged in the first instance and were banned. If they took place, anyway, I had to step in. Deal with it, somehow."

"I'm conducting an interview with a church minister in Kentucky next week. I'll be getting his perspective on it, too."

"Horrendous and unfair. And that's me understating it."

"I concur," she stated.

"This breaks my heart, but I'd rather talk to you about some of the other things. Which do you want to know about, first?"

"You mentioned in your list, as we called it, the database first. Shall we start there?"

"Sure." Abruptly he stopped, looking pensive. "That reminds me of something more important first. May I?"

"Be my guest."

"My own exemption. I was informed that I'd be exempt, and sure enough, they got me into one of those red bracelets. But my staff weren't exempt. That's neither of my deputies nor the two office girls. I can't run my department with my staff being unable to perform. The girls, Clara and Becky got together and talked. A lot. They came to me one day and said *"Sorry, boss, but we are off. Leaving. We have to hide and even here in the police station, we just aren't safe".* Turns out they talked to the deputies, as well. Got them riled up, too. They became just as scared; whether or not they had guns and permission to use them didn't seem to count for much."

"What did you do?"

"We had a proper meeting to discuss this. Talked of all the options and bish, bash, bosh, the solution fell right on my lap, just like that."

Constance raised her eyebrows in expectation, encouraging him to continue.

"You see, we are first on the scene at accidents, incidents, fights, murders, you name it. That very morning, we got a call of an RTA. That's Road Traffic Accident. Two people had stuffed their Buick into a tree about a mile from the police station at quite some speed, by all accounts. Both died outright. We went there in a hurry. Recovered the bodies, got them back here. A middle aged woman and her 20 year-old nephew."

"What happened next?" she asked.

"We staged a scene where one of the deputies had intentionally picked these two people to be his own killing targets. You know, the people you have to kill to gain your immunity. So, Deputy Taylor took the necessary photos, making it look like he killed them intentionally. We then processed that through the database I was about to talk to you about a few minutes ago. It gained him immunity. He got his green bracelet. First one I got around to issuing. Then we gave the bodies to the morgue for processing."

"Uh huh," she muttered as a form of encouraging him to continue, as he had paused for some reason.

"Did you know, all morgue workers are red bracelet exempt?" She obviously hadn't known this. "I figure they'd have to be. After all, what sort of mess would we be in if they weren't around?" A rhetorical question that she knew she should avoid trying to answer.

"Sorry. Back to those two car occupants I was telling you about. We decided there's no point involving the hospitals or ambulance service, either. We dealt with it ourselves. We often had to, so there was no suspicion raised. Clearly, Deputy Taylor was going to say nothing. And Clara, Becky and Deputy Mactavish wouldn't either. Because obviously, they realised that sort of solution would eventually be their way through this conundrum, too."

"I like what you were thinking."

"You can't underestimate how relieving it is not to have to kill anybody just because some diabolical politicians order you to. And if you grew up as a church-goer, as I did, you can sleep slightly better at night than if you killed indiscriminately."

"There's an understatement if ever I heard one, Sheriff Canley. So I'm guessing you managed to do the same for the others?"

"Over time, yes. We had a kid die of a drug overdose. Recovered her body pretty quickly, we did. With a bit of fancy staging, Becky nabbed one of her kills. Later she got the other from us after we simply collected an elderly guy who had died in his sleep of old age. Now, normally, we'd involve a coroner. But when you're the sheriff of a place like this, you'd be surprised how easy it is to... how shall I put it?"

"Cheat the system?" Constance offered.

"Get the best out of the system is how I'd put it. Yes. That's what it is, knowing how to do things the best way. Even if it's not above board."

"So that's Deputy Tayor and Becky immune. What about the other two?"

"We had two guys, who were apparently best friends, have a brawl outside a bar in town. It got very serious and one stabbed the other. He didn't even know he had done it, so drunk was he. We got them both back here and the one who got stabbed died in the cell overnight. I've got great photo of the deputy holding the knife like he had just done it, himself. Used that one for one of the immunity kills. The drunk guy was released the next day and though he raised questions about where his pal was, we lied to him and said he met with an accident. Said we had no time to investigate. After some complaining, he must have realised we were ignoring him as best we could. I guess, to this day, he lives with unanswered questions buzzing around his head. But that's none of my concern now."

Constance was intrigued by the story and the manner in which he told it. She allowed him to continue, uninterrupted.

He said, "The other kills the team needed came this way and that. There was a fire someone was killed in and a drowning in the pond. Some vagabond who probably fell in when inebriated. Can't recall all of the details. But these unfortunates got my team all the immunity they needed."

"Do we call that lucky?"

"We call it what we want. But you have to avoid publishing their names, ma'am."

"That's part of our agreement, Sheriff. I'm going to make sure none of the details get published when this goes to print."

"I want to move onto something else now. That database we almost talked about earlier."

"Yes, indeed."

"They came installing a scanner on the desk over there and some special software on the police station computer."

He pointed at a flat-screen monitor that stood above a grey-topped desk near the back of the office, the scanner having been boxed up ready to be returned now it was no longer needed for anything.

He continued by saying, "They did all this a couple of weeks before Day One. Showed me how to use it all and gave me a *'personal access code'* which I was told *'not to forget, or else'*. One of my jobs was to use this every time I switched any of that equipment on and when prompted to do so."

Constance Brighley was obviously taking notes fast enough for him not to hesitate.

"To get peoples' immunities sorted and to process the known dead, I had to access the computer, type in my code number, KT68644VL and another couple of letters, and access the victim's details first. So I scan John Doe's image from the pic or video I should have been issued. And once the scanner and computer recognises the person, he or she will come up on the screen. I then get asked to *'Select action option'* and Invariably I select 'D'. The computer then says *'Link victim to applicant'*, whereby I'll open up that person's record and then press the *'I'* button which gives them instant immunity if it's their second killing or awards them 1 credit if it's their first. Boys between the age of 10 up to adult age girls 13 upwards got instant immunity with their first killing. Adults had to get two."

"I think the Enforcers get this link, too."

"Apparently not. They don't have the mechanisms to issue immunity after they process a 'D'. They don't have the *'I'* option. Just us authorised officials."

"If instant immunity is granted, the system then asks me to enter the serial number of the green bracelet I'm told to issue there and then. So I type the number in where prompted. The applicant gets the bracelet which I have to personally install onto his or her wrist using this fancy bit of kit I keep locked away."

"Fascinating. I never did understand the process. I'm sure the readers will be equally intrigued."

"Please don't forget. Keep any incriminating detail confidential," he implored her.

"Guaranteed! You know that. Did you have to record how people were killed? Like by gunshot, knives, poison, etc?"

"No, that would make me a coroner. And all that aspect of the accounting was suspended. The government knew that the number of people who were going to die was going to inundate the system. All they wanted, the evil motherfuckers, was for as many killings to happen as possible."

"How many killings happened in this County in the time the atrocities were happening?" she enquired.

"Lost count. If I had to guess, in just this county, you're looking at about four thousand five hundred. And this is just a small county without any large towns. And no cities. We are tiny here. Goodness only knows what happened in the likes of Atlanta, Augusta, Columbus. Rumour has it Atlanta lost 71,000 people. That's madness."

"The government wanted to reduce the population of the USA by the killing of about a third, I believe. And 71,000 is not even 10% of today's population of Atlanta. I'm glad it all came to an end when it did," she said, offering her opinion.

He could only shrug at the vast numbers. She went on to ask about the killings a bit more. "Except for the obvious, like guns and knives, in what other ways did people die? What did you have to deal with?"

"You name it, I dealt with it. But one that comes to mind is," he hesitated to think of the right way to put it, "almost funny."

"Funny?"

"You decide for yourself. Near the canal walk in town. One of the school kids, a boy of 14 was stalking a girl who was normally in the same school class as him. She was 13, so just old enough to be his target. He followed her up this long flight of steps. Concrete ones that ran up the side of the canal path. Knife in one hand and camera recording in the other. I heard from his friends that this kid was going to post the killing on his social media site like lots of kids chose to do. Evil little shitheads. Anyway, he followed her up the steps, filming away. She heard him behind her, turned around and just caught a glimpse of the knife coming at her in time to duck to the side. He missed. She swiped out at him with her shoulder bag, catching him round the ear. He tumbled all the way down the steps and broke his own neck. Dead by the time he hit the ground. His hand hadn't let go of the camera and ended up filming his own death. Right up to the point his frozen image was front and centre on the screen. The kid died looking at the screen of his own death."

"Rough justice."

"And I'm not finished. She took his camera, saw what was on it and used it to get her own green immunity bracelet. Now, is that funny, or what?"

Constance Brighley was indeed smiling and holding back a chuckle. So yes, she considered part of it to be funny.

"We also had snipers who used their fancy assault rifles to make kills, but they didn't have usable film or photos. Too far for the cameras to record acceptable detail. It's one of the rules of The Objective. A burden of proof."

"A death for no reason?"

"You could say that. But I even had to process the application of a guy who snatched the dead body from somebody else who had *sniped* him from 300 yards, hastily taking the body away to his own place somewhere and claim he had made the kill, himself. I can only imagine how confused the sniper guy would have been when he got to where he thought the body would have been only to find it missing, or just a pool of blood."

"How do you know that happened?"

"This guy showed me a photo of a dead body and claimed he had done him with a "Two-two', which is a small-bore pistol. Well, the hole in this corpse was not, shall we say, commensurate with a little pistol."

"The outcome?"

"I used that database and gave him his award. Who am I to talk? Don't forget I did the same for the deputies some time before."

Constance Brighley didn't offer comment for this.

"Deputy Mactavish had a guy turn up with two bodies under a tarp in the back of his pick-up truck. These corpses hardly resembled people. Faces destroyed beyond our ability to ID them. So a terrible waste in more ways than I care to mention."

"What happened to the two?"

"Nothing I could do with them, personally. I told the guy to take them to the morgue. And you know what he said to me?"

"Can't even guess."

"He said *"I risked bringing these two here. I'm in mortal danger. I need my immunity."* Which I couldn't give, of course. He refused to take the bodies to the morgue and drove them home quick as he dared instead. Back to where he felt safest. I saw him again three days later with two completely different bodies I *could* use the system to identify. Killed them the exact same way. Only this time he had the common sense to take photos first. Neither of us spoke of the other two. Once his bracelet was fitted, he broke down in tears. I had to harden myself to what was going on, ma'am. Just ignored him and told him to be on his way."

"You must have suffered inside."

Ignoring that particular bait, he asked, "What's next on the duties you want to know about for your readers?

"You mentioned detention centres. Taking people there."

"I had to take *non-compliants* to the detention centres."

"Why, or under what circumstances?"

"My remit was to make sure people played fair. In a world where nothing is fair, I had to enforce some sort of parity, if that's what you'd call it. Some controls, too. If I discovered that somebody had tried to steal someone else's green bracelet, not that they could be removed without the proper kit, they went to detention. If I thought it wrong that somebody was trying to gain immunity unfairly, off to the detention centre they went, too. I let others make the judgement, to decide if anything was wrong and to what extent it may be. I merely took people there when there were suspicious circumstances."

"Do I anticipate you didn't know at that time that Enforcers at the detention centres sent many of these people to their own deaths?"

"No, I didn't ma'am. No way in the world. Had I known I'd have turned a blind eye to some of it. I'd have turned people away, tail between their legs, sulking. Sending people to their deaths for no good reason is not what I'm on this good planet for. This is exactly why I'm leaving Consetta County and heading as far from here as possible. I know there's folk who hold grudges on me."

"They must know you were just doing your job."

"Whilst they've still got guns and the knowledge they have about me, I'm not staying. And I'm never coming back.

Part Three
The Hunters and the Hunted

Chapter 28

Steevo Baxter hopped into the shotgun seat of Wolf's pick-up truck. Wolf turned up a minute or two later, having brought with him some guns and ammo. He wedged them behind the seats in the cabin. He also had a notebook and pen. He put those into one of the pockets of his camo jacket.

They drove for thirty miles, into Kansas, and stopped on the outskirts of a small town.

"You can come with me if you want. Just watch and listen. Don't do anything else."

"You got it."

Wolf, with gun in hand wandered down the street, surveying the houses all around. "No, don't like this street. We are moving on," he said.

"What are we looking for?" asked Steevo.

"You'll see. I'm off to earn some money."

They walked around a corner of a street, alongside a house with a short front garden, bordering onto the footpath by an eye-level hedge.

"This one may do." He readied his gun and his camera. "Stay back here and just observe." He told Steevo. He walked up to the front door and knocked.

A girl of about nineteen answered the door but the visitor was unfamiliar. She just stood there while he looked down at her bare left wrist. Before he could react, the girl's twin sister came into view as well. She didn't have a wristband either. He shot both in the chest. Two bullets each. A double-tap for each, as cinema-goers often heard this referred to in the movies. He slipped the gun back into his chest holster, got out his smart phone and hastily took two photographs. Eight seconds after knocking on the door, he was now descending the steps, walking down the short footpath back to the sidewalk and ushering Steevo away from the house.

As they left, they could hear the girls' mother calling out. "Who's there at the door, Cheryl? Is that your school friend?"

They were fifty yards away, heading back to the truck by the time the mother's calls had turned to screaming.

"You can't do that," Steevo protested.

"I didn't."

"I saw it with my own eyes. And it was twins. Same demographic. That's a hundred percent not allowed."

As they walked and as he was listening to Steevo trying to quiz him on what he had just seen, Wolf took out the small note pad from his pocket. He checked a couple of entries and then found his phone. He pressed a few buttons, hit a send button and put the phone back into his inside pocket.

"You see, Steevo, I didn't do anything. John and Mary White did that. One each. They just received the photos of their kills. They're half-way to immunity, now."

Steevo now fully realised what he had just witnessed.

Wolf added, "And I'm $20,000 richer too once I get them their second kills!" I did it for them. It's simply business. Tomorrow, we go to another town and get them their next two kills."

Steve Baxter made a mental note not to keep Wolf company on that trip. He was a hardened hunter, but having just seen what he had, even he thought it a bit too cruel. Yet there was no way he would say this to Wolf. He knew the man was callous and would not take any protestations. Steve would act like the normal '*Steevo*' in front of him but make up some excuse not to go along tomorrow.

Despite Steevo not going with Wolf the next day, he felt obliged to sit with him and Wex in the clearing by Wolf's cabin, while Wolf told them both about the four kills he made that second day. On behalf of paying customers.

"Yeah, I've done it." Wolf said while cracking the ring-pull on another beer. "But it's boring. I want a proper hunt."

"Nobody to stop us. It's not deer hunting season yet, but the wardens ain't about. There'll be no witnesses."

"I'm not after deer. I want a man-hunt."

"Like a real person?"

"Yes. Torment him. Pursue him. Then kill him the old-fashioned way. With an arrow into his spine as he's running away."

"It'll be a first," said Wex with more enthusiasm than Steve secretly felt.

"I'm going to promote and sell a man-hunt on our site to the club members. Most of them loved the buffalo hunt we did last time, but I know there's some who'll cream their jeans if I told them what's about to happen."

For the next few hours they talked about the idea. Many beers were finished, there were cold meats in the cool box and Wolf organised some music to keep them company through the evening.

By the early morning hours they knew the basics of the plan but were missing one vital ingredient. A target.

The next morning Wolf woke to find Wex prodding the embers of last night's fire with a long stick. He was just managing to get the first new flames to lick their way along some kindling when Wolf asked him, "Are you cold, or something?"

"No, just scrounged some eggs from inside and I was going to scramble them into a pan for us three. You want breakfast?"

"No time today. I'm having a tattoo done. Back of my calf. A racehorse. Always wanted a racehorse tattoo."

Later that afternoon, Wolf returned to his cabin all excited. Steevo and Wex were both still there. Hanging around, flinging pebbles from their catapults at tree branches and yelping with joy if one of them hit a point-scoring target.

"Guys. Gather round."

They pulled up beer crates to sit on and got ready to listen.

Wolf continued, "I've got a target for the man-hunt. Whilst I was at the tattooist, he told me some guy's been asking around for information as to who killed his family. Said he's looking for two guys who could be tree specialists."

"Why is he a good target?"

"'Cos he's a fighter. And we like a good fight. But he can't cope with fate and now he's sobbing into his beer at night, I don't but wonder. He's angry and he wants a fight with someone and I'm willing to oblige. And if he's a real fighter, he'll make good sport out of it. Just think how excited the club members will be."

"Where does he live?"

"I've got the exact address. The fuckwit has told everybody where he lives. Shared his address. What a fool."

"What else do you know about him. Is he young or old? Is he a white guy or black? What's his name? Is he..."

Wolf interrupted. He said, "No idea about anything else at the moment. You guys can help me find out what we can. Starting tomorrow first thing. In the meantime, I'm going to start making the hunt advert for the website."

Four days later, after Steve and Wex Baxter had found out what they could about Spencer Dexton, Wolf had completed the hunt advertisement.

He forwarded this to his usual band of reprobates. Along with the usual welcoming messages, the *details* page on his Dark Web Site read as follows:

Target: Decided and located.

Location: Oklahoma (North East). Further details to follow.

Status: Under surveillance when possible. Periodic temporary loss occurs.

Gender: Male

Age: 45-55

Appearance: Medium height / well built. Dark hair. Fit and is deemed capable of defending himself.

Known circumstances: This man has been asking around about the killers of his family. He is vengeful and seeking to find these killers for probable retribution. This makes him dangerous and adds to the excitement of our hunt, and his current state of mind will put him on high alert. This also adds to the value of the target.

Hunt notes: This is to be one of our high-octane no-guns hunt. It has been awarded 'Gold Label' status.

Allowable weapons: Bows and arrows / Crossbows / Hunting knives / Axe / Machete / Any other bladed weapon / Catapult / Slingshot. No guns to be taken anywhere to the hunt. Leave them at home. No hunting dogs allowed.

Rules (1): Kills made by any other means will result in disqualification and exclusion from this club.

Rules (2): As this is our 'Gold Label' private hunt. No uninvited attendees. See application details further below.

Rules (3): No advance attendance at the location until the published commencement date / time. See details below. Anybody witnessed attempting to obtain any unfair advantage over any other participant with this regard will be excluded from the hunt and club membership revoked.

Entry fee notes: Increased since last hunt due to nature of preparation work by my team.

Hunt fee: $8600 per person.

Payment: Payment in the usual way. Only cleared funds will confirm a place on the hunt.

Prize: Normally we do not offer a prize. However, on this occasion, we will be prepared to donate 20% of profits made to the winner.

Date/Time: June 16. Meeting briefing 1700-1800 hrs. Hunt commences 1900 hrs.

Meeting place: In North-East Oklahoma. We have an abandoned car-lot available to us. Exact location to follow in first main (forthcoming) briefing.

Application: By advance payment only- See details above. Applications must be in by June 10. Sorry about short notice. But we have to move on this one, and quick.

Judges' decision: All evidence will be reviewed to ascertain who made the final kill. Judges' decision is final.

Janner wanted applications in, paid for and completed by June 10th. He was not disappointed and had a full contingent of hunters by that date. It was a popular opportunity, quite clearly. There would be three women and eleven men.

Janner promised applicants they would receive the usual two briefings. The first to inform them of the meeting details and the second, which would give them the details of the target and his whereabouts, on the day of the hunt itself.

The message each received to confirm their attendance laid out some of the ground rules.

It reminded participants of key things from the hunt advert. Wolf was keen to make it clear that that this was an old-fashioned hunt. No guns allowed anywhere, at any time, so they were to be left at home. They were told not to bring their own walkie-talkies as, like always, these would be issued to each hunter on the day. They were all told to bring video recording equipment; with bodycam being the most popular choice and were also told that special prizes would be given for things like the best film footage posted after the hunt was over, or the best still-shot which may one day feature on the website to help promote future events. Another special prize would be awarded to whoever radioed into Wolf the most useful hunt update information during the time the hunt was progressing. Wolf reminded applicants that "*we all help each other out*" with live reporting as the hunt progresses.

Wolf was truly excited and couldn't wait.

Chapter 29

The Chronicle Interviews-
Post-Disaster Era- Interview Six

Martindale O'Toole was driving on his way to Franklin near Nashville to visit his latest interviewee, Arthur Beatley. He mulled over what he had found out from his Chief Editor at the Chronicle.

Constance Brighley told him that he was an elderly gentleman who not only suffers from hyperthyroidism which makes him twitch a lot, but his recent experience has made him into an even more nervous person, and so he would need to be sensitive to both conditions when interviewing him.

"Why did you select him, all things considered?" he had asked her.

"He's unique, as you'll find out. Not many people have gone through what has had to. It took me ages to find somebody like him."

"Tell me more."

"No, sorry, Marty. On this occasion, I want you to do it blind, to hear some things with no pre-conceived ideas."

"I'm intrigued. Let's do it."

With the day having arrived, Marty was now finally driving up to the sidewalk outside Arthur Beatley's home, a very plain single-story dwelling that looked like it would fall down the next time the wind blew.

However, once inside he was delighted to see that the home was very loved and well-tended to. Cute ornaments were nicely displayed on the shelves and mantlepiece, pictures of his family adorned the walls, and the place smelt beautifully fresh like a spring morning.

Arthur's wife met him at the door. A charming lady of a similar age. Both in their mid-seventies, he would guess.

"Hello Marty. It is Marty, isn't it, or would you prefer Martindale?"

"The only time I see '*Martindale*' is when I read it on the utility bills they send me. So just Marty, please."

"Well, I'm Arthur, but my friends call me Art, so feel free to do the same. And my wife's Babs, but she's Barbara on our utility bills." That was enough to have Marty creased up laughing.

Having settled into a very plush armchair, Babs brought Marty a coffee in a big mug and she brought Art something to drink in a beaker with a straw sticking out of the top. Marty reckoned it was so he could drink it without spilling any on account of his hands shaking; as he noticed they were prone to doing.

They made a start.

"Art, I have a confession to make to you," Marty said.

"Ooh. That's interesting."

"Normally, I do my homework before arriving at the places I do these interviews. But today, I come here blind, as I was told nothing and also not allowed to ask questions before I met you."

"Oh, I see. I thought you'd have known everything."

"I'm running on empty."

"Goodness. Where to start? Well, there's two parts to my story. One is how I escaped death right at the end, and the other is the mistake that put me in the mess in the first place."

"I figure we start at the beginning."

"Fair enough. Like most God-fearin' folks we couldn't believe what we were hearing when they made that *Announcement*. You know the instruction to kill other people. Ridiculous."

"99 percent of people thought the same, Art."

"So we got to talking about it and decided we would simply not do it. We would hold out, keep our heads down and wait for it to all change."

"Another common thought and approach. But it was a dangerous choice for many."

Babs joined in. She said, "And a bad choice for many, too. Easy targets. You were stuck indoors and if you tried to go outside? Well, you just didn't dare."

Arthur continued, "Very easy to meet your maker. We lost five neighbours in the space of the first few days and I think maybe the same number again in the couple of weeks after that. People got more and more scared. If you got clumsy, you could get a bullet, or a knife."

"I'm guessing you closed the curtains and simply tried hiding," the interviewer suggested.

"At first, but we ran out of food. I had to go out. I knew where I had to go. Round here, you ring up this number. It's a grocery store. You sort of ask them what they've got in stock and they prepare a box for you to collect. You drive up to and arrive at the back door and swap your payment for the box. That way there's hardly any contact with anybody else."

"Sounds like a good system," Marty suggested.

"We got used to it over the weeks. It became very easy and sort of second nature. To just place an order and collect it when they said."

"I like it."

"One time, I had just collected our box and I was coming home. A teenage boy stepped out right into the road from between two parked cars. I hit him with my car full on. 35 miles an hour and I killed him, Marty. Outright. He stood no chance. He wasn't looking, just staring down at his mobile phone. He never knew what hit him."

"That's most unfortunate," he agreed.

"That's what I thought at first. Anyway, I waited for a bit, trying to think what to do. I had my own phone with me. A mobile thing, a bit like that kid had. Our daughter made me buy one some time back. So I rang the police but couldn't get through. I tried calling the hospital, but same thing. Then I thought about the National Order and I thought *'well, I've killed someone. They didn't say how you had to do it.'* So, I took a photo of his face and took it in. For processing," but Art was clearly saddened at this point in the story's rendition.

Babs took over for a while. "We simply didn't know all the rules. After all, we weren't going to participate anyway. So we didn't know what you had to do, or how."

Arthur joined back in. "So I reported the kill at the local school. That's where they were taking details. It was late in the afternoon. The guy at the desk looked at what I'd given him and asked me to have a seat in this office just behind him. I figured that was the process, so I sat in there and then I heard the door lock behind me. Like I was captured, or something."

"I've not heard that happen before, to anybody."

"I was very scared by now. I mean, I'm not a well person, anyway."

"I can tell by your shaking. Oh, sorry to be personal."

"No, no, not a problem. It's pretty obvious my shaking and all that. People think it's that Parkinsons, but it's an over-active thyroid in my case. Makes me shake, gets my heart rate up, makes me sweat a lot sometimes. Anyway, where was I?" he said to himself.

"In a locked room," Marty reminded him.

"Of course. So, I'm there for about thirty minutes and this army guy arrives. He was as stern as you can imagine. No greeting, no smiles, no humanity. He tells me I've done something very wrong. He says I've killed a green bracelet immune person and I was now in BIG trouble. He emphasised BIG, like I had killed the President, or something."

"I wish you had," Babs said. "You wouldn't have to have gone through all of this."

"So, you were in the hands of the army."

"Yeah. And they whisked me off in the back of a secured van. It only had two little darkened glass windows. And a screeching siren. I had no idea where we were going."

"I had no idea where he was. He'd been ages by this time." Babs had started sobbing by now. Marty wasn't far off joining in. This did not sound like a good news story at all.

Arthur continued again. He announced, "I suppose about 30 minutes later, we stopped. I was frog-marched out into this building. It looked like a business used to be run from there. There was some faded lettering on a wall sign which I think said Nashville Thread... something... but the place was empty except for some chairs, a couple of desks and a computer. Someone they called an Enforcer came to see me. She was a woman, not much younger than me."

"Army woman?"

"Oh no. I got the impression she was a librarian, or a parishioner. Somebody nice. Or used to be. She looked incredibly stressed and not wanting to be there at all."

"What did she do?"

"First, she got an army guy to sit with us while she asked questions. Apparently, the army guy was there as an independent observer. But he was like a judge. Staring. Listening to every word. Concentrating. It was most unnerving."

"What happened next?" Marty enquired.

"She took my details and recorded them on this keyboard fixed to the computer. Then she simply said to me:

"Tell me exactly what happened. In your own words."

So I did. I tried to tell her the reasons I hit the kid, explaining it was his fault and I couldn't avoid it. She then said:"

"Why didn't you just drive away? Why did you try to claim it as one of your kills?"

So I said I was a God-fearing type and if fate got me to kill someone, then fate was going to get me this immunity. She reminded me that I was not allowed to kill a green bracelet person."

"It wasn't intentional."

"But then she said to me, *"Because I can only work with facts, I deem you to have violated the rules."* She wasn't happy telling me this, I can tell you. But I didn't have time to dwell on this, because that army guy escorted me away, through another door. Right away, to a new room. Like, three seconds later. Told me I had to sit in there and wait."

"Another locked room, I'm guessing," Marty enquired.

"Last one I ever intend to be in." And Art, though telling a very harrowing story, started laughing uncontrollably. Babs knew why but Marty was taken aback."

"Art. What's going on?" he asked.

"Well, do you remember I had two parts to my story?

"I sure do," he replied.

"The army guy said he was obliged to read me a statement. Well, once he started, I was in so much shock and disbelief, I can hardly remember the exact words. But I remember the underlying message, no problem."

"Go on," he encouraged him.

Arthur mimicked him a little.

"It is my solemn duty to inform you that due to rule violation XYZ123, or some such number, the US government sentences you to death by firing squad."

Art set aside his beaker, stood shakily to his feet and saluted like some army officer saying "yessir" to a senior. "Oh the words were a little different, but you get the gist," he added.

"I certainly do. But you're here, at home. Safe."

"I almost died instantly from a heart attack, I can tell you. They almost didn't need a firing squad. They said something about a priest. Told me to write down on a piece of paper the contact details of who they should inform afterwards. None of it made sense and your mind is racing by now. Your thoughts are like the ball in a pinball machine, bouncing all over the place."

"When was it going to happen?"

"Immediately after I had seen the priest, apparently. But I sat in that room. And it was getting on for midnight. It was like a torture, of sorts, this waiting in fear. Anyway, I was saying my prayers even before he arrived. Then there was this whooping and hollering and one heck of a commotion from outside."

"What was it?" Marty asked.

"It turns out that the government had just that very minute announced they were putting an immediate halt to the killings. The NCCO thing had been... what's the word...?"

"Rescinded." Barbara helped out.

"Rescinded, yeah. And not a moment too soon. Word had just got around. They received it at the desk that very moment, so it seems. They let me out. And one guy drove me home. I sat in the front seat with him. Crying with joy all the way back. We both were."

The rest of the day at the Beatley house was spent chatting about the good times. Marty was glad he had met this lovely couple. Victims of circumstances from both ends of the spectrum.

Chapter 30

Spencer Dexton and Frankie Canetti agreed, with Jo Lechie acting as intermediary, to talk in the first instance on the telephone. A conference call between all three.

She thought planning a face-to-face meeting as their first point of group contact would be hard to organise. Currently, she estimated, the two men were about a thousand miles apart. Domestic flights were exorbitantly priced and very seldom flew nowadays, anyway. One had to have a very good reason to fly by plane and have a pot of gold available to afford a ticket. She, herself, just a few days before, had been summoned down from her Fort Worth home office to Conway in Arkansas where the KXHB outside broadcast team were often stationed.

She had started working on a new story with her tech team and collectively, they were stuck at their desks trying to hit a broadcast deadline. She realised she would be unable to leave her desk for the foreseeable future.

Because of this, she was no longer anywhere near where Frankie Canetti was; although not too far from Spencer in Oklahoma.

Therefore, all things having been considered, the first contact between all three of them would be best conducted by telephone. When this was proposed, all three were in agreement.

The call happened on a Thursday evening.

"Hello to you both." Jo started the group chat going.

"Hello," they both said, one after the other.

"You've not met or spoken before," she said, "and so I'd like you to take it in turns to briefly explain to each other who you are, share something of your background and suggest why you think this call is important."

They duly obliged. Spencer went first. He told Frankie about his job as a researcher and how Jo had asked him to help find him at his Pittsburgh location.

"So, you're the swine who's forced me to run away?" Spencer could hear in Frankie's tone of voice that he wasn't being serious. There was some fun in the accusation.

And Spencer retorted, hopefully with an equal tone of light-heartedness. "And you're the swine who's apparently told the whole of the USA to go and knock each other off."

Frankie attempted a forced chuckle. But it was obvious that this remark of Spencer's hurt a little too much. He tried to defend himself straight away.

"That's what our esteemed White House Chief of Staff and his favourite Attorney General puppet would want you to believe. And every bloody member of the press, so it seems. I'm at a loss to understand why they are trying to pin this on me, specifically."

"I gather you want some help clearing your name, Frankie?" he speculated. "Turn the tables on these guys. What are their names, again?"

"The former is Jeremy Weinstein and the latter, the A.G, is Robert Gently."

"Oh yes, I remember now."

Frankie turned the table with his own question. "And I gather you want some help approaching them both so you can give them merry hell for what happened to your family?"

"That was my original intention, certainly. However, now I've given it some serious thought, I want to do something else, Frankie."

"Which is what?"

"I want to do whatever it takes to force them both into rescinding this NCCO."

"Though I like your thinking, I really doubt you'd achieve that, my new friend. But tell me how you'd try."

"Not over the phone. Let's meet. I have a cunning plan brewing," Spencer offered.

Jo interrupted. She said, "It sounds like you two are getting along rather well, all of a sudden. Three minutes ago you had only vaguely heard of one another, trading insults too, and next thing you're planning a pow-wow to plan to overthrow major government decisions."

"When you put it like that, I guess that's just about it. A great summary," Spencer remarked.

Frankie said, "I guess you know I'm still holed up in Washington, having had to escape Pittsburgh for the time being, but where are you staying, Spencer?"

"I'm currently in Steerwagon Falls in North East Oklahoma but I live in Archville, East Iowa, so will be travelling back quite soon. We can meet somewhere up there if you so wish."

"I'm not specifically familiar with either of those two towns but hold on and stay where you are, anyway.

I've got access to Gently's schedule for the next couple of weeks. He's going to be working in Memphis quite soon and visiting a Three-Star Army General in Texas shortly after that. Memphis isn't too far from where you are now."

"There's a logic that says if we are going to approach Gently, we should do it where he turns up, not where we'd want him to be."

"Of course," Spencer agreed.

"I'd certainly favour trying to get to see him in Memphis. He doesn't tend to travel with personal security staff. But when he's back in his offices in Washington, you can forget seeing him there. It's like Fort Knox. And doing it anywhere near army personnel isn't particularly appealing, either, so Texas is out of the question, too."

"What dates are we looking at?"

"If we are going to plan something, we have to meet as soon as we can. When are you free, Jo?"

"Not for ages," she sadly admitted. "You two will have to plan what you want to do next on your own accord."

"And what about Weinstein? How do we get to him?" Spencer asked.

"That will be a major challenge, I fear," Canetti said. "He's as hard to get an appointment with as is the President, himself. We'll have to work on that completely separately and at a later time."

The conversation drifted about a bit, discussing a multitude of things, but the most important thing to come from the call was Spencer and Frankie would be meeting three days hence, in Jo's KXHB office in Conway, Arkansas. They all worked it out to be about 2 hours from Memphis. Close enough to where they would be aiming to be at a later time.

They all grudgingly decided to meet early on the Sunday morning, with Frankie planning to drive down from Washington over the course of the Friday and Saturday. He knew they would be very long arduous days' driving but that was alright with him.

"I'm a bit concerned with being able to get about. Steerwagon Falls to Memphis, via Conway, etcetera. Fuel's an issue…"

"Consider it solved. I'm the Transport Minister, don't forget."

"So what? Oh, sorry. Not trying to be rude."

"Don't fret. Okay, here goes. Us government guys travel all over the place. We can't simply fill up our cars at the gas stations the public use. We need a reliable supply. So I'm going to mail you a list of hundreds of locations all over the USA. Most of these are gated warehouses with shutters on the doors. You give me your licence plate number and the make, model and colour of your car and I'll enter it on the main-frame computer. Your car will be cleared for entry into any of these and you'll get free fuel. The operatives who work at these places don't ask questions. And in reality, you'll be working on government business, so it's not underhand," Frankie told him.

"I can't believe that."

"Well, it's a hundred percent what happens and what I'll do."

"I can't thank you enough."

"There are obvious rules. You don't unscrew your licence plate and lend it to anybody else for them to use on their car. In fact, you tell nobody about this."

"Of course," Spencer agreed.

"And lastly, when all this is over, I'll change the status of your vehicle on the computer to '*Invalid*'. You got that?"

"Couldn't be any clearer. Thank you."

Jo started asking. "Frankie, can yo…."

"NO." Was all he had to say. And he said it firmly.

Chapter 31

It was Sunday morning, and after Jo met and welcomed both men, Spencer Dexton for the very first time on a face to face basis and Frankie for the second time, she surprised them both with a hearty breakfast that she had managed to prepare in the broadcasting studio's little but well-equipped kitchenette.

Twenty five minutes later they gathered around a glass oval table the studio staff often used when planning programmes, interviews, schedules and suchlike.

"Gentlemen," she started, "you'd think my interest in all of this would be for the potential news story. But Spencer's a long-time acquaintance whom I'm trying to help. And you, Frankie, are sitting on a bombshell of a situation. You need help with it, too. I honestly believe you'd be good for each other."

"Well, we've agreed to meet, and we can start making our plans, in earnest." Frankie offered the chance for Spencer to respond.

"I'm all for it," he agreed.

"But, guys, before you get to planning stuff, I've a much more pressing situation to tell you about. Big-time worse, perhaps." She looked toward Spencer with a sternness he found unsettling.

"I don't like the sound of this at all."

"In fact, you both have. That's you too, Frankie, but in a different way. So I'll come to that shortly. Guys, I have to tell you the things in the right order. So please be patient." She glanced down at her pad of notes.

"Where was I? Oh yes, I'm lucky in so much as I have a great research team here at KXHB. They find stories, they research facts, access data and give us reporters every bit of support we need."

"Sounds like a good team."

Jo continued. She asked, "May I swear you both to secrecy?" They both agreed. "They have access to questionable sources. Some low-level government sites, foreign aid entities, charities' servers, results from hacked phone records, and the Dark Web which is still used today all these years after the internet was invented. It's not quite as secure as it used to be, but nonetheless very popular with low-lives and reprobates."

"Your guys and girls are resourceful people."

"They love what they do. I swear they'd even do it if we didn't pay them. But we do and it makes that job the best in the world. In their eyes. So, I get to hear about all sorts of juicy things from time to time."

She paused for a moment, taking in some water to keep herself from getting a dry mouth.

She continued by saying, "It all started when we were researching Gently's forthcoming trip down here. I was trying to get the background on what's about to happen. To be ready for this meeting. We didn't get a lot at first. So we did what we call *Parallel Checks*. This is research into anything else that may be going on that isn't directly associated with the event in question, but anything his name may be linked to. Then we discovered the name Gretson."

Frankie was taken aback. "Tabitha? Where does she fit in? She's a friend of mine."

"Who's Tabitha Gretson?" Spencer asked.

"She's the Chief Scientific Officer. I've worked with her a very long time."

"Gentlemen, please." They both hushed up. "The reason her name came up is because one of the team was on *transmission duty*. Oh, sorry, it's a stupid term we use. Anyway, we tapped Gently's phone."

"Impossible. It's government issue," Frankie cut in.

"Actually, you're right. We didn't tap his phone, we intercepted the signals at the transmitter aerial. We capture everything for the period we want and put it through the *Sorter Box*."

"What's one of those?"

She said, "Your call will have a carrier signal with it. Let's say, in the simplest analogy, it's wearing a blue hat. The next guy's call will have a different carrier signal. Let's say it's wearing a red hat. At the same time a girl is calling her mother. This carrier signal wears a yellow hat. The Sorter Box puts all off the blue hat stuff in one box, the red had stuff in another and the yellow in yet another. We tell the Sorter to keep the blue hat stuff and get rid of the rest."

"A nice analogy," Spencer offered.

She continued. "Consequently, we have all of the messages sorted and the stuff we want ready for us. The digital set of bleeps and blips are converted back to a conversation for us. Essentially, we don't tap their phone, we tap the transmission. The airwaves, you may call them."

"How easy is it?" Frankie asked.

"Incredibly difficult if either party is mobile because you're not guaranteed to use the same transmitter for the full duration of the call. It only works, really, when both parties are stationary," she said.

"How does Tabitha Gretson ring your alarm bells?"

"We intercepted a call from Gently to somebody called Claude. No last name. We don't know who he is yet. Do you want to hear the recording?"

"I'm assuming you want me to, from your body language."

Over the next half-hour they listened to a call between Robert Gently and this unknown person whom, it was becoming apparent, was a hit-man for hire. An assassin. No other way to put it. He had clearly been requested to conduct surveillance on Gretson and wait for the instruction to carry out her subsequent killing.

"All because she authorised the facial recognition technology for the NCCO. Devastating." Frankie Canetti exclaimed.

Jo summarised his predicament. "Frankie, both you and Tabitha are being set up. Tabitha is possibly going to be eliminated for being somebody with evidence against Gently. And you're being set up for the fall. To be the scapegoat. Do you have any evidence against him?"

"No. It would all just be hearsay."

"In that regard, he wants you to be alive. For sure. But as for Tabitha. She's a direct threat to him. So therefore, expendable."

Spencer interrupted. "May I?"

"Sure."

"You said a while ago that my predicament may be worse than Frankie's. How can it be worse?"

Jo looked him squarely in the eye. "The research team accessed everything they could to find anything about Claude. They didn't find out any more than we've already discussed a minute ago. But they went onto the Dark Web and did searches for assassins, hit men, murderers; any number of similar titles. They had to initiate a filter to narrow-down what they were seeking. So they put in an area search around where Gently was suspected of being. The radius was about two states in each direction.

"We discovered a thoroughly unsavoury character called Wolf Janner. He organises and conducts wildlife hunts all over the South. Illicit ones. Anything from out of season deer hunting to stalking and killing prairie buffalo. He sells these hunting opportunities to his accomplices, let's call them, fellow hunters. A secret band."

Spencer commented. "Plenty like him all over the place, I assume."

"Not like this guy, Spencer, no. You see, since the NCCO came in, he's taken to offering his services to kill people to sell video or photographic evidence of the kills to paying customers so they can pretend it were they that made their necessary kills and who may then apply for their immunity bracelets. There are, after all, a plethora of people who want immunity but who don't want to kill."

Both men looked at each other with concern.

Jo said, "He operates out of Oklahoma as best we can tell, but we have no idea where, exactly. He may even be in Kansas or Texas. We simply don't know. The area filter on the web search had wide geographical boundaries."

Spencer listened intently, leaning forward on his forearms resting on the glass table. He did not interrupt her.

"He has decided to offer a man-hunt. Not deer, pheasant, geese, or normal game anymore. Not protected buffalo, nor out of season shoots. No, this time he wants a man-hunt. A real person."

"And this person is?" Spencer was still looking in her direction. She turned ashen-white and stared right back at him.

"You must be absolutely fucking kidding me. This must be some form of joke." But as he said this, he got the distinct impression that it was not.

Even Frankie was beyond being able to speak. He was in his own form of shock.

"Why? Why me, any idea?"

"Yes. I think I do." She had regained Spencer's full attention.

"Earlier I said Wolf Janner lives in Oklahoma, Kansas or Texas. I gauge that on what happened next. It seems he was near, but probably not in, Steerwagon Falls and came across a tattoo parlour owner who had overheard there was a guy in that part of Oklahoma state who was looking for two guys who had killed his family. Wanted to track them down."

"Oh, shit. That *was* me."

"Said he was looking for tree specialists and did Wolf know any tree specialists who had killed a family in the town? Janner told him he'd look into this."

"He knows about you and may even know your name, though we can't be sure."

"And you can be aware of that how, exactly?"

Jo said. "I've got the tech guys here at KXHB monitoring what goes on in the real world almost all the time when they're not fixing this, installing that, or loading software upgrades."

"Where are your guys?"

"They work from home, predominantly. They are all over the place. Nearest one is Shreveport."

"Can we get them on a call, to speak with them?"

"Whilst I've agreed to be here on a Sunday, I'd not be able to even get them on-line with me today. Those guys need a day off, too."

"How do you know all this stuff? The detail, I mean?"

"Janner has his own blog on his Dark Web pages," she said. "It's how he drums up interest in his hunts."

"This hasn't been a good day at all," Frankie Canetti stated. "First, we hear my friend and colleague Tabitha Gretson is on a hit list and now we have Spencer who's the target of a hunt."

"Is that going to affect your plans for Gently?"

"I don't know. Let's talk, Spencer." It was clear that he was in agreement with this. Jo went off to make some hot drinks and clear away the cooking utensils she had used earlier when she made their breakfast; now many hours ago.

When she came back Spencer said, "We've agreed to press on. We are going to get Gently. He may be the only way to put things right and to stop this hunt, too."

Jo clicked about with her laptop mouse. As she was so doing, the image of a man came up on the screen.

"Who's that?" Spencer asked.

"That's Robert Gently, himself. You've not actually ever seen him before?"

"No. Never thought to ask," Spencer said but was distracted by the face of the man who had been ultimately responsible for the death of his girlfriend, her daughter and his future in-laws. People he called his own family. "He's a bit different to what I was expecting. He's my age. Thought he'd be older."

"He is older by a good ten years." She remarked.

"But he looks younger. Does he dye his hair?"

"No. Same colour as yours. Do you dye yours, Spencer?" This was enough to have them laugh just a little. "And get some of his designer wear and you two could be models on a catwalk. You're very similar."

"Shut up. Right now. If I ever bump into him in a dark alley...." But he let that trail off. Better to be calm and relaxed.

"The plan for tomorrow? Monday?"

"Get to work," Frankie exclaimed. "How far is Steerwagon Falls from here, Spencer?"

"I did it in about 4 and a half hours," Spencer replied. "Not a crazy distance and certainly much nearer for me than you."

"We've nowhere else to go to do our work, Spencer. What say we move the show to Steerwagon?"

"I don't see why not. I've an empty place and we obviously can't stay here."

Jo added. "That's right, guys. This place will be heaving with the editing team first thing tomorrow."

"Jo, would you do something for us whilst we get set up back in Oklahoma?"

"What's that?" she asked.

"Just keep the monitoring going, please and keep us updated on this Janner thing and anything from Claude and Gretson, if and when you get it?"

"Sure thing."

Chapter 32

The Chronicle Interviews-
Post-Disaster Era- Interview Seven

Marty O'Toole started writing the interview even before he arrived at the BroadTree Condominium, a building in the town centre, comprising of eight floors with five apartments on each floor; and inhabited by 93 people before the atrocities commenced. The building overlooked the train station to the north, the direction in which the front of the building faced, a sprawl of urban office buildings to the west, run-down shops and equally run-down tenements to the south and predominantly industrial units to the east which ran parallel to the rail lines that headed off into the distance in that direction.

BroadTree Condo was known as BTC to just about everybody in the town whether or not you lived therein. It was built 46 years prior to *The Announcement* and, thanks to its new-found fame and fortune would probably be well looked after by its residents for the next 46 years, at least.

BTC was a unique building in so much as it was the only building of its design for miles. They hadn't built any in the same style as this since it was first opened. Though considered ugly by many, it stood tall and proud and on sunny days cast its shadow over the station and its platforms.

This was one interview he was particularly looking forward to.

He wanted to impress the people he was going to interview with a snazzy opening. One that would mirror the incredible achievement of their victory over the authorities.

He decided to start with a simple headline and followed it with an introduction that read as shown.

Victory for the Little People

The Homeland Chronicle is pleased to introduce you to a group of 56 people. These are incredible people who beat America. They challenged authority and they won not only their own battle, but the whole war.

Though he couldn't interview the whole group, he did manage to find four of them who were more than excited to talk with him.

Firstly, there was Miles, the condo's caretaker and live-in warden. He had managed the building since he was 30 years old, now well into his 70s, nothing seemed to stop him. He put it down to eating his favourite Jamaican food, a recipe he had inherited from his grandmother and to drink at least one shot of Jamaican rum a day.

Next in the group of interviewees was Agnes. By far the oldest interviewee Marty had ever had the pleasure to talk with. She lived on the second floor when the atrocities started in earnest but was keen to tell Marty all about the wonderful people who were her neighbours.

Thirdly, he recalled the name Thelma. A single mother of six, four of whom lived with her on the third floor; the other two having moved into their own apartments in the town's growing sprawl. He had wanted to interview those two boys of hers, but she previously informed The Chronicle that they decided not to participate. Nonetheless, this wasn't going to stop Thelma telling the world of their heroics.

Last, but by no means least, was little Sophie. A nine-year old daughter to a young couple who lived on the sixth floor. Marty had yet to interview one so young, but if these interviews were to be complete, he not only had to involve the young, he thrived on the idea of meeting her and getting her version of the story.

"Ladies and gentleman. I always start with saying thank you for meeting me and agreeing to have this chat," he said while facing a line of beaming smiles. Lots of white teeth and, at the moment, just silence. Nobody wanted to go first out of politeness. Marty pressed on.

"I have to start the interview by setting the scene, and that means I have to describe the place we are in, the building we are in, and even the room we are all sitting in. So, Miles, I'd like to start with you first in this case. You know the building best and have lived here even longer than Agnes, who I believe has been here for about 25 years." Agnes nodded, but she knew it was Miles being asked to speak, so kept quiet for the time being.

"That's right," Miles stated. "Came here with my Mammy and Pappy on a boat I can't remember because I was too young. My Pappy went to work at the car place. He fitted the engines."

"And how long have you been caretaker here in BroadTree Condo?" Marty asked.

Miles said, "BTC took me in the week it was finished, 46 years ago. I helped work on some of the final fixings. Doors, skirting boards, kitchen counters and cupboards. I was a carpenter by trade. The management kept me on temporarily in case anything went wrong in the early days but I just stayed on ever since."

"Would you be so kind as to tell the reader what room we are in and where it is in the building."

"This is the conference room. Didn't used to be though. The building was originally designed to have a big dining hall. Not used for that since the day we opened the building. Had a big party in here, then. Long tables filled with all manner of good food. Things nobody sees anymore. So then we used to let it out to businesses if they were running events. We sometimes have wedding receptions in here. Dances when the community is celebrating stuff, too."

"It's a fine room. We'll come back to how you managed the building during the big lock-in soon," he said. Marty then looked toward little Sophie who knew what was coming. "So, Sophie, can you tell me what happened five days after your last birthday?"

She almost burst with excitement. She said, "Mummy said we are going to make the building into a castle. She said I wasn't going to go to school for a long time and we were going to fight anybody who tried to get in."

"I love the way you describe it. Such an adventure." Marty smiled back at her. "And just so the readers can get an idea of who won the battle, can you tell me if anybody got in during all that time, or did you keep the baddies out?"

"Nobody got in. Ever. So we won," she announced with pride.

"That's so good. And, if I'm right, I think you're friends with Thelma who's here with us, too. Have I got that right?"

She replied, "Yeah. Thelma's girl, Latitia, is my best friend. I love them both, even if they don't live on the same floor as me."

Marty smiled back at her. They chatted about this and that for a while. He wanted to know all about her skipping school for such a long time and how she managed to study at home. They discussed pop groups and her favourite bands, though Marty was clearly well out of his depth on the topic of current chart-toppers. He got her to confess the thing she missed most was going down to the local ice cream parlour to get her favourite milkshake, when the shop had it in stock. She reminded him that milk was in short supply just like everything else. Some of this would go in the newspaper but this article was predominantly reserved to report upon the security and isolation lock-in the residents organised for themselves for their own protection.

Marty said, "I'm going to ask Thelma some questions now, and then I'll chat a lot with Agnes and Miles. There's going to be a lot of adult talk. Do you want to stay here with us or go and play with Latitia?"

Seemingly, Sophie preferred the idea of finding Latitia. This rather pleased Marty as some of what he intended to talk about with the other three may not have been appropriate for a nine-year-old. Once she had left the large room, he turned a little in his chair to face Thelma.

"Lovely young lady," Marty said. "Reminds me a little of my niece, though Sophie smiles a lot more than her."

Agnes replied, "She's our little princess. If ever we are sad, she cheers us up."

Marty addressed all three. "It's great that she gave me her perspective of your decision to lock yourselves in to protect yourselves and to try to avoid having to participate in the atrocities. But I need a lot more of how you went about the process of organising it. Or deciding what to do and how. And how you managed to gain agreement from all that were here."

He suspected Thelma would volunteer herself to explain and he was proved right in his guess.

"As soon as we heard *The Announcement*," Thelma said, "we reacted like everybody else. Shock followed by denial at first. And there's so many of us in here. There were arguments, shouting, doors slamming, a lot of crying, too, I can tell you. But we got together. We came here as a group. Into this great big room." She looked around it as if to reminisce.

Miles said, "I got as many chairs out as I could. At first, I lined them up like a big theatre."

Thelma continued, "But that suggested we were going to listen to somebody at the front. You only have a front, and a big table up there, if you are going to be lectured to; to be told this and that. That would have put somebody in charge. Not good for participation."

Miles took the initiative again, and said, "So we arranged about a hundred chairs in three huge circles. One inside another. Facing one another mostly."

"Concentric, that's called, I think," Marty offered.

"Sure, well, it worked like a dream. Everybody was close to one another and if one person talked, all the rest listened."

"Very clever."

"We got to discuss our concerns. The biggest one was from a guy called Terrence."

Agnes joined in again at this point. "He simply said:

"Some of us won't kill. Some of you will do it to protect yourselves. That's the game."

We didn't like the word *'game'* but we knew what he meant.

He then said "We can't have killing in BTC. Not within the walls. I suggest if you want to do that, you do it outside. Not here."

This was a popular thing to hear, I'll say. Nobody wanted any killing in here."

O'Toole was fascinated. "So what happened?"

Thelma seemed most comfortable with summarising the plan they had devised. So she took over.

"We asked for a vote on who agreed with Terrence. Nobody, and I mean not a single soul said they didn't. 100% agreed vote. No killing in BTC."

"Did everybody agree to renege on *The Objective*? Not kill at all?"

"Oh, no. Some said they were going to get in trouble with the authorities. They said stuff like *"Perhaps its best to comply"*, or *"Though I may agree with Terrence,*

I'm not staying here", or *"I'm man enough to look after myself in the outside world."* Stuff like that."

"Bravado, I call it," Agnes remarked.

Thelma continued, "Before long we agreed that if you stayed here, you agreed not to kill. If you left, you couldn't come back. Until it was all over."

"We took another vote on this," Miles said. "Hundred percent agreement, again." He clapped his hands together sharply as if to say it was a done deal.

"And you were okay with that?" Marty asked.

Miles said, "We seemed to operate as one from the start. Same good ideas. Same clever plans. Same worries. Nobody takes credit. Nobody takes blame. That's the only way this was ever going to work. We predicted arguments, but they didn't really happen. Looked like we were set to fight from the inside out."

"And I guess the only way to do that was to do what Sophie said. Make BTC a castle."

"You got it," Agnes agreed.

"That can't have been easy." He addressed Miles, again.

"We knew we had to act fast. We asked those who intended to go, to do so quickly. Though some were reticent, I think they saw the need for this so that the rest of us could make preparations and changes. We had to shape up to defend ourselves properly." He looked toward Agnes, for it was clear she wanted to say something more.

Agnes said, "Well, there's normally 93 residents in this block. 37 decided to leave. That's 56 left over. 31 adults and 25 children. Of course, some of them is not quite an adult but a bit older than a child. But the numbers are approximate for you Mr O'Toole."

He said, "Please, it's just Marty. Otherwise it sounds like I'm being interviewed for a job. And I kinda' like the one I've got, thank you." They all chuckled at this.

"Back to the main rule," Thelma interjected. "We said to each other, it's *stay* or *go*. A full duration agreement. Then we devised some rules that we could all abide by. Told ourselves to keep it simple.

1. Nobody comes in for any reason.
2. Nobody goes out unless medical emergency, for example. But Rule 1 still applies, so you stay out.
3. No guns. Guns means the potential for danger. No guns equals no danger. Oh, we know that's not true as there's more knives in the town than there are cars. This town is growing so fast it's almost a city. But there's a different type of threat or danger when there's guns about. So, we all agreed to pass them on.
4. We share everything. Food. Water. Medicine. Whatever.
5. We share all the work. Cleaning. Maintenance. Again, whatever.
6. We persevere. It only works if we stick with it.

"And I guess it did," Marty exclaimed, hopefully.
"Eventually, yes."
"What did you have to do first?" he asked.

'Scavenge. We needed torches, batteries, candles. We thought we also needed equipment such as water butts to store water if the supply was switched off. As it transpired, it never was, but we didn't know that at the time. Food. That was the difficult one. So, we sent out a search party to get anything. We didn't care if it was cans of corn, dried cookies, old tins of beans. It's all going to be needed."

"And,' Agnes said, "we told everybody who was leaving BTC to give us anything they had, too. Most were very happy to help us. We got corned beef, rice, pasta, packs of dried meats. All manner of stuff. Very welcomed it was, too."

"But didn't those people need it for themselves, where they were going?" Marty asked.

"We got a bit clever, there," Miles confessed. "We said if we get hungry, we can't guarantee we won't take a look around *your* apartment. And they know I had a Master Key. Anyway, they were happy to help. We are all friends here deep down. They could look for new stuff out there, wherever they were travelling to or where they finally settled down. We had…"

'Scavengers.' Thelma proudly announced. "My two oldest."

"That sounds interesting," O'Toole smiled back at her.

"My two boys live out in the run-down part of the town. I'm not going to hide the fact, but when the atrocities started, when we were told by the government to work to their *Objective*, my two boys did what evil they had to do."

"So, they got their immunity?"

"Yes. They did. But I'm sticking with the good things they did, Marty, not the bad."

"I applaud you for that. I truly do," he said.

"Whilst we were locked in here, they used to get us supplies. If and when they could. They'd come along to the wall under apartment 1b and we lowered a rope with a hook on the end. And a big basket that hung from that. We winched it up and stored the goodies they found for us in the main store. Over the weeks they did us proud."

"They did indeed," Agnes agreed. "They brought us fresh chicken sometimes. Vegetables. Bread very often. Milk, but that was hard to get. Soap powder on a few occasions."

"Innovative boys, Thelma."

"Like gold to me, they are," she agreed.

"But, you said *"Lowered a rope"*. That's not as easy as opening a door or even a downstairs window." Miles started laughing. Marty knew he'd explain shortly, so didn't attempt to ask.

"We bricked up all the ground floor windows. There's no apartments down there anyway. We bricked up the back door, too. All that was left was the main front door which we fitted bars across on the inside. Secured a sort of cage in place with great big padlocks. You couldn't get in or out without some sort of effort."

"All for safety?"

Miles agreed. He said, "All for safety and security. Both were equally important. There were questions on what would happen if we had to evacuate quickly. Like in the event of a fire. But we all agreed there were some compromises we had to take."

"I'm impressed. Did anybody try to get in? Storm the castle, Thelma?"

"There were a few times they tried it. But we persuaded them away. We claimed there was nothing of any worth. Minimal food. No incentive for them to get in, all things considered."

She said, "You see, Marty, the town may have been growing before *The Announcement*, but right afterwards it froze. Like it had hibernated. And while the town slept, the gangs roamed the streets, making sure that each of their members did enough to get their green immunity bracelets. Always hunting for their next hit, or drugs score." Marty was nodding in agreement to what Thelma was saying.

She continued. "We didn't realise at the time that the atrocities kept drugs usage much lower. The supply simply wasn't there. The gangs were uncontrolled. None of the police were willing to patrol the streets. We often heard gunshots, alarm bells going off. You name it."

"Your safety within the walls was paramount, no doubt."

Agnes beamed her infectious smile and said, "We did it. And boy did we do it well. Came through the other side without any killing or death. All of us in the building are safe and happy. We can pray to our Gods again with thanks instead of worry."

Miles joined back in. "People drifted back home here soon after. 56 is now 70 or more. Some were lost to the atrocities. But that was on the outside. In here, we won!"

For the next hour or two, over refreshments, snacks, a restroom break or two; Miles complaining of possessing a small bladder and disappearing often, they talked of how they occupied themselves. They laughed at the memory of some of the party games they devised in the conference room. How they tried playing various sports in the hall, too. They confessed that basketball didn't work, the ceiling being too low, and tried to tell of how one resident attempted to make an indoor golf game which turned into a farce; but was resurrected the next day as crazy putting. Birthdays were always celebrated one way or another. Residents wrote and performed mini plays. The kids dressed up and acted their parts as often as they could. Indeed, life during their lock-in was far more enjoyable than before it all started.

Martindale O'Toole later confessed that what he did next would turn out to be one of the biggest journalistic mistakes of his life.

He said to the group of three, "Normally, I like to hear a funny story to finish, a bit of good news to trump all of the doom and gloom, but your story is so creditable, of how you all pulled together that maybe just this time, one of you could tell me a bit about your turmoil. Tell me something sad so I get a full understanding of what you had to go through."

Thelma looked at the other two. They knew what was coming.

She started, "One evening, a girl ran up to the front entrance. She found it barricaded with bars, of course. She was screaming and covered in blood. Especially her hands and one side of her face. She was perhaps 17 or 18. Then we saw three young boys, a bit younger. They emerged from behind the old railway station wall. That's about 100 yards from the front of the building. Lots of us heard the commotion. Some of us had gathered in the lobby by now and it was obvious the boys had been searching for her. They soon spotted her here. She continued screaming, battering at our door."

"You could have let her in," Marty suggested.

"No. Rule Number One, Marty."

"But..."

Agnes swiftly stopped his protest. "Suppose she was faking it so that she could get those three in the door, who could then block it getting closed again and their gang appear from around the corner, forcing their way in, too? Food is scarce and there was a rumour we were well stocked. Which we weren't, of course."

Miles was clearly in agreement with Agnes. "It's how Rule One was set up. For *our* safety and security, not the safety of others."

Thelma continued, "Within moments our very own Antonio appeared outside. That's Antonio from Apartment 1e. To start with we didn't know how. We since found out he shimmied down the supply rope after tossing one end out the window. Anyway, he was outside, chasing the three boys away. He's just the same age as they were, I figure. He was trying to be a hero. But then it got messy. More kids arrived. He was in danger.

"He knew he was not getting back in the front door. He knew he'd never get her back up that rope he used to climb down. He also knew we couldn't help them.

But we watched him usher the girl away to somewhere. Could only hope he survived and was safe."

"Did you ever find out?" asked Marty.

"Just a matter of days later, yes. One day he came back to BTC. Spoke to his sister through the glass. He told her he was safe now, as he had gained his immunity the hard way. And sure enough, she saw the green bracelet on his wrist. And he told her he was learning how to survive on the streets. Said it was hard." Thelma started crying.

Agnes took over the story once more. "His sister asked him, *"Who did you kill to get your bracelet?"* but he said to her, *"I'm not going to answer that. I'm not proud of what I did."* Yes, indeed, that's what they said to each other." Agnes, too, took a big gulp of air before being able to continue.

"His sister asked, *"What had happened to the girl, Antonio?"* And he refused to reply to her."

Marty couldn't help but flinch with the anguish that hit him hard.

Chapter 33

Spencer and Frankie moved their working partnership to the Verlano house in Steerwagon Falls, about 250 miles west of Jo Lechie's broadcasting studio. They followed one another and it took them about six hours, arriving mid-afternoon on Monday.

The night before had not been particularly comfortable, getting a few hours broken sleep on a sofa that was too small and some cushions strewn across the studio's office floor.

Upon arrival at Independence Lane, Steerwagon Falls, Spencer gave Frankie the tour of the house and grounds, showing him where he lost his family and pointing out the plot he had dug for them. Frankie noticed the flowers Spencer had laid and the makeshift wooden cross. Before settling into the house, and though fed up with being in a car, Frankie asked Spencer asked if he didn't mind giving him a quick drive about the town. He wanted to get a feel for the location and amenities, to get an idea of the place before they got down to planning.

He got to see the community areas, the school, an abandoned church and some recently vacated houses, a few of which looked to be derelict. Not a surprise, he considered, based upon what some of these poor families have clearly gone through. Spencer took him on a route to see various other places he had spotted previously. A working mill, the municipal centre, courthouse, and the police station with all of its office light blazing away therein, even though it was quite early in the afternoon. He then took him along the row of shops which included a boutique coffee shop but which displayed a *'closed until further notice'* sign. They also saw the library, similarly closed.

And finally, Spencer had an idea. He took Frankie to see what he thought was an abandoned cabin, about a mile and a half outside town. The rear of it could just be seen from the road. Although featureless from the rear, the entrance must be out of view to one side or the opposite wall. On the way back to the house, they also noticed a repurposed coal distribution depot. Coal hadn't been used for a long time, having lost its popularity with users and sustainability do-gooders. But the depot had become a form of builder's merchant. A place one would buy construction materials for DIY or trade work.

Now, back at the house, sitting in the living room, they slowly edged into a conversation on getting control of Robert Gently, Attorney General of Maryland. It became apparent to them both that he should be the topic of a new day, Frankie being a bit too tired to concentrate fully on the challenge.

Instead, Frankie collected from his car a box of things he had brought with him on the journey. From within, he took and laid out a big map of the USA on the table. He folded it in half so just the eastern half of the country was visible. He knew where Gently was now and where he would be going over the next few days. He need not concern himself with anything west of Kansas. He reached into the leather briefcase he had brought with him and took out various printed pages. These, too, he laid out across the table. There were schedules, lists of government buildings in the Arkansas and west Tennessee areas, he had copies of some e-mails he thought he may have to reference, there were pages of hand-written notes and a well-thumbed booklet on legal precedence he referred to often.

Once finished with the now empty box, the living room table looked like a war room.

"We need more space, Spencer. Have you got another table?" he asked.

"Look, I've a reel of sticky tape, and once I leave this house, I doubt I'll ever come back, so stick things up on the walls, with tape. I don't care if the wallpaper gets a few marks. It won't matter in the slightest."

"Okay, if you don't mind." And with that, Frankie started displaying various documents on the walls, mostly at eye level.

Spencer said, "Whilst you're doing that, I'm going to drag the small desk from the next room into here. I'll put the laptop onto it. After all, this is now *'Frankie's Nerve Centre'*, and give me a few minutes and I'll get a big pink neon sign that says so." Both men laughed.

It was now well into the evening and they decided to spend the rest of the evening chatting about their lives before the NCCO was passed. A bottle of supermarket brand wine was found in a cupboard and some oat cookies, too. Not quite a gourmet feast, but they'd seek something better tomorrow.

They exchanged chats about hobbies and realised both enjoyed jogging for fitness. Frankie was a keen chess player, whereas Spencer had never tried to learn. Their taste in music was also shared with them both preferring music from the Rock 'n Roll era of the 1950s and 1960s. Spencer was also keen to hear how much Frankie knew about the way the 1970s shaped music for decades to come. They spent some time trying to remember the more obscure pop group names. Finally, Spencer showed Frankie which room he should use as his own for the night.

But their night didn't last very long, as in the early hours of the morning, their telephones were both being called. One after the other. Whoever it was, was trying to get their attention.

Chapter 34 - Hunt Briefing One

The pre-attendance hunt briefing, sent electronically to each confirmed hunt attendee, was presented almost in the form of a set of step-by step instructions.

Wolf Janner intended the briefing to be succinct and unambiguous. Designed to be followed, to the letter, without question. No need to seek clarification.

The unwritten message was: '*If you do not understand, you will be excluded from the hunt. If you do not comply, you will be excluded from the hunt.*' An electronic copy was sent to each participating hunter. It read as follows:

- Locate the abandoned car sales lot at New Hayling, Oklahoma. You will find this in the vicinity of the E 441 Road.
- Arrive at the lot between 1830 and 1915 hours on Thursday June 16th.
- Park any vehicle you arrived in within a half mile, but not at the lot, itself.
- Walk to the car lot.
- Leave any guns and ammunition in your trucks.
- No hunt dogs allowed. This is a skills hunt to test your own hunting ability.
- Fully obscure the flashing green lights on your immunity bracelets. Use opaque tape or similar.

- Make sure you have memorised your callsign. You will be referred to this at all times.
- If contacting the organiser, use his callsign "Animal".
- If contacting the support team, use their callsigns "Blocker" or "Chalkie".
- You will be allocated a walkie talkie upon arrival. They are numbered. Your number was issued to you when your application to attend the dig was confirmed.
- Do not forget your number.
- If you do not comply with the rules above, or any previously given, you will NOT be allowed to attend. Club membership may also be revoked.
- No vehicular use will be allowed until the hunt is concluded.
- Further briefing upon arrival

Chapter 35

The phone call was from Jo Lechie. Still working from Conway. Spencer answered his phone first. Frankie was still searching for his. He was in an unfamiliar bedroom and took a few extra moments finding his own bearings. He overheard Spencer taking the call from Jo.

She said, "You're in trouble, Spencer. Wolf Janner is committed to this hunt of theirs. You're still their target. And what's worse is they knew you were here in Conway on Sunday. Somehow, they must have contacts in this area, or a way to track you. You'll have to abandon your car in case it has a tracker in there. They followed you to watch you, to gauge your habits, have a good look at you. That sort of thing."

"That's disconcerting to know," he replied.

"The hunters have been instructed to arrive in your area on Thursday afternoon. That's in just two days. I suggest you get out of there."

"Where do I go? It seems pointless if they were able to follow me to your offices a few days ago. It'll just mean I won't know where to defend myself."

"Can you defend yourself there?"

He said, "I've got a shotgun. Hardly enough against a marauding horde."

"The local police," she offered, "you've got a police station there, surely!"

"I'll be locked up as a crackpot. I'd not know how to explain that to them."

"I see your point." Jo agreed.

"Anyway, what details have you got? What am I facing?"

"Janner and crew are in Oklahoma, ready to start. I understand the hunters are gathering in either an abandoned diner or car lot a couple of miles out of town. There was a discussion about a disused wood mill. Or lumber yard. I really can't be certain of which; the intercepted messages were not completely clear and obvious. I don't know which they've chosen. Sorry. But I remind you it's two days from now. Thursday. I can't be sure because there's no confirmation, but I think the briefing is the final part of their build-up before the starting hooter blows. I think we can confidently say that as soon as the briefing is complete, you're in the spotlight."

"What about other things? Like numbers of people, if hunt dogs will be used, guns, whether I'm the only one being hunted? Shit, I've got a million questions!"

"No guns. It's an old-fashioned hunt. Bows, arrows, spears, lancers, crossbows. Hell, I don't know. It sounds medieval to me. But there's no guns to be used on their hunt."

"Holy crap," he exclaimed.

"I've told you everything I know at this time."

"Jo, thanks for the call. I'll speak with Frankie," who by now was dressed and could be seen wandering around the house, "and I'll get back to you as soon as I can if I need anything else."

"Okay."

"And Jo?"

"What is it?"

"Thank you. Thank you for being there. For doing this for me whilst you could have been doing anything else. You didn't have to, you know."

Chapter 36

Having been unexpectedly awoken at five O'clock on that Tuesday morning, they decided they may as well make an early start. And sleep would be impossible after hearing the news that the hunters were closing in fast. They had to decide what to do.

Spencer told Frankie, in no uncertain terms, that if the hunters were upon him, Frankie had to escape. Disappear. There would be no chance to negotiate his own safety and as a potential witness to the event, would almost certainly be killed, too. Frankie was given little choice but to agree. But they had to try to find a solution for Spencer's sake, however.

Their initial ideas were limited. They considered the ideas Jo had had; escape, defending himself, involving the police. But to no avail. Nothing useful came to mind immediately. But they'd re-visit the problem in due course.

Talk soon resumed about Gently.

"What are we going to do with him once we have him in our hands?" Frankie asked.

"Confession and repent," Spencer suggested.

"From Gently? You must be kidding. He's a dangerous person. He'll say *"Yes, okay, good idea,"* one minute, and the very first time he's elsewhere, he'll say *"Hell, no. I'm going to fight that,"* about the same thing and then plan ways to get back at you thereafter."

"So, you're suggesting he'll never see sense."

"Precisely," agreed Frankie.

"What do we do?" Spencer asked.

"Make him regret it." Frankie offered.

"How?"

"I have absolutely no idea, whatsoever."

"Threats?" Spencer considered. "We may have to revert to threats."

"Only if you're prepared to carry them out," Frankie stated.

"I'm never going to find my family's killers. Gently is the next best thing. He is, after all, the ringleader."

"That's true. So, what you're saying is- it's your turn to be superhero vigilante?"

"If it comes to it, I'm not ashamed to say *"yes"* to that," Spencer admitted.

Frankie was adamant when he claimed, "We have to lure him somewhere. You can't kidnap him. You'll get nowhere near him."

"I'll give it some thought."

Frankie went off to the kitchen to make some hot drinks. When he came back, Spencer had a suggestion.

"We need to coax him into our domain. Here. Not Memphis. Get him away from territory he finds familiar. We need to be in total control. We need full ownership of this. A place we can force him to talk to us. Where he'll finally confess and, if we keep the level of threat high, perhaps even repent."

"Why Steerwagon Falls?" Frankie asked.

"Familiarity. Of a sort. I know no other area to any great extent, except perhaps the urban roads around my Archville home. How about you? Do you know of anywhere between here and Memphis we can spring our trap?"

"No. Not at all."

"Then here has got to be as good a place as anywhere else. Although I'm not sure how we could get him here, though."

After a brief delay while he thought about that, Frankie said, "I think I may have a solution to that one."

"Do tell."

"Tabitha Gretson. She's a friend and fellow government partner. Well, she's obviously got an interest in this, too, what with that Claude guy on her tail. I should have called her as soon as Jo told us, but I've been so tired and distracted. I owe it to her to try to help her, as well."

"What's Tabitha done to deserve that threat?"

"She's a witness to what Gently has been doing, deciding, planning and initiating since the very start. When it's all over, Tabitha could tell the media, "*Gently instructed me to...*", or "*Gently told us he was going to...*" or "*Gently is fully at fault for everything that's happened and I can prove this with evidence, so here goes...*". They are some of the possible ways she'll unwittingly get into trouble. Consequently, I suspect we can get her on-board, too. She's got her own name to clear and a threat against her that we have to help extinguish for her."

"You think we can help her, too?" asked Spencer.

"If we involve her, we can. If she knows nothing, we can't. And I'll tell you something else Jo let me know about; by car phone as we were travelling here. My Pittsburgh house is bugged. They've been scheming behind my back."

"Shit! By Gently or by the press?"

"I'm not sure," Frankie said, "but I'm going to find out."

"It's something we can ask Gently once we get him."

"Well, we've been able to confirm his schedule for the next week or so. That means, if we know where he'll be, we have the chance to get to him. Figuratively and literally speaking."

"Can you get Tabitha here. To talk and join us?"

"Leave it to me. She doesn't know about the hit-man thing so I'll use that to tell her to get herself here so we can work out how to keep her safe. I'll ring her later."

"Thank you," Spencer said.

"In the meantime, we have to decide precisely where we are going to do it."

"I think I know. But first I have to ask if we're at the same conclusion regarding our strategy options."

"Explain," Frankie demanded.

"Option 1- We get him to admit his errors and retract the NCCO."

"Little chance of that." Frankie commented.

"Option 2- We force him to do it."

"What, like torture? Don't be daft."

"Option 3- We put him at risk of humiliation which should give him some decent incentive."

"That might work." Frankie looked hopeful.

"Option 4- Listen carefully, it's a bit complicated. A last resort option. And it ties in with my other little problem, too."

"By *little problem*, you mean Wolf Janner, of course."

"Him and Claude. It may solve both problems."

Over the next hour, they discussed the Option 4 and agreed to carry it out but only if the other options failed.

"Do I take it we have our plan, then?" Spencer asked.

"Yes. But that means we have to be fully committed to getting Gently here. And we'll have to check out that old cabin, thoroughly. The one we saw on the tour of the town," Frankie suggested.

"You ring Tabitha and get her here. Make sure she brings the equipment we need." He was referring to the Option 4 possibility and he saw Frankie nodding in agreement. Spencer added, "Then we go check out that cabin. I think that'll be secluded enough. Could be ideal."

He busied himself with household chores whilst Frankie was on the telephone with Tabitha. It was a somewhat heated conversation. But it sounded to Spencer like he was successfully getting his message across. On one brief occasion, he saw Frankie give him a thumbs up signal, so knew things were fine.

Most of the afternoon was given over to further planning.

Spencer called it *'putting the meat on the bones'*.

After they had agreed some details, Spencer ran around gathering some supplies, tools and equipment, stacking them in a cardboard box. He went into Bruce's wardrobe and selected a couple of garments he would be using, too. A very bright yellow shirt and a pair of denim dungarees that Bruce would use to decorate in or perform DIY around the house. He also found some very plain clothes which he would need, too.

"I'm popping into town, Frankie. Theres a store where I have to buy some thin rope and a couple of electrical items. There's none of that in the garage here I can use."

"Okay."

Whilst in the town, getting the rope, Spencer also managed to find basic food supplies at one of the trade-through-the-door establishments he was getting used to having to deal with.

Once back at base, after enjoying a couple of helpings of eggs and ham Spencer had bought, they continued gathering resources. They found Bruce's Beretta, eventually, on the garage shelf and Frankie admitted he had a pistol in the trunk of the car. Between them, they created the fundamentals of a plan and most of the equipment needed to carry it out. Tabitha would help with a couple of things the storekeepers in Steerwagon Falls would never have in stock.

Chapter 37

In the early hours of Wednesday morning, before normal activities around town began, Spencer and Frankie went to check out the cabin to firstly see if it was still vacant and then to prepare it for their forthcoming meeting with Gently if it was.

With Spencer's Volvo being out of action for fear of a tracker possibly being hidden somewhere within it, they took Frankie's Mazda for safety, and made sure they were not spotted leaving the house. Upon arrival, they parked the Mazda in a secluded spot and made their way to the cabin, approaching it from the rear. It was only about eighty yards from the road, but up a steep embankment and the terrain was unfriendly. There were plenty of rocks and uneven ground, so it was not the easiest access. Their difficulty climbing was compounded by Spencer having to haul his now quite weighty cardboard box, filled with tools and equipment with him. Nonetheless, they got there unnoticed.

They found the door on the opposite side of the cabin, so positioned, one would presume, because the approach to it from a path through the woods was easier than the direction from which they arrived.

The surrounding woodland ensured they couldn't easily be seen when at the door as the front of the cabin faced into the woods, as did both sides. It was only the rear of the cabin that was visible from the road, over eighty yards away. Nice and secluded and very quiet.

A cheap low-quality padlock managed to keep the door from opening on its own but was not strong enough to survive a determined blow with a rock which they found close by. Later when they left the cabin, they would loop the broken padlock back through the latch to help the door remain closed but which could easily be removed later when they came back.

Inside, they found it sparse of contents. There was only a small stack of chairs, a table with a broken leg, an oil lantern which was all dried up and a few empty cardboard cartons strewn across the floor. There was a single electric lamp hanging from the ceiling and to their surprise it worked when the switch was flicked on. There were also two power outlets one could plug things into. Spencer had brought a small electric drill and after plugging this in, confirmed there was, indeed, power at both outlets.

"Yes, or no, Frankie? Do you think it'll work?"

"Looks perfect to me. There's so much undisturbed dust that I don't think anybody's been here for months and I'm quite sure nobody will be here in the next couple of days, either."

"Scout about outside and do a reconnaissance of the immediate vicinity. Look for any obvious issues. Check there's no other dwellings nearby, within earshot. Or roads further in which we didn't expect."

"I'll do that," Frankie agreed. "You install the equipment."

Whilst Frankie was gone, Spencer fitted a burglar alarm siren under the eaves of the building, facing into the woodland. He disabled the motion detector part of it and wired up an on-off switch that could be triggered from inside the building. He tested it was working but made sure it didn't sound during the test. He then proceeded to mount four super-bright flood lights that faced outward into the woodland once again. He fed the wires back through one of the walls and plugged their circuit into the socket. He switched them on and was in the process of going outside to see if they worked, when he saw Frankie coming back.

"Crikey, they are bright," Frankie exclaimed as he arrived. "Switch them off, quick."

"How was the area?" asked Spencer.

"Rugged and secluded."

"Perfect."

"How're the installations going? As successfully as the lights?" Frankie asked.

"All done except for the spy-holes." They went inside and drilled four small holes in the walls; one in each wall thus all facing in different directions. They were just wide enough to see out from, but subtle enough not to be seen from afar. They covered each hole from the inside with black tape to block light escaping, which could be easily removed and replaced when they wanted to look out.

The box with the rest of the equipment was put in the corner and covered over by the old empty cartons that had been there since long before.

On the way back to the house they stopped at a parking lot near the Municipal Centre and decided it was nicely secluded from through traffic and prying eyes. It would serve as a great place to meet Robert Gently.

They returned to the house with as much care as possible so as not to be spotted, parking well away from the house and returning on foot separately. They didn't want anybody who may have been watching that they had gone far from the house. And it was best that Frankie's car was no longer parked at the house, itself.

"May I play Devil's advocate?" Frankie asked later on, over coffee. When Spencer nodded, he continued by asking, "What if it all goes horribly wrong? So many things could."

"At any stage we can simply get in a car and drive away. Keep going, never look back and create a Plan B from Iowa or Pennsylvania in the near future. Don't worry. I'm ready to drive away if anything gets ugly."

Chapter 38

On Wednesday evening, with Tabitha Gretson previously having suspended everything relating to work at the drop of a hat, she now sat with Frankie and Spencer in the living room of the Verlano home and was now listening to a string of things that concerned her greatly. She had no idea just how scheming Gently had been and was horrified to hear that there was a hit-man due to visit any time soon.

"What do you want from me to fix all of this?" She asked.

"Your help in luring him here, to Steerwagon Falls."

She looked at Frankie and admitted, "I don't think I'm very imaginative. I don't know how I'd do that."

"Tabitha, we already have a plan and a strict timeline, and you need to follow both to the letter."

"Depends what the plan is, of course."

"Right, sit down, make yourself comfortable," Spencer said.

The two guys took her through the concept. She seemed comfortable with the basics but was concerned that if she made any slip-ups at all, Gently may not play along.

Spencer suggested, "Would you allow me to script it? Write it out like a script from a stage play. It would help you stick to the main things to be said so you don't forget."

"Anything to help. So yes, sure."

Over the next hour while Tabitha and Frankie sat in comfortable chairs away from the desk over which all their notes, plans and diagrams were strewn, Spencer typed out a script for Tabitha to follow. Finally, he printed it off onto paper.

Eventually, he said, "Okay, I've got it here. Time to practice."

Tabitha took a look at it and said, "It's only got my lines. You haven't typed anyone else's."

"That was intentional."

"Why?"

"Two reasons. One, we can't predict what Gently will say and two, if we tried to predict it and I had typed it, you'd be put-off when he says something different to what we guessed."

"A fair point," she confessed.

"So, this is what we will do. Frankie can leave the room, so he can't hear us. You run through your part of the script and I will pretend to be Gently and play the other part. I'll respond to what you say as best I can and we'll see if the script works. Then afterwards, Frankie can do the same. So you get two different possible reactions."

"Why can't I sit in the same room when you're doing your turn, Spencer?" asked Frankie.

"It may well influence what you say or don't say to Tabitha. You need to treat it like a surprise phone call."

'Very clever. Yes. Of course."

Over the next hour they practiced the script and were pleased to realise that it didn't seem to need much tweaking.

"But knowing Gently as I do," Tabitha said, "he'll come out with something completely different to you guys."

"I'm sure he will. But the way you handled our two different examples was very impressive, so I'm sure you'll cope just fine."

"I hope so."

Rehearsals over, when the actual telephone conversation happened, mid-afternoon the next day, it went exactly as follows.

"Good afternoon, Robert. It's Tabitha Gretson."

"Tabitha. Good to hear from you. What brings you to call me?"

"Robert, I'm working in Oklahoma at the moment, with the laboratory technicians and we've discovered some problems."

"Problems?"

"The facial recognition software we developed following your instruction, carried with it some background code. It highlights your name as Chief Designer and it's clearly an error."

"That's both confusing and unfortunate. Why would this be?"

"Possibly because you instructed my department, via me, to carry out this work."

"Why was it recorded at all?" asked Gently.

"Any development work can only go ahead if the requesting department is recorded, otherwise it can't proceed. When I instructed the team we were doing this, they didn't pay much attention to what they recorded."

Gently didn't seem particularly perturbed. "I don't see this as much of a problem."

"Well, unfortunately it caught the attention of one of the members of the team. A very disgruntled member who has lost two family members, I hasten to add. Anyway, she has been in contact with the press with the view to do some whistleblowing. Scaremongering, you and I would call it. But she's already contacted the press and I fear is about to link your name to a good number of things you wouldn't want it to be associated with."

Gently's pleasant demeanour had obviously taken a seismic change. "You have got to be fucking kidding me."

"I don't think it's too late to fix this. I think there's ways we can nip this in the bud."

"How?"

"We meet. In person as soon as possible."

"I'm just west of Memphis, Tabitha. A town called Lonoke. I don't have anywhere here that's appropriate."

"I do. Here."

"Where are you?"

"Steerwagon Falls, Oklahoma. Its virtually on the border with Arkansas, so about two and a half hours. Not far at all."

"Steerwagon Falls? I've never heard of it."

"Look, I wanted somewhere quiet we can meet. And it's not too far from the laboratories here in Oklahoma and just far enough to be remote but close enough that I've been able to sneak away to. I hunted for a place like this carefully. Somewhere safe, secure and private. A good quality office where I've set up good links to my laboratory systems where I can demonstrate everything that could be problematic."

"Couldn't we have done this somewhere else?"

"We've no time to waste, Robert. I didn't have the luxury of time to find somewhere nearer to Memphis. There's nothing wrong with this town, except it's smaller than the cities. Small is good, sometimes."

He asked, "When are you there?"

"I'm here now. Would appreciate it if you could be here at your earliest convenience."

"Can't do tomorrow. Meeting with a group of foreign dignitaries about something or other. Something the Chief Justice of the USA has set up. Not flexible. It's a two-day event. The pleasantries may go on for another day."

"The longer we delay this, the..."

"Oh, for goodness sakes! I'm leaving now. I'll be there in three hours. Damn it! Where, exactly, do I head for?"

"The Municipal Centre parking lot. Slap, bang in the town centre. It's well signposted. The office is round the corner but you'll not find it, so I'll meet you at the lot."

They ended the call and Gretson smiled at Canetti.

"It went as planned. He's on his way. I figure he'll be there by 8 O'clock this evening. I'll let you listen in if he makes any calls to me whilst you're here, or ring you straight after when you're at the parking lot waiting for him. I hope you're both properly ready."

"Tabitha, I can't thank you enough."

"You can thank me by making sure I don't get in any trouble for this and stopping that Claude person from carrying out what you told me about."

Frankie said, "Believe me, when all this is through, it'll be sunshine and blue skies forever."

Without the luxury of time to relax, they took her through the rest of the plan once again. They called it Phase Two. She fully understood her new role.

They tested and double-tested the radio frequency monitoring equipment she had been asked to bring along, and it worked absolutely perfectly. It was suitably high-powered that it would pick up signals up to 3 miles away, so long as there were no major obstacles in the way. Between the cabin and the house on Independence Lane, there were very few. Mostly trees and low buildings. Most of Steerwagon Falls was unimpeded by significant obstacles, too. She should hear radio activity all around as and when it was transmitted.

Chapter 39 - Hunt Briefing Two

Wolf Janner, callsign Animal, 6 foot 7 tall, stood well above normal eye-level on a makeshift platform consisting of two stacked wooden pallets so he could look down upon all of the participating hunters and so that each could see him and make eye contact.

They had gathered around the portacabin that served as the salesman's office at the used car lot. This was where Wolf had set up his platform.

"Great to see all you guys and some gals with brawn, too. You are all welcome." He held aloft a walkie talkie. "Y'all got one of these?"

Apparently, they had.

"Each of you will have a different and fixed frequency. You will not be able to hear each other. I will monitor each and every transmission. You are to keep me informed of any relevant information about the target. That way we cannot lose him. Anything that I feel the whole group needs to know, I will transmit and you will all hear it at exactly the same time.

"I repeat, you will not be able to hear each other. Just me. You will not be able to adjust the frequency of your own walkie talkie. They are fixed to the frequency you have been allocated. Is that understood?"

There was a collective grunt of agreement, some nodding and the occasional, "Yes, boss," from one or two participants.

"I cannot monitor all the frequencies if they are encrypted. Consequently, these are open-band walkie talkies. So name no names. I do not want to hear the name of the target. You will use your callsigns. Those are the ones you have been issued when you received your confirmation of attendance. Has everybody remembered their callsigns?"

Another affirmative grunt, nod or "Yes boss."

"And if anybody. I repeat anybody, transmits my name, you WILL be the next hunt target. "Do I make myself clear?"

There was a very positive affirmation of this from all parties.

"You all know my two closest friends, callsign Blocker and callsign Chalkie. They are both in situ, monitoring the target and making sure we are kept informed of his position when you arrive. We will let you know the starting position but have no control over where he goes thereafter. That's part of the fun for you.

"Once we start, he will remain in the general area. Blocker is going to stay on the road a few miles south of the town and Chalkie a few miles north. If either spot him trying to leave, they will simply turn him around. They, unlike you, do have guns.

"The latest update is as follows: The target just left his house a couple of minutes ago. We are monitoring his movements.

"I will keep you fed with clues or further instructions. Do not be put off if the instructions and clues are missing a bit of detail. That, too, is part of the hunt fun. To do something for yourselves. I ain't here to wipe your asses." There was a lot of laughter at this.

"The time is now 1945hrs. The first instruction for you is as follows: We leave here at 2015hrs. On foot.

The first clue is: Steerwagon Falls. That's a 30-minute hike ladies and gentlemen. Mostly on trails. Very few roads. Don't get spotted getting there."

Chapter 40

Constance Brighley and Martindale O'Toole sat around the conference table, pondering over what to do with the recorded conversation Marty had had with Squirty McFee, real name Norman.

He had picked up the nickname Squirty following an accident he suffered when young which involved leaking hot oil from a hydraulic press at his lumber yard.

The interview not only failed to go to plan, but Squirty McFee cried and sobbed his way through just about every minute Marty was with him.

Constance was saying, "It must be very difficult losing your business the way he had. Running a business is like caring for your own baby. You have to nurture it and ride a bunch of hard times every so often."

"I can well imagine," Marty replied. "Not that I know anything about running a lumber yard, I can't help but think he could have cleaned up the mess and continued regardless."

She asked, "What would you do, if one day you walked into your own yard and you found numerous dead bodies dismembered and jammed into your main lumber saw?"

He replied, "After vomiting profusely, which I'm sure I would have done, I guess I would have asked my local Sheriff's office for advice. We know from past interviews that the army removed bodies. I'd like to think those army guys would have a stronger stomach that I've got."

"Sounds logical," Constance agreed.

"I'd have asked the police to contact them on my behalf, in the first instance. I don't think I'd be able to find a phone number for the army on my own. So, yeah, contact the police."

"And then?"

"After the bits have gone. Oh, sorry to be graphic, I'd get a jet washer and simply spend a few hours spraying everything," he said.

Constance caught herself doodling on her pad of paper. Her mind had drifted from the conversation momentarily, remembering the days she, too, had trouble keeping her publication going. It had been a difficult time.

Shaking herself from her reverie, she said, "Squirty was saying there was blood all over the fresh timber. You couldn't use that ever again."

"It sounds like we are interviewing ourselves. Speculating on what to do."

She remarked, "I'm sure Squirty will come around, eventually. It's early days and he'll man up. He'll probably pay his staff a whole bunch of extra money to do the clean-up for him."

"So, what do we do with the article for the paper?" asked Marty.

The article went out as follows.

The Chronicle Interviews-
Post-Disaster Era- Interview Eight

Dear readers.

It is with regret that the scheduled interview for this edition has had to be cancelled. We hope to be back to normal in the next publication.

We offer our since apologies to those of you who look forward to reading this regular feature.

Chapter 41

Tabitha was alone at the Verlano home when Gently called her.

"I'm still en-route, Tabitha. I've just stopped for a comfort break. I should be with you in about 45 minutes."

"That's good progress," she said. "Well done. So about 8 O'clock, great."

"Maybe 10 minutes after 8. So sure, see you soon."

Tabitha called Frankie and relayed the news. He and Spencer had parked the Mazda close to the entrance of the parking lot at the Municipal Centre, but away from where they chose to hide until Gently arrived.

"Thanks, Tabitha. From now on our phones are on silent/vibrate. So messages only, as the plan, please."

"Sure, Frankie."

"And how about the monitoring? Any activity?"

"Plenty. Mostly people sending test messages which seem to get acknowledged by just one master handset."

The forty five minutes seemed to drag on for much longer, but eventually a car pulled into the lot. Frankie Canetti recognised him right away and told Spencer Dexton to keep hiding and wait for their pre-arranged signal before stepping out.

"I've got him spotted," the hunter callsign Bullseye announced over the walkie-talkie to a listening Wolf Janner.

"Location, please?"

"Municipal Centre parking lot."

"Do you have a clear shot?"

"No and I'm too far away, anyway. Maybe 350 yards. Also, my crossbow isn't that accurate."

"Other status details?"

"Denim dungarees. Yellow shirt. Too far away to see much else."

Wolf Janner transmitted to all of the hunters simultaneously: "Animal calling with a group update- Approximate location is the town centre. Wearing dungarees and a bright yellow shirt. No additional detail. Listen for further updates."

———————————

Gently stopped his car in the parking lot, switched his engine off and got out. As he climbed from the driver's seat, he shook the creases from his pants, straightened his necktie and reached into the rear of the car where his Italian designer jacket had been hanging. He ran his fingers through his hair while trying to see his own reflection in the door window glass.

Canetti met him halfway across the lot.

"What are *you* doing here, and where's Gretson?"

"I'm working with Miss Gretson, to help get this sorted."

"She never told me."

"And *this* gentleman is working with us, too." He encouraged Robert Gently to turn around where he saw Spencer Dexton walking toward him. A stranger dressed in a pair of decorator's dungarees over a disgustingly bright yellow long-sleeve shirt, scruffy shoes and most concerning, all of a sudden, was the gun he spotted this man holding and which was clearly being pointed at him.

As he approached, Dexton was studying Gently closely. Mid-sixties but could easily be mistaken for 10 years younger, no grey in his hair, same as his was. Another fit guy who had clearly looked after himself. Expensive clothing, designer glasses.

"What the fuck is going on here?" Gently turned back to Canetti who was now also holding a gun, and similarly pointing it at him.

"We'll explain soon. But for the time being we strongly suggest you cause no fuss. We are going for a little ride."

They virtually pushed him into the rear of Canetti's car. Dexton sat next to him and kept the gun pressed tightly into Gently's ribs.

Three minutes later they arrived at their chosen parking location a few hundred yards down the road from the log cabin. It was still ten, maybe fifteen minutes hike by foot, but they needed to leave the car some distance from the cabin. With two guns pointing at him, Gently realised he better not try to run, and so complied in silence. The light was fading fast so they used torches in short careful bursts to illuminate the terrain if it got too tricky.

Spencer felt a vibration from the phone in his pocket. He checked and saw a message from Tabitha, that read: "Walkie talkie activity all around. I've intercepted various messages. Just one critical at this time. I believe you have been spotted." Spencer typed "OK" and returned the message.

"Status update required, please, Bullseye," Janner demanded.

"He was with two other men, Animal. They got into a car. Red Mazda. Have attempted to follow. The headed south, toward the woods. They may be armed. I think I saw one of them with a pistol, but I couldn't be sure."

"Roger. Thank you. Out."

Wolf Janner transmitted a further group update: "Animal calling with another group update- Target heading south from town in red car. No further detail. Listen for further updates."

Dexton opened the door of the wood cabin. It was just as he had left it last time he was here. Nothing had been touched, including his box of bits and pieces he was starting to suspect he would be forced to use.

They encouraged Gently inside.

"Take a seat, Gently," pointing at a choice of old wooden arch-back chairs.

The hunter callsign Viper transmitted to Wolf. "Red Mazda spotted. Parked just off road on the main route from Steerwagon Falls toward Oklahoma City. Almost a mile from town. Empty. I have no idea which direction they have gone."

"Roger, Viper."

"Anything else to report?"

"Negative, Animal."

Group update from Janner: "Target's vehicle spotted parked and empty. South of the town. Approximately a mile. Listen for further updates."

Another phone vibration. Tabitha sent a message stating: "Mazda identified when you moved away and additional sighting but I've no details at this time". Spencer acknowledged in the manner they agreed. He knew he'd have to be on the lookout for any movement, now.

His attention went back to their unwilling guest.

"What is all this about?" Gently demanded.

Spencer responded, "Care to take your jacket off? That chair looks mighty dirty to me."

Taken aback by this modicum of hospitality, Gently did indeed remove his jacket after having seen a relatively clean coat hook just to the side of the door.

"Sit back down."

"I'll not take orders from some fucking hillbilly in dungarees, thank you."

"I've a gun," Spencer said. "And because my family are dead, courtesy of you, I'll not think twice about using it. So sit down and shut up."

"Oh, such a big man, so you're after retribution are you?"

Dexton checked Canetti was still pointing his own gun at Gently, then satisfied he was covered, he walked around the chair until he stood behind him. He then deftly looped a nylon rope around Gently and around the frame of the chair. Gently didn't have much time to react and by the time he did, the rope was somewhat too tight to struggle. A minute later and it was sufficiently tied so that Gently could hardly do any more than breathe and talk.

"Retribution? No, not necessarily," Spencer finally answered the question. "I'm more of a gentleman than that. I want you to do some listening now. And then you'll be offered a choice."

"A choice of what?"

"You'll see. Over to you, Mr Canetti." Making the gesture sounded very formal.

"Thank you Mr. D."

"Robert, I'm very disappointed in you. We both know that you're one of the two masterminds behind this NCCO."

"So what?"

"So it's time to call it off. To realise it's diabolical, inhumane and cannot be allowed to continue. Furthermore, by blaming others for the concept, and the very idea of doing this, you're inadvertently admitting it's wrong and want others to take the fall. Namely, me."

Interrupting Canetti, he said, "It's a personal grudge then?"

"No. It's an attempt to do the right thing for the people of the USA. To stop it before it goes on any longer. To…"

Gently interrupted him again. "Suppose I don't want to? I sure as heck can see the benefits for the country even if you can't. I'm not changing my mind, you deluded fool."

"Mr D, I think we have to face up to the fact that he doesn't like the first choice."

"Option 4?"

"No choices left."

Dexton started to prepare. He went to the box they had brought to the cabin earlier. He took out a pair of black slacks, a dark blue tee shirt and a black sweater. He took off all of his clothes and put these new ones on. He hung the dungarees and yellow shirt next to Gently's designer jacket.

Next, he retrieved the pair of scissors they had put into the box.

Hunter callsign Defender made the next transmission to Wolf. "Activity spotted at the old ranger's cabin. There's light coming from a gap under the door. Visible by binoculars. Distance 500 yards. Moving shadows visible through gap, also."

"Any sounds?"

"Distance too great. But it's possible I heard a shout."

"Roger and out."

Janner transmitted to the whole group. "Animal transmitting with important details, so listen very clearly. Head into the Reservation Woods. Approx location map grid reference 36.37, -94.81. Note this is approximate. Unfair to give exact coordinates. Listen for further updates."

Wolf anticipated any hunters who were previously and frantically travelling to Steerwagon Falls town centre would now re-route into the woods just a few miles away. It was part of the hunt entry contract promise that all hunters would get sufficient clues to keep them in the game. It maintained interest by all participants.

Janner, himself, was merely 400 yards from the cabin. He had absolutely no line of sight at this time and the terrain between him and the cabin wasn't particularly favourable, either. It would be slow going.

Spencer was momentarily distracted by another phone vibration. He passed the phone to Frankie. "Your location known. Be prepared."

Meanwhile, Dexton proceeded to use the scissors to cut the remaining clothes off Gently's body. First his shirt, which was soon a pile of shredded cotton on the floor by his feet. Then he attacked his trousers in the same manner.

"What do you think you are doing?" he started off by saying but within a minute or two longer this had become a shout. "I said what the fuck are you doing?"

"You had your chance."

"So you're trying to humiliate me are you?"

"That's not my intention." Spencer said and carried on cutting the clothes off until the only bits he couldn't get to were the areas being covered by the ropes. And his boxers. He left him his dignity. A confused Robert Gently was, by now, looking very uncomfortable. He was also very cold, as he kept reminding Mr D, whom he did not know as Dexton.

"How's it looking outside, Mr Canetti?"

"I believe there's something going on out there now. I'm sure there's torchlight. Way off in the distance but getting closer."

"Shit. We have to hurry." Spencer remarked, and then walked over to where Gently's expensive jacket hung, rendering it unwearable by cutting that into several pieces, too.

Whilst this was going on, Canetti took from the box a bracelet installation and removal tool. That was an advantage of working with the Chief Scientific Officer who designed and made them. He used it to remove Robert Gently's red exemption bracelet. It took just 25 seconds to accomplish.

Spencer then handed the scissors to Canetti.

Frankie Canetti took Gently's glasses off him, much to his annoyance and protestations. He then looked very closely at Gently's hair and then back to Dexton's buzz-cut style. He started snipping chunks off Gently's long hair, who had to be gagged at this point as the shouting was getting too loud. A strip of tape did the trick, at least for the time being. Canetti continued shaping his hair until it was about the same length as Spencer's.

"That's gonna have to do." He announced. "I'm no hairdresser."

"Looks pretty good. Not unlike my own. Now for me."

Canetti then started taking off as much of Spencer's hair as he could and a shaver they had stashed in the box did the rest. Within just two minutes he was as bald as he could make himself. He pressed the prescription glass lenses out of Gently's spectacle frame. He tossed the lenses away and slipped the frame into his pants' pocket to be used shortly.

From their spy hole, they could now see multiple torch lights. Getting closer by the minute. Whereas before the light was dim, being obscured by hundreds of yards of trees, they were now brighter and obscured by very little.

Time to get busy.

Keeping their guns pointing at a now shivering Gently, they untied him and removed the gag.

"Why don't you put those on, Gently?" Dexton gestured to the yellow shirt and dungarees. For the want of having nothing else to wear, he grudgingly put the dirty hillbilly clothes on. He put this own shoes on too but noticed one of the two men had well and truly scuffed them up by treading on them with mucky boots.

"I have no fucking idea what you're playing at," he complained to the stranger.

"I'm playing you at your own game, Gently."

"Which is?"

"Being a sneaky bastard. You'd know all about that because you've had years of practice. But you have now got one last chance to rescind the NCCO. I have your phone here. I took it out of your jacket pocket. Do you wish to make a call?"

"You'll pay for that jacket, you fuck heads."

"If it's a '*no*' I'll take your telephone access code, instead, please."

"No chance. It's biometric, fingerprint only. There's no way I'm going to oblige," he declared.

Janner announced to all hunters: "Approximately eight hunters within killing distance of target. Advise your last chance to arrive at kill zone is now. No further updates. Kill expected imminently."

The next phone vibration was ignored completely. Tabitha had been brilliant, keeping them informed as she intercepted their transmissions, but from here on in, whatever she informed them would not be of any use. They were on their own.

Canetti took one last look through each of the four spy holes they had carefully drilled through the wooden walls. He made a speedy assessment of each direction from the cabin. He realised that whilst most of the hunters had been lured through the woods, at least one was certainly working his way up directly from the road. Struggling with the loose rocks on the uphill approach from that direction. A latecomer.

"Plenty of lights now visible, Spencer."

"Now or never. Go, go, go," he exclaimed.

Canetti pulled open the door and Dexton thrust Gently out into the open air, closing the door again straight after. Gently was immediately illuminated by two or three beams of bright torch light.

"Who the hell is that?" he shouted. "Are you more fuck heads like th..."

He was silenced forever by a crossbow bolt that hit him from the side, entering his neck from his right hand side and ripping just about every tendon, vein and artery it found as it shredded his trachea and left a gaping hole upon its exit on his left side.

"Now!" Spencer said, excitedly.

Canetti pulled the wall switch they had installed and the woods around the cabin were suddenly awash with a blaze of light and the sound of an intruder deterrent alarm they had also rigged. It was deafening.

———————————

Janner became frantic. Having just witnessed one of his hunters taking the target out with an exceptionally fine crossbow shot, he was suddenly very confused. He did not expect alarms and flood lights. Not at all.

"All hunters disperse. Now. I repeat. All hunters disperse now!"

Fearing for his own safety and determined to avoid being spotted and identified, he made his own escape as fast as possible. He vowed to go straight home and walk away from this hunt completely and forever. It was in danger of going horribly wrong. He would have to wait a long time into the future before he ventured into Steerwagon Falls again, just to protect himself.

———————————

Spencer quickly exited the building, having just donned Gently's spectacle frame. With pistol in hand, he managed to catch one of the hunters before he made his escape. A somewhat overweight and unfit specimen of a man. He fired a warning shot which stopped him in his tracks. The sound of the gunshot boomed out in the clearing. Everybody else scarpered.

"Who are you?" the man said in panic.

"I'm the guy with a gun. You've got an unloaded bow and arrow. No match from this distance."

"Uh.."

"Nice bow, though. Is it a Crestway Carbon Fibre?"

Surprised by the armed guy's apparent knowledge of hunting bows, he was confused as to what was happening. And didn't know how to respond.

"A Crestway?" Spencer repeated.

"No. Erm it's. Er...."

"A Dougdale?

"I can't afford either of those. What do you want?"

"Something simple. And you get to go free."

"What?" The man looked quite scared by now. He was not used to being the hunted and felt like a hare trapped in a lure.

"I just want to know if you filmed the kill."

"What if I did?"

"Just yes or no."

"Bodycam with memory card inside and simultaneous Bluetooth download to my phone. In my pocket."

"You simply hand over your phone to me. I will forward the clip to my own phone. Then I delete the message and you go free."

"Damn. Is that all? I thought you were going to turn me in," the man said.

"Nope!"

Spencer took the phone from the man, had a quick look at his footage and was pleased with what he saw. Nice, clear footage. He selected the 'Forward To' option and sent it to himself, to his own phone, in the depths of his pocket. He heard the tell-tale 'Ding' noise. A quick glance to see if it had come through successfully and he then asked for the bodycam unit. The man duly obliged, and Spencer put this in his own pocket. He then shattered the man's phone with the heel of his boot.

"Better safe than sorry."

"I, uh..."

"One last thing," Spencer said, "Give me your arrows. I don't want one in the middle of my back when I walk away."

The man, now shaking with a form of disbelief, thrust the arrows at Spencer, turned and ran away. Clumsily.

The lasting memory of that little encounter, Spencer would think about many times in the months to come was the would-be archer had not recognised Spencer as the real intended target. His bald pate and round rimmed spectacles had served as a very effective disguise. That and because he was no longer wearing a bright yellow shirt and dungarees. It would seem, to a whole bunch of hunters that the intended target had, indeed, been hit and taken care of. Game over, they would later claim.

Canetti called Tabitha who immediately got the state troopers to drive along the road nearest to the cabin with lights and sirens blaring.

She had warned them that one of the Attorney Generals had become lost in the area and was feared to be at risk. Would they please just do a drive by with lights and sirens to scare off any undesirables.

Confused by the instruction but seemingly compelled to oblige with a government order, they did precisely that.

Any hunters who may have been hanging around would have been chased away.

The plan must have worked because Canetti and Dexton made it safely back to the Verlano house by daybreak.

They watched the film clip on Spencer's phone so many times that his battery went flat.

Chapter 42

Robert Gently's mobile telephone could only be accessed by using his fingerprint. Fortunately, he had been lying in a very convenient spot for them to borrow his finger for a few moments before they left the cabin.

Firstly, they accessed the phone, using his lifeless finger. They then swiped through the applications until they found the Settings tool. With a few clicks and options chosen, they had changed the password security to match Canetti's fingerprint.

They now had permanent access to his phone. All the records, the contacts, message trails, photographs and anything else they should find useful.

One of their first jobs in the morning was to contact Claude, whose phone number they easily located.

The call was answered within three rings.

"Robert, what brings you to call me today?" he said as his greeting.

"Claude, I am a former colleague of Robert Gently. You are the first person to hear that Robert Gently has been assassinated. I now control his phone, his contacts, his call records, and all communications evidence. We know he employs you to do unsavoury work on his behalf and, in particular, I bring your attention to the matter of Tabitha Gretson."

"I'm familiar with that name."

"If you continue to try to threaten Gretson, we will pursue you and bring you to justice."

"I was never paid up front, so there's no need for me to continue with any such issue. Besides, my first remit was surveillance and monitoring. And what's more, she disappeared a day or so ago. I've no idea where she is, even! Furthermore, I was not yet given any final instruction you would describe as '*termination*'. So, consider the matter closed. I have no interest in taking any further action."

"We are watching you, Claude. Any sign you are lying to us, and we have teams who will track you down."

"Message received and understood. Can we say goodbye to one another, forever, here and now?"

"Let's treat this situation in that manner. Don't give me cause to come looking for you again."

"Then it's goodbye. Forever. Thank you for letting me know."

"Goodbye to you too." He pressed the end-call button.

Chapter 43

Jeremy Weinstein sat at the dining room table of his country retreat, having just finished his evening meal. A dish of Clam Chowder followed by Lobster Thermidor. With a glass or two of a 2031 Domaine Louis Moreau Grand Cru Chablis, he felt like he had just tasted a soupçon of Heaven itself. He was rather full, not even having room for a third glass of wine and could hardly move when he heard the telephone tinkling in his drawing room next door. He just managed to get there in time before it rang off.

"Weinstein speaking," he answered as he always did.

"Sir, let me introduce myself. I am Chip Wesson," Frankie Canetti lied, fabricating the name, "I work as one of your junior ministers, a communication officer in The House of Representatives. Yet you could say my role relates more to my NSA status than it does to my House status. I have a dual role." Another lie, but part of the plot.

"If this is anything to do with official business, not only will it wait, but I'm quite sure you'll have a superior who can handle any issues at all. They are well paid, you know," Weinstein offered.

"Invariably, Sir, that's how I would handle it. But I have sensitive information relating to the late Mr Robert Gently, which I believe would be for your eyes only and information that is linked to us ensuring your own continued safety."

"My safety?"

"Mr Gently, having been assassinated recently, appears not to be the only target we are concerned about."

"Do I detect I'm somehow included?"

"This could well be the case, Sir. We need you to review some communications. I have had them printed and they are with me now. There are photographs I think you should see, too. And I need to ask questions, Sir. Ones which are best posed face to face," Canetti lied but maintained the subterfuge.

"And where, precisely, do you propose this to take place?" Weinstein was becoming most uncomfortable. The rich lobster sauce had started repeating on itself. Thoughts of that third glass of Chablis were, by now, well and truly banished.

"We could come to your place of residence, or have a car meet you and take you somewhere familiar. Such as your Washington office, your golf club, even. Anywhere you'd feel comfortable and a public place is quite acceptable to us."

"Golf club's fine. But I'll have my chauffeur drive me. I'll be there in under an hour."

Two hours before this call was made, Frankie Canetti and Spencer Dexton had had a very private meeting with Jeremy Weinstein's chauffeur. A man called Quentin Jacobs.

Jacobs had lost six close relations in the atrocities. A set of twin girls, both just 14 years old, their older sister, 18, and their father, Quentin's only brother. Jacobs had been doing his best to tend to what was left of the family. He tried to be confidante, provider and a decent uncle to the kids that had survived.

Neither Jacobs nor his brother's widow had any idea who had authorised *The Objective* all those weeks before. Little did they know that the very same man wrote Jacobs's pay check each month. They didn't understand how Weinstein could be so dismissive of his questions. *"Why is this NCCO necessary?"*, he would ask his employer, the White House Chief of Staff, or *"Surely there are better ways?"* But each time he asked permission to talk with him, he was treated with often little more than a dismissive waving of his arm. Unacceptable distain.

"We will talk about it later," he would be told regularly. But later never came.

And now here were two men, Frankie Canetti and Spencer Dexton, proving to Quentin Jacobs who had devised the abominations, who had made the very decisions underlying why he had lost so many of his own family members.

"We need your help, Quentin," Frankie Canetti confessed.

"Anything you want. I'm not working for him again. I'm leaving immediately."

"No, you're not. We need you. You'll be part of a revenge plan. Are you with us?"

"I like the sound of that," Jacobs agreed.

"We need you to act normally for the next two or three days. One day shortly, and we'll organise it for about 7.50 one evening, so you know it'll be us, Weinstein is going to ask you to drive him to his golf club or his Washington office. You are to willingly agree."

"Okay. What next?"

"On the hill, just a mile or so from the house, there's a fork in the road."

"I know it well. Pass it every day. Left for Washington and the gold club. Right goes only to a farm and a set of abandoned warehouses and storage units."

"You take the right turn. Hopefully he won't notice, but it doesn't matter even if he does. You'll pull into the turnout that's only 80 yards down that road."

"I know it, too."

"We'll be waiting. So as soon as you arrive, unlock the passenger compartment of the limo and Spencer will get in the back with Weinstein. Open the front and I'll take your place," Frankie said.

"What do I do?" he asked.

You said it, yourself. "You don't want to work for him anymore. So walk back to the big house, get what you want, call a cab and just go. Believe me, after what we are going to do to him, you'll want to distance yourself from him as much as you can."

"I'll take his other car. He can look for it at another time."

"Are you okay with all of this?"

"More than you think, now."

"Just one more thing, does Weinstein have any guns in the back of the car?"

"Never."

Jacobs answered the ringing phone in the servants' quarters.

"Yes, Sir,' he said, "How may I help?"

"Jacobs, I want a car, please. A quick trip to the club. Right away."

"Certainly Sir. I'll be ready and out at the front within five minutes."

Five minutes later, Weinstein got into the back of the limo. Five minutes after that, Dexton was let into the back after Jacobs met them where planned. Weinstein was more than a little surprised to see he suddenly had an unwanted guest. Something was happening up front, too. The driver got out and a new one got in.

"What the blazes is going on?" he demanded.

"Just like the call you got half an hour ago. We are taking you somewhere to discuss Robert Gently's death and the danger you are in."

"You're not FBI or NSA. Those guys don't wear chinos and a bright red lumberjack shirt. So, who is 'we'?"

"No, that's right. I'm just a lowly member of the public. Never been a government man, nor a serviceman, nor have I had any role in public office. I'm just a regular guy. You can call me Smith."

"Not your name, I'll bet,' and when he saw Dexton/Smith shaking his head he realised he was right in that regard. "I'll have you arrested. You're in big trouble, Smith."

"Sir, I think you'll find the boot's on the other foot. I'm in control and you're the one in trouble."

Three minutes later they had arrived outside one of the abandoned warehouse units. Canetti, known by Weinstein as Wesson, pulled up outside the Unit, walked to the limo's rear door, opened it and ushered Weinstein inside. To the rear of the vast space was a very comfortable but makeshift office. Well lit and warm. It even had a leather sofa, two armchairs, a coffee table, and a big television at one end of the office.

"What is all this?" the White House Chief of Staff gestured to the furnishings. "Who are you guys?"

Without a smirk, Canetti said, "He's Smith, and I'm Wesson, who spoke to you on the phone just a short time ago."

"Smith and Wesson." That's not even funny. "You consider yourselves funny people? Do you?" He was shouting at this point. "Well, do you?"

"Sir, we are respectful people. And there's no reason that harm will come to you. We want you to watch a short film, and then listen to our proposal. Nothing more."

"Nothing?"

"We'll see."

The room was carefully laid out. A good deal of planning had gone into exactly where everything was precisely positioned in the room. Hidden from view, high in the ceiling space, was a very expensive ultra-high-resolution video camera. It was aimed to capture Weinstein, full face. It would also capture the images and film footage that they'd shortly show on the screen. On the coffee table was today's copy of The Washington Post. This was so positioned so that it, too, would be seen by the camera. If questions were later raised as to when the film was made the newspaper would help verify the date, to some extent. The angle and direction of the camera lens would also capture no more than the back of Dexton's head or his right shoulder. At the most. Dexton didn't intend it to capture any of himself if he could help it.

Weinstein had no idea he was being filmed. None whatsoever.

Canetti was both out of shot and, it had been agreed between the two, not on audio either. He would remain silent throughout the meeting. Later, after he joined the conversation, his appearance on film would be edited out.

"Are you sitting comfortably, Mr. Weinstein?"

"Are you being sarcastic?"

"Actually, I'm trying to be a suitable host. But let's play the tape."

Weinstein's attention turned to the screen, where he watched Robert Gently, dressed for some reason in casual clothes, his hair was shorter too, exiting from a log cabin in what looked like a wooded area. The sound had been muted so Weinstein could not hear what Gently was shouting. Though it was an unusual scene, the evidence that it was Gently was undeniable. Just five seconds after Gently had exited the cabin, something suddenly happened. He was almost flung to his left side. Initially, it was hard to see what had occurred. But Canetti/Wesson then rewound the tape with the remote control and let Weinstein watch it again. A few times.

"Was that a crossbow bolt?" he asked Dexton/Smith. "That looks like he was shot with a crossbow."

"That's correct, Sir. Robert Gently, former Attorney General of Maryland, was shot and killed by an assailant using a crossbow."

"Shot? That's an understatement. His neck was obliterated by the crossbow." His comment was akin to a narration.

"The entry wound would have been no smaller than half an inch wide, Sir. The exit wound several inches across. Tattered flesh, bone and sinews." The brief but graphic description seemingly had its desired effect on Weinstein who was turning pale.

"Where did you get that film?" he asked his interviewer.

"Your own rules say one has to have video evidence of kills to gain immunity. This film was taken by one of the men who killed him." We intercepted it five minutes after it was taken. We were lucky, really, that the person who made the film of himself killing Gently didn't make their getaway before we got there first."

Weinstein asked, "Why was it filmed, Mr. Smith?"

"The killer wanted to donate it to his nephew, so that he could '*claim*' a kill of his own and use it to apply for immunity." This was a lie, of course, but added credibility to proceedings.

Weinstein understood the process, Dexton/Smith noticed.

"That was horrendous. You can't make me watch horrors like that."

"Millions of people have been watching their loved ones being killed in equally horrific ways, Mr Weinstein, *White House Chief of Staff*." Dexton/Smith emphasised the job title as clearly as he could; for the benefit of the camera. "They've watched abominations, murders, dis-memberment sometimes, killings in ways you and I have never even seen in horror films. What you've just witnessed is often less horrific than what they had to watch in real time. Up close and personal. Are you not aware of what people have been asked to do?

"Of course I'm fucking aware. Who do you think organised it?"

"Gently, obviously, at the behest of you, I'm led to believe."

"He was my puppet, man. He did what I told him to."

"May I ask you the question I want answered, just for me. The one that's puzzled me throughout all of his?"

"Try me." Weinstein challenged him.

"Why?" he put simply.

"Why?" Weinstein mimicked him. "Why?"

"Yes, what was it all about? What for?"

"Money."

"I'm sorry, I don't understand."

"The country's running out of money. We can't afford to seek any more oil, which is running out at a rate you can't fathom. That takes investment. Food production costs money which we have to supply to the farmers by way of subsidies. Yes, we pay them to farm. And what are they giving us right now? Not enough. That's what! And health care. You've the do-gooders who think we should pay for part of their health care! That means we have to find money."

"I can see the benefit in that!"

"Oh, let's see shall we little Saint Smith'. He gave him a derisory look. "Mr X smokes all his life, eats too much sugar, doesn't care for himself and makes himself sick. Not short-term ill, but proper long-term sick. He comes to us and says *"I know I've not cared for myself, so I want you to pay to fix me."* So, you think the government should finance it all? Huh?"

"People still pay most of their own bills. You're only expected to meet part of it. You're the politicians. Isn't that your job to find the best solution. Maybe not to fix people but educate them not to get sick the wrong ways in the first place. Saves money in the long term."

"People will still get sick," Weinstein hit back. He added, "They'll cost us money, any way you look at it. The older they get, the more expensive they are to us."

"It's not your money,' Dexton/Smith tried to argue, "Just spend what you have on who needs it."

"We estimate population reduction on the scale we envisage will save the country $380 billion a year for the next three years, reducing a bit each year for at least 10 years. But overall, we save the equivalent of 50 to 70% of the current National Debt."

"By killing your taxpayers?" Spencer was confused by the logic of this lunatic.

"A high proportion of who will die don't pay tax, Smith. They are a burden on society."

"They are our society, you lunatic."

Weinstein ignored his interruption and continued regardless. "And think what the government can do with $32 billion a month. That's what it works out as, or $8 billion a week. That's better than old people wanting free healthcare, unemployed people wanting free food, single mothers churning out expensive children."

Spencer was starting to feel sick. Deep down in his stomach. He wasn't sure if he would stop himself throwing up.

"Money makes the world go round, man. Can't you see that?"

"And I suppose you get to decide where it goes?"

"I'll have some say, yes."

"All good causes?" Dexton/Smith asked him.

"That and other projects," Weinstein said.

"Other projects? Are you trying to admit you're financing some personal projects?"

"Well, if some of it gets, shall we say, '*redirected*', that would be little more than unfortunate, wouldn't you say? It's the way of the world."

Canetti, trying to keep quiet in the shadows, couldn't stifle a choking sound. He hadn't realised that for the last minute or so he must have stopped breathing. He spluttered a cough.

Spencer continued, "So let me get this right. You ordered people to kill themselves so you could, what, buy a new speedboat, install marble worktops in your kitchen?"

"I had to control the country's finances, Smith. Some of it may have to be used to reward me."

Spencer wanted to look away. In disgust. But he had to be sure the camera didn't catch him. He fought the urge to do so and kept his gaze forwards, toward this vile and evil man sitting almost smugly in a leather armchair in front of him. A man showing absolutely no remorse whatsoever.

"Are you satisfied, now, Smith? You've got the answer you wanted."

"I may have got the answer, but I'm about to make a deal with you."

"A deal?"

Dexton/Smith said, "I want your resignation. You are to step down immediately after you rescind this National Order. I'll tell you now, you won't be receiving your bonus."

"Like fuck I will."

"Mr. Wesson. Do you care to join us again, in conversation?"

"My pleasure," he called from the shadows.

"What do you have to say to our esteemed Chief of Staff?"

"I'm disgusted."

"Don't care."

"Shut up," Canetti/Wesson growled at him. "And just listen. Firstly, I'm disgusted not just because you're a sick, twisted, self-centred psychopath, but secondly, because you attempted to blame this on others. Do you even remember who you requested to attend that first ministerial meeting?"

"Which meeting?"

"The meeting chaired by Gently when you claimed you were overseas at a global fuel-supply summit. I can see it fully for what it was, now. It was a gathering of people you could blame. You didn't want to hear other peoples' solutions to national debt, resource concerns or population control. You already knew what you were going to do. You just wanted names to blame."

"So what?"

"You don't even remember who attended it, do you?"

"I don't give a fuck who was there. And if any of them are implicated, then great, because I don't give a fuck about them, either."

"Haven't you figured out yet why I seem to know so much about that meeting, Weinstein?"

"I'm sure you'll tell me." He said sarcastically.

"I was one of them. I was there. I represented the Transport Ministry. You and Gently tried to pin all of this on me, you bastards."

"Oh, so that was you? Oh well. Shit happens."

Canetti added, "And we've met before. Don't you even recognise me? We had a meeting about fuel rationing some months ago," but he could see that Weinstein obviously looked blank. He found this to be somewhat insulting. "No recollection at all, you swine?"

Angered by the man merely shaking his head dismissively, Canetti shaped to strike him, but Dexton got in the way, prevented it happening.

"Let's keep focused, shall we?"

"Yeah. I suppose."

"You'll simply have to let me go. I'm powerful. I can do what I want. I can make you two disappear. Just like that."

"Consider these factors first. Firstly, we organised Gently's demise and, as you've noticed, we got to you too. That was so easy. We'll do it again if we have to. I know how to employ men with crossbows, if I so wish."

"Is that a threat?"

Spencer put his nose two inches from Weinstein"s, invading his space and staring at him from as close as he dared. "Yes, it's a threat." He stood back.

"Secondly,' Canetti joined in, "We have your confession."

"Hearsay. I'll deny it."

"Don't be naive. This isn't just a chat. This whole evening has been caught on camera."

The colour in Weinstein's bulbous face turned from a jovial rose tint to a shockingly pale grey. The blood must have drained from his whole head. For a moment, it looked as though he was about to faint.

"Where, how?" he asked. And he looked all around but couldn't see the camera.

"It's back there, above the ceiling tiles." Frankie temporarily left the room and came back in with a flash drive. He plugged it into a port to the left of the colour screen and after pushing one or two buttons, the interview was playing in full colour on the screen with perfect audio. Every word was clear, every image was sharp. Weinstein's face was there for all to see, and his identity could not be mistaken. The copy of the newspaper could be seen thus supporting the date the film was made. And Spencer was pleased to notice his own image was suitably obscured. The most one could see of him was the back of his head, just the right side every so often, and from time to time his right shoulder, the red shirt covering that shoulder being visible periodically.

Weinstein tried to argue, but the futility of his situation hit him hard.

"What do you want from me?" he asked.

"I've told you already. You'll rescind the National Order then resign your position of White House Chief of Staff as soon after as is practicable."

"How the hell do I do that?"

"Use your imagination. Perhaps you'll tell your favourite press officer *"The Objective isn't achieving the benefits the country expected and so, with immediate effect, we shall cease any further action,"* or similar."

"My colleague said *immediate*, Mr Weinstein. And we will have you back in your country retreat in the next half hour. You have telephones available to you. A computer. Access to multiple departments, I'm sure."

"Half an hour! You must be kidding."

"I'd like to remind you. We saw to Gently. We got to you very easily and could do the same any time we want. Any. There are still people out there with guns. And I could easily remove that red bracelet of yours, put you in a pair of dungarees and throw you into a small remote town in West Virginia without any ID or money. See how long you'd last. And we have your full confession recorded. And plenty of copies. That camera is linked to our computer in the next room, which has been making several copies. They could go anywhere we want.

"So, half an hour from now, we'll be tuning onto FOX, CBS or ABC, or wherever, and we'll be listening to the '*Breaking News*' story, along with millions of others hearing the same messages.

"Why are you doing this?"

"I'm changing the government. In the only way that works. It's a sick entity that is growing like a cancer." Dexton/Smith was animated in the way he described it.

"So, vote for another. That's the system in this great country of ours." Weinstein attempted to argue.

"Voting put the likes of you in power. The country deserves honest people who fight *for* them, not *against* them. In 1861, Lincoln said in his inaugural address: *"When the people shall grow weary of their constitutional right to amend their government, they shall exert their revolutionary right to dismember and overthrow that government"*. Looks like a form of overthrowing may be happening."

"You're not big enough," he said to Dexton/Smith.

He replied, "It starts with one person doing the right thing. Let's see how that applies here. We voted for your lot. All 435 of you in the Senate. You got together with your own opposition and devised a way to eliminate the very people who chose you. You all agreed to it. All of you. In my opinion, that's pretty damning. It says, *'we don't like the people who voted us in'*. So now, the people who voted you in see fault in the normal constitutional manner in which you were chosen. You, Sir, give me no option but to conduct myself in the way President Lincoln, himself, suggested would happen.

"And so, I choose to turn your own weapon against you. As I did with Gently," Dexton/Smith concluded.

"Time to get you a telephone," Canetti exclaimed and frog-marched him back to the limousine.

Chapter 44

Jo Lechie was on the telephone to Spencer at 11pm sharp. She knew what he had been up to all evening with Weinstein and figured he and Frankie would probably have concluded their business by now.

"Talk to me. I hate being left in the dark."

"We've got him. He's a broken man. But until he puts word out, officially, I don't trust him as far as I could throw him."

"What happens next?" she asked.

"He and Frankie are in his drawing room, next door, discussing how they are going to do the right thing in the right way."

"All he has to do is ring the press. And I'm one of them!"

"You know you can't be the first, Jo. It would be more than a little suspicious if KXHB got the story first, and it would imply you've had something to do with the threat we made to him, too. You could get in a lot of trouble."

"Well, I want it just after ABC, FOX and CNN get it. What was he like? How did it go?"

"He hated every moment of it but had to accept the inevitable. And there was a bit of disagreement between the two of them as we drove back to the house as to which establishment to inform first. Weinstein wanted to tell his contact at the New York Times, or his contact at the Washington Post. Frankie would have none of it. Reminded him they don't essentially publish their news until the papers hit the streets later in the morning. That would be hours away. We had both demanded instant action. To the TV companies. We weren't going to change our minds."

"Why the delay? Tell him to get on with it."

"Just hang on, Jo. I can hear something going on from the room where Canetti and Weinstein were arguing over semantics. Just hold on patiently."

"Okay, but if you leave me waiti..."

"It's in. I suggest you tune into one of those two channels. They both know."

"I want the video."

"You'll get it, but not now. We talked about this, Jo. You'll be the first to have it, but in a couple of weeks."

"Remind me why so long. I'm itching to see it."

"I have to see what Weinstein does over the next few days. I have to witness him sticking to his promises. I have to make sure he doesn't try any back-stabbing or reneging on the deal. I'm using this as a bargaining chip. If he behaves and does everything he's promised to, I'll delete the film."

"You what?" she asked incredulously.

"I'll delete it just after I send you a copy."

"You're golden, Spencer. If I wasn't already married, I'd give you a great big kiss."

"Is your television on?"

"Sure is. And something's coming up on the screen. Oh boy, here we go!" she said.

"Enjoy it, Jo. I'll speak to you soon."

"Sooner than you think. I'm coming round to your house tomorrow night. I've scrounged a few cans of beer. Try to find a pizza, or something we can make

317

one from. And it's film night for us. Even if I can't take a copy away, I'm going to watch it."

"You got it. See you tomorrow."

Chapter 45

It was 11.15 on a Wednesday evening. The TV stations were a hive of activity. Camera crews were told to stay by their cameras, they were on overtime and should be prepared for a long night ahead. Off-duty reporters were being told to come into the studio. Immediately, no exception, no excuses. The editors and senior staff were running around like headless chickens, barking orders, cancelling programmes, continually making and receiving telephone calls and glorifying in what was happening.

At one of the major stations, the TV Anchor, Cassie Parnick, normally reporting at this time of night on repeat stories from earlier in the day, sports round-ups and unimportant local interest programme fillers, was suddenly handed the hottest news story to have hit the screens in many weeks. She was delighted and could hardly contain her excitement.

"Ladies and gentlemen. We bring you the following breaking news. And we will also shortly play you a recording of a telephone call we received just minutes ago that shows just how it was that we just found out, ourselves. But put simply, the news is the atrocities are finishing. The government's objective to reduce the population numbers by the National Order is being rescinded. I repeat. No more killing. Stop now. We are safe. We have survived."

A still image of Weinstein, the White House Chief of Staff was projected onto the screen. Reporters had been sent to his country retreat and office to try to get a live shot and to stay there until they can get him on camera. *"Get an interview"*, they were told. But they soon realised he wasn't receiving visitors. Consequently, a well-known library shot of his was being broadcast.

The red Breaking News Banner started scrolling across the screen.

Breaking News- Atrocities End With Immediate Affect

The editors watched on, thinking. She's doing as good a job as she can. But she's being a bit emotional. "Play the telephone call," one barked to the Director, "before she breaks down in tears."

They gave her the signal to introduce the call.

"We are now going to play a recording of the call the White House Chief of Staff made to our offices just minutes ago. We can confirm this is authentic, ladies and gentlemen. Do please enjoy the following."

The call was played in its entirety. As this was happening and off-camera, two seasoned reporters had taken up their positions alongside Cassie Parnick. As the call concluded the cameras focussed on them to discuss what they, along with tens of thousands of viewers, had just been listening to.

When the call was played for the viewers for the second time, the viewing numbers were in the hundreds of thousands. By the next morning during what was commonly known as the Breakfast Show, viewing numbers were running in the millions.

Also by early morning, the call had been discussed by many studio reporters and a plethora of roving reporters now camped outside Weinstein's address. Unbeknown to them, he was not there. He had travelled under the cover of darkness to meet with the President to try to get himself out of the mess he now found himself in. The President, as friend, pacified him under the ruse of helping, but in reality was more concerned about his own legal position, reputation and political standing. He had summoned his own advisers into emergency meetings and did not re-surface for many hours.

The people of the USA didn't care much to know what pressures the weak and nowadays a thoroughly unpopular President or his Chief of Staff were under. They simply revelled in the knowledge that it was all over. They could put a stop to the atrocities and make a start to get back to normal. Many were already making plans to come out of hiding, return home, or to reunite with long lost loved ones.

Most, however, realised it was not the time to just run out into the streets and start jumping up and down with joy as they were likely to be shot by somebody who hadn't yet seen the news. Word spread by telephone in the first instance, or by shouting from windows. It was not long before the street parties began, unsurprisingly.

In more rural areas, word spread more slowly. Not as many people watched television or listened to their radios. But eventually, the whole nation got the message.

Six days after the broadcasters' announcement, the blame game started in earnest. People wanted answers, apologies, and confessions. Some people even spoke of seeking compensation. Generally though, people were happy. Better to be free again with questions than hiding away, dazed and confused.

ABC ran a programme that invited anybody to call in with ideas as to (1) who swayed the decision, (2) where Weinstein was now hiding and (3) who was going to pay for the mess.

The invitation attracted more crackpots than useful callers and was disbanded almost as soon as it commenced.

Politicians were still hard to find though their Press Officers started taking calls again and some even agreed to appear on television, but not to discuss the atrocities. One State Governor wanted to prove she was *on the side of the people*', *'working hard for change'* and other clichéd buzz phrases. She sponsored an hour of one of the major networks to demonstrate how she was going to get her state cleaned up and moving back in the right direction. With an agreement in place, the reporter made sure the questions were all about re-building and not once did they look back at the atrocities of the previous weeks.

Chapter 46

Spencer fussed over the idea of making pizza dough, but Jo took control, claiming it wasn't difficult, although she'd have to make her own Polenta, too. She was hoping to have found it in one of the shops she frequented, but neither had had any for some time. She nabbed a couple of cans of sweetcorn, instead.

"Have you got a food processor?" she asked Spencer the moment she arrived at his duplex and was pleased to see him nodding.

She also added, "You said you'd get toppings, Spencer. What did you find?"

He opened one of the pine eye-level cupboards to the right of the sink and took down a selection of goodies.

He said, "I managed to find three tomatoes and a little cheese. No pepperoni, so we'll have to use a bit of sausage meat which I found in the freezer."

"A feast fit for kings!" she exclaimed.

As the pizza was baking, they managed to watch the video clip no less than four times. From start to finish, each time without stopping. But during the last play-through they kept pausing the footage and making comments about Weinstein's demeanour, his reactions when challenged, the colour of his skin when he realised he had been caught out and anything else that was noteworthy.

After viewing the film on the screen in the living room, they returned to the kitchen. The aroma was delightful. Spencer served up the pizza in slices as Jo laid a couple of places with beer poured into glasses.

They sat opposite each other at the counter on tall chrome-legged stools.

Conversation over dinner was understandably focused on the events within the warehouse and when they returned to Weinstein's country retreat; the latter topic raised a big question in Jo's mind.

She drained the last of her beer, put the glass back on the counter and asked it of him.

"Didn't his security team confront and arrest you when you arrived there? You are, after all, not his chauffeur or bodyguard. They would not have expected you to be in the car with their boss."

"Jacobs can be thanked for that. Did I mention him?"

"You said he was part of the kidnapping plan. But beyond that, nothing else was said," she remarked.

"Do you mind not using the term kidnapping?" Spencer asked.

"What was it, if it wasn't kidnapping?"

"We invited him to his golf club for a chat. He went along willingly but his driver took a detour on the way. So, I'd call it an organised meeting with an amended agenda."

"Won't fly in court." They both laughed.

"Jacobs," he resumed, "after having returned to the house, spread the word to the staff about what he'd discovered Weinstein had been responsible for all this time. He reminded those closest to him how devastated he had been to have lost his family and now he knew who to blame. The security team were split on what they should do.

"On the one hand they were supposed to protect their boss. But on the other hand, he had been the cause of several of them having lost family members, too. The servants, he has two, I believe, were not inclined to stay after hearing this, either. All in all, the eight employees, that's security guards, chauffeur, cook, servant and somebody akin to a butler, had all but abandoned the sinking ship before it went down. Two of the security guards vowed to stay on to ensure no harm came to him once he'd returned to the house. They figured this was a good way to keep from being blamed for his apparent abduction. But when they discovered what was, indeed, going on with regards him confessing the way he did, they too let him fend for himself by jumping into their Jeep and were away in a flash.

"When we left, we were the last. He was completely on his own from then onwards."

Jo listened to every word. Intently. As only a reporter would, and wondered if she'd ever be able to broadcast any of it from the KXHB studio. Common sense prevailed and she knew that would never be accepted. She asked, "How do you know all of that, if Jacobs wasn't there?"

He replied, "One of those two security guys told me about Jacobs, just before jumping in the Jeep. Also, I contacted Jacobs at his home address the next day and advised him to say nothing about this, otherwise it may implicate him in anything that went on regarding our...*kidnapping*... of him, to use your term. He said he wanted nothing to do with it and as far as he was concerned, the less he knew the better. He was still mindful of the threat to his adopted family's safety. The rest of the servants didn't know any of the details either, so they would not be an issue for us, he assured me."

"Essentially, then, the only people who know about this tape are you, me, Frankie and.... Who?"

"Nobody else. At all," he admitted.

"What are Frankie's intentions with the film?" she enquired.

"He wants nothing to do with it. He got me to promise him that the section at the end of the film, where you hear him talking to Weinstein, is not only edited out, but permanently deleted. And I've no problem doing that before you get your copy of it. He wants to go back to the comfort and familiarity of his own house in Pittsburgh, finally. He's looking forward to working properly again, too, and to resurrect his ministerial career in earnest. I even doubt if I'll ever see him again."

"I don't blame him at all. It must be reassuring to think he's helped bring this horrid experience to a close and he can walk away completely free of it."

"Lucky him. I'll live with it for the rest of my days," Spencer declared.

They returned to the living room. Spencer switched on two standing lamps which cast a warmer glow across the room, far less intense than the ceiling light which he then turned off. They made themselves comfortable in the brown leather armchairs.

The next couple of hours were spent reminiscing about the days before the atrocities began. The happier, innocent days that were full of hope and joy.

Jo told Spencer how her kids were holding up and because they were just five and seven years old, were unlikely to remember too much of these difficult times.

Spencer tried expressing how much he missed Jenny and Marianne. Jo could still feel their presence in the house and Spencer had disposed of very few of their possessions. Most were still where the girls had left them all those weeks before. But there again, Spencer had only got back here a matter of a few days ago from Oklahoma; via a detour with Frankie to Washington to deal with Weinstein. Consequently, he had had little time to do any major tidying or make changes.

There was still a bit of business to discuss before Jo left to head home. A two-hour journey in which she would replay the film she watched over and over in her mind. She knew Spencer would only give her a copy of the film in a couple of weeks, but until then, nobody else would get to know it even existed.

"I'll broadcast your tape, to get the story out there, but you have to do me a favour in return," she demanded.

"What?"

"You agree to be interviewed Martindale O'Toole."

"Why?"

"He's a very good friend of mine. He has to conclude his interviews and I know he's looking for one last story. I think it'll be your chance to lay your own ghosts to rest."

"Who's to say I have any?"

"Spencer, darling, I may be no shrink but let's lay out the facts. You lost everybody that was dear to you. You tried to hunt for the killer and failed. That in itself is eating you up. You got hunted by a gang of psychopathic loonies in camo gear. You kidnapped. And yes that *is* the right term for it. Kidnapped the Attorney General. You made sure he was slaughtered. You *sort of* kidnapped the White House Chief of Staff, too, and forced him, with a threat I hasten to add, to confess to the greatest crime in human history. And you think you have no ghosts?"

"When you put it like that...." his comment trailed off.

"You deserve some peace."

"There's no way I'm telling that to a small-time reporter."

"He's not small-time. He covers several states. Lots of people will hear your story. People who talk to somebody important manage to clear the air. They sleep better at night. Are you having any nightmares?"

"Maybe I am, maybe I'm not."

"You can use it to pay homage to your family. Help them rest in peace even if you can live with your nightmares," she said.

"I like the last idea."

"So treat this as a tribute to their memory. You owe it to them."

Chapter 47

The Chronicle Interviews-
Post-Disaster Era- Interview Nine

Martindale O'Toole met Spencer Dexton at the library in Archville, Iowa. Dexton's home town. O'Toole had rented an office on the top floor of the building, well away from the quiet area where the library members came to read books and study in silence. The room, like the whole building, had the wonderful aroma of antique oak and, as he walked past the area where the tens of thousands of books were neatly stacked, this had a slightly different but wonderful aroma that cast his mind back to his student days. He used to love studying in libraries.

He wondered how students were coping in these early days after the atrocities had abruptly stopped. Were they still studying? Were colleges still teaching the same things and in the same manner? He promised himself he would find out in the coming days. It may make a good newspaper article.

He suspected it may be too soon to investigate. Nothing had gone back to normal yet and it was still too early to tell the extent to which America had recovered. He was all too aware that fuel was still in short supply and still being rationed. Food supply was similarly slow to recover. Welfare services were decimated and hospitals were in a mess. But there were promising signs here and there and that was very welcome.

People struggled to come to terms with what had happened. Most of the burials, having taken place in mass graves, caused great consternation with those who had lost their loved ones. How could they grieve properly if they weren't sure which part of the plot their own relative was buried? Sadness and confusion would take a very long time indeed to subside.

And while all this was going on, the big TV networks and national press still had more questions than answers. The articles they ran were thin on substance and heavy with conjecture.

He and Constance Brighley had had a discussion on the success of these interviews. They agreed that it was time to move on, to return to the old days where they met kids at pageants and interviewed them about their costume design. Where they met ladies cooking Grandma's apple pie recipe to help celebrate their town's 200th anniversary. Where the school prom in SomewhereVille was bigger than ever and the teachers wanted the interview to showcase the kids' efforts to design the best stage set their county had ever seen. Yes, it was time to return to the good-old-days.

But there had to be one more. One to finish. He wanted the best good news story he could get. And as he and Constance searched for a suitable subject, he got a call from Jo Lechie, Roving Reporter for KXHB TV, a dear and old friend. She knew his dilemma and had, she claimed, a solution for him. A guy she knew from Iowa. He had spent the last few months in Oklahoma where he had lost his family. But he's a tough one and he's got a story to tell.

She had said, *"You own me a favour, so do it."* But what was even more sinister is she had added, *"And after you have, you'll owe me favours forever. He's sitting on a juicy secret or two, I'll have you know."* He asked her what this was, but all she said was, *"A good interviewer may be able to tease it out of him,"* and left it at that.

That last part of the message was a bit confusing but his mind had already drifted. He was immediately in *'planning mode'*. He would interview this fellow, Spencer Dexton, and get his story on how he rebuilt his life after such a loss. He could only presume Jo was suggesting that after he dealt with such adversity, he must have a great recovery story to tell.

As it turned out, Martindale was in for a rocky ride.

He shook hands with Spencer in the library's room where they met.

"We have a mutual friend, so it seems. Jo Lechie," he said.

"So we have. Lovely lady. She's the one who told me to agree to this interview," Spencer replied.

"Told? That sounds like you don't want to do it."

"Oh, that wouldn't be accurate. Let's use the word advised. She thinks it'll be good for me."

Mindful that Jo had said he was *'sitting on a very juicy secret'*, O'Toole was now hunting for a sign. Some sort of *'Tell'* as a poker player would say.

"I gather from her that you're a freelance researcher and work for the press from time to time," Marty said.

"That's right. But not exclusively so. I've worked for advertising companies, movie set designers, crop farming research into yield optimisation, I've done some TV stuff in the past and just recently I've taken on some work for a museum. But don't tell them when I say, it's not as interesting as I thought it would be."

"I don't tend to put people's CVs in the newspaper when it's published, so I'll just say you research for the arts, if you don't mind."

"That sounds very fair, Martindale."

"Just Marty, please."

"You got it."

"I'm hoping you're familiar with the interviews we publish in The Homeland Chronicle?"

"Jo made me read the full series. Love the stories. Some made me very sad."

Marty said, "Unfortunately, we've lived through difficult times. And it's my privilege to be with you here so you can share your experience with our readers. You'll become one of our special family of interviewees."

"I'm not sure what Jo's told you about me. I really don't think my story is different enough to warrant an interview. I'm meeting more out of politeness to Jo than for any other reason. That, and because you agreed to come to where I live. For me it's a five minute walk. For you I dare say you've travelled some distance." Marty didn't disagree.

After talking to him in platitudes and tautology for an uncomfortably long spell, Spencer was getting a little frustrated with Marty's approach. "I'm no reporter, Marty, but it seems to me that you've not done your research."

"How so?"

"We've chatted about nothing much for ages. Banal nothingness. I'm sure your time is precious. You've not asked me a direct question yet. I don't think you know what you're going to print in your paper."

"Interviews are open affairs. I let you tell me what's on your mind. And I create a story from that. So, please feel free to tell me whatever you want."

"Now you're sounding like a shrink. Should I lay back on a couch and tell you all about my mother; my first pet, or when I was bullied at school?"

"Have I upset you, Spencer? I didn't intend to insult you. All I'm hoping for is an honest discussion about your journey through these atrocities. We should start by reminiscing with your stories. Which are you most comfortable with?"

"Okay, I'll go along. But first, I've a question for you, Marty."

"Fire away."

"How many members of your close family did you lose to the atrocities?" asked Spencer.

"Just one. A niece."

"And who killed her?"

"A woman I don't know. I'm not even sure how it happened. There was a witness who found my niece dead on the ground and woman walking away. With a camera-phone in her hand."

"How easy is it to talk about it with a stranger?"

"Not at all."

"So what makes you think I'll be comfortable telling you, a stranger, all about the way the only four members of my family were brutally killed? And, before you answer that, what's worse is you want to put this in a newspaper for thousands of strangers to read it!"

"Our stories are anonymised, Spencer. For one thing, you're not baring your soul to strangers, because they don't know who *you* are, so there's no come-back, whatsoever. Secondly, not for a minute would I expect you to describe the brutality of the attack. I do, however, want you to realise I'm much more interested in learning the wonderful things about them. I could describe them in a few hundred words and then say *"John, Jane and Jackie are sadly no longer with us, but very precious because…"*. That way the story is a good news story and not a morbid passage which will turn readers away from the newspaper. I'd not last five minutes as a reporter if I tried to do that."

"So, without detail, how do you want to write my story?"

"I want to publish something like this…

"Today, I have with me a freelance researcher who works with the arts, called Xavier (or whatever name we agree to print, Spencer). He has so kindly shared wonderful stories of his family memoires, and although his family members did not survive the atrocities, like so many readers out there, he wanted to revel in reminiscing about good times. Xavier particularly remembers the weekend they all went to Lake SuchAndSuch…"

Marty was sure he saw the first vestiges of a smile appearing on Spencer's face.

Spencer opened up for the first time and said, "Funnily enough, we had a weekend trip to Lake Chippenhoe where my girlfriend's father fell off the end of the jetty. It was slippery. You reminded me of that, so thank you."

"You see, the interview is for you to enjoy. Not to fight me."

"You're right. I've been on the offensive."

For the next couple of hours, Spencer and Marty exchanged family stories. Though Marty's wouldn't find their way into the paper, of course, many of Spencer's memories were destined for the printing press.

After a while, the two men went down to the cafeteria to see if there were any sandwiches available. Disappointingly, the range of snacks extended only to cookies and flapjacks. There was no bread in the local shops, apparently. Nor potato chips. But milkshakes were on the menu.

"Oh wow. They've got milk," Marty noticed. "I haven't had me a milkshake for many months. Chocolate for me. How about you, Spencer?"

"I'm a black coffee man. Perhaps I should have a shake just to be rebellious. But, no, I'll let somebody else enjoy one later while the milk's still available. But I will have a flapjack."

After the rest break, they returned upstairs to carry on. Spencer talked of little Jenny and how she would have grown up to be a lawyer. She was forever watching every episode of those crime-buster law series on the cable channels. She loved a good 'Whodunnit' mystery, and often solved the riddle well before the end of the first half of the show. He paid homage to the Verlanos and told Marty how much he had wanted to become their son-in-law officially after he finally found a way to persuade Marianne to marry him. Alas, this was not to be. None of it.

Marty had to work very hard to keep him up-beat. But the truth was slowly dawning on Marty. Spencer came across as just an ordinary guy. Why did Jo Lechie almost demand Marty interview him?

Her words rang in his mind once again. *"You owe me a favour, so do it. And after you have, you'll owe me favours forever."*

That proved it. There was something big, here. He was going to get to the bottom of it before Spencer left the library. Only one way to do it, he mused. He dived headlong into the conundrum.

"I can't help but think Jo asked you to do this interview for another reason. Something very specific. Something only you have done. You're unique, Spencer. And you're hiding it from me. There's a bond of trust between me and Jo. As I'm sure there is between you and Jo as well. Ipso facto, that bond of trust should exist between us two."

Spencer gave the "Poker player's tell'. He looked away. Almost shamefully.

"I want to know what's really going on," Marty demanded in a forceful manner that surprised even himself.

Spencer jabbed a finger into Marty's chest. "If this goes any further, I swear, you'll regret it."

"You know how confidentiality works, Spencer. I'd be a blithering idiot if I bit the hand that feeds me."

"This interview's killing me. It's been like a dagger to my heart." His ghosts were laughing at him, and he was desperate to exorcise them. He knew that more than anything else at that very moment, he wanted to tell. He needed to share. He had to get it off his chest.

"It's not my intention to..." Marty was not allowed to continue.

"Whatever happens from here, between you and me, it gets nowhere near my Chronicle story. Not a single thing. Got it?"

"Uh, sure. Erm...' Marty felt most uncomfortable now. He was certainly no longer in control of this interview.

"Do you watch television, Mr. O'Toole?" Spencer headed toward the door.

"It's just Mar... yes I do. I do watch television occasionally. Why's that?"

"I own a very bright red checked shirt, that may be famous one day."

"Excuse me?"

"Tune in on Tuesday mid-morning to KXHB. Good day." The door swung closed behind him.

Chapter 48

"Where the hell did this come from?" the TV station Executive Officer, Archie Hewlen, demanded of Jo Lechie, pointing at what was now a frozen image of Jeremy Weinstein on his computer screen. "This.. this... crazy shit!" His volatile temper had surfaced once again.

The nature and content of the video clip he had just watched twice had caught him unawares.

"You know I can't reveal my sources. Under any circumstances. For anything."

"Don't you dare throw that *'protecting my sources'* card at me, you bitch. That's what we tell everybody else out there. In here, we share information. Especially if it's as nuclear hot as this."

"No. A flat NO. You can use it if you want, or I'm taking it somewhere else. But wherever it goes, my source is protected."

"You can't. You're an employee of KXHB. You're ours."

"Not if you refuse to use it. I'll simply walk down the road to that other broadcaster. You know, the one run by the guys you don't get on with. Don't think you've got the only copy, there. Oh, and that version you've just seen is incomplete. There's more."

"Incomplete?" Hewlen looked like he had been robbed of something precious.

"You get the full version when you sign a contract which protects my property and my rights."

"And if I don't like your contract?"

"I'm off down to…'

"Don't you dare mention their name in this office," Hewlen said.

"Well, do you want them to have it or not? If the answer's '*No*' then you have to air it."

He looked defeated.

She added, "And I'll tell you something else, boss. Two hours after you broadcast it, it will find its way on the internet, anyway. So make the most of it while you can. The person who made the film knows we are not a national broadcaster. They want everybody to see it. No exception. You get the chance to broadcast it before anybody else. One chance for exclusive rights. Just one."

He submitted to her demands and they laid out how the programme would pan out. Presenters were called in to anchor the story, to set up the broadcast. In rehearsal they watched the film footage with incredulity.

"Can we be sure it's authentic?" A collective concern, so it seemed, judging by the nodding of heads around the briefing office.

"My source, the person who owns the film, pored over the footage for some time in the safety of their own home. They couldn't decide, at first, whether to edit it or send it out uncut. They settled on the uncut version to prevent anybody accusing the footage from having been fabricated or 'Selectively edited'. The only bit that's been cut is when the cameraman talks for a bit at the very end. We cut that out to protect his identity. Get our Tech team on it first to verify this, by all means. I'd expect nothing else. I'm mindful that your station's reputation is on the line, and you have to ensure the authenticity. So go ahead, put it through the necessary process."

Consequently, after the specialists analysed it as best they could in the little time they had, the film was deemed to be authentic and was given the green light to proceed.

"And one last thing," Jo Lechie said to the Chief Executive. "You don't ever call me a bitch again."

On a murky summer's day just over two weeks after the atrocities ended, with the rain lashing down across what seemed like the whole of the country, an exceptionally strong wind felling trees here and there, and people reluctant to go outside, most of the nation tuned on their TV sets for something to do. They watched the normal channels: ABC, CBS, FOX, ESPN, a film network, some brand new sports channel that had popped up on most stations, the cartoon for kids channels; and so on.

Suddenly, telephone calls such as these started to happen all around the country:

"Janet. You have to switch over to KXHB. Don't ask why, just do it!."

Or *"Boss, turn the T.V. on. Now! KXHB."*

Or *"Stop what you're doing and tune into KXHB, Mike. No time to lose!"*

The broadcaster was clever. They didn't show the footage until they figured they had an audience way in excess of the numbers they had ever had before. All morning the following headlines featured in their 'Breaking News Banners' that ran along the foot of the news screens, alternating and teasing the viewer to want to know more:

'Breaking News- Presidential Blame for Killings'
'Chief of Staff Gets His Just Desserts'
'The Truth Behind All of the Atrocities'
'Jeremy Weinstein, Personal Friend of the President Confesses'

At long last, the programme began in earnest. Over the next three hours, the TV presenter took viewers through the film Spencer Dexton had made. Jeremy Weinstein was big on the screen. Front and Centre. Telling it all in his own words. It wasn't supposed to be a confession, but it could not be interpreted as anything else.

Nobody recognised the voice of the other man in the footage though the camera sometimes picked up a glimpse of his shoulder, the back of his ear, or the nape of his neck. On one or two occasions, you could see the back of a bright red checked shirt. He never faced the camera at any time.

The one viewer who found a particular interest in seeing that shirt was Martindale O'Toole, sitting at home with his jaw wide open, staring unblinkingly at the screen. He recognised the guy's voice, too.

The presenters speculated on who the mostly obscured man could be, because the viewers would have been doing this as well. They correctly figured he was the source of the footage, but there were insufficient clues to come to any definitive conclusions. They invited experts into the studio to verify the authenticity of the footage; to which they gladly did. They invited calls from government offices or calls from Senators and Congressmen to answer for their actions, or lack of the same. One or two senators attempted a call to say *"Hey, it had nothing to do with me, I was set against it"*, but each and every one of these served to do no more than to make themselves look culpable.

Jo Lechie was interviewed, by the presenters, also. She claimed the film was sent anonymously thus protecting herself and Dexton. Nobody disbelieved her, it seemed. The presenters took her at her word.

In the days that followed, the public went into a frenzy of protest against the government. Figuratively speaking, heads rolled, Senators went into hiding, buildings were vandalised. Freedom flags and banners flew on flagpoles outside Town Halls across the country. One office was set alight with an effigy of the

President tied to a lamp post outside the building. He, too, was set alight once a local film crew had arrived.

The last thing anybody knew of Jeremy Weinstein, after word had got around that he tried to escape somewhere on his luxury yacht, was he had been caught and subsequently taken to the Smithsonian National Zoo. As it transpired, he had been put into a cage of lions with a popular brand of handgun containing one single bullet. Not enough to kill all of the big hungry cats that had caught his scent. Enough of him was found the next day to make a positive ID. The Coroner, in her subsequent inquest, declined to speculate as to why the kidnapper had hung a sign around his neck that said *'You Wanted Gun Killings. Let Smith and Wesson Help You Have One Last Hurrah'*.

———————

Acknowledgements

Normally, one would expect to see a list of all of the people a writer would wish to thank first and foremost.

But I'd rather start with an apology. A massive one.

I sincerely apologise for taking you on a journey into a very dark place. It was a place I had no idea my own imagination was capable of going into until I started writing this novel.

There were times I hated writing parts of it and on numerous occasions I told my friends that I simply couldn't continue. And for four weeks, at least, during the spell I was writing this, I refused to continue.

But then I changed tack, and approached the challenge from a different direction and it took me to a better place. One where good wins over evil.

And so, I hope you'll forgive me for taking you into this dark place and are relieved by your return to some form of normality again.

None of the characters are based upon anybody I know. Consequently, any similarity between any of them and any living person is purely coincidental.

And now, the thanks.

I wish to thank Lorna R, for telling me "you should write a book about that", after we were chatting about the concept of the story. Had she not, there would not have been a book. Her feedback was invaluable too, especially in the early days as it gave me the motivation to get past the first few chapters.

I also wish to thank Mick O and Steve C for giving me similar encouragement during the times I was writing and editing.

My eternal thanks to my lovely lady, Sue, who seems to have copious amounts of patience with me when I tell her "I'm going to try a new hobby", or "I'm going to replace the roof on the house", or "I'm going to write a novel". Quite frankly, I've no idea how she puts up with me sometimes.

And finally. My thanks to you for reading this novel. I hope you'll forgive me for having taken you on this macabre journey.

***Number 1 in the
Spencer Dexton
Trilogy***

In this series:

The Killing Interviews

The Prisoner Interviews

The Survivor Interviews

Printed in Great Britain
by Amazon

36772151R00195